Prequel

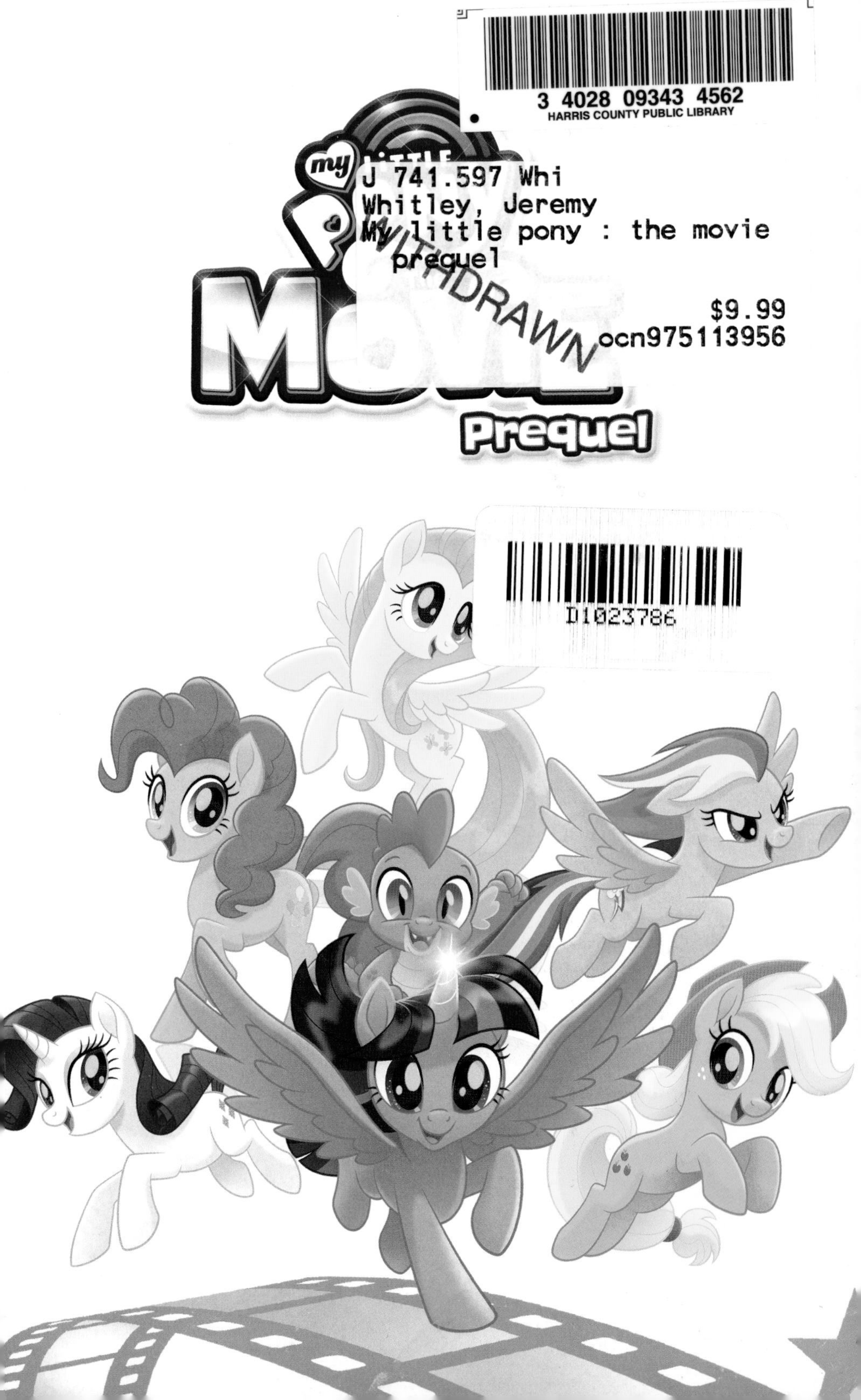

 Licensed By:

Special thanks to Meghan McCarthy, Eliza Hart, Ed Lane, Beth Artale, and Michael Kelly.

ISBN: 978-1-68405-107-6   20 19 18 17   1 2 3 4
SCHOLASTIC EDUCATION ISBN: 978-1-68405-214-1

Become our fan on Facebook **facebook.com/idwpublishing**
Follow us on Twitter **@idwpublishing**
Subscribe to us on YouTube **youtube.com/idwpublishing**
See what's new on Tumblr **tumblr.idwpublishing.com**
Check us out on Instagram **instagram.com/idwpublishing**

Ted Adams, CEO & Publisher
Greg Goldstein, President & COO
Robbie Robbins, EVP/Sr. Graphic Artist
Chris Ryall, Chief Creative Officer
David Hedgecock, Editor-in-Chief
Laurie Windrow, Sr. VP of Sales & Marketing
Matthew Ruzicka, CPA, Chief Financial Officer
Lorelei Bunjes, VP of Digital Services
Jerry Bennington, VP of New Product Development

For international rights, please contact licensing@idwpublishing.com

MY LITTLE PONY: THE MOVIE PREQUEL. AUGUST 2017. FIRST PRINTING. HASBRO and its logo, MY LITTLE PONY and all related characters are trademarks of Hasbro and are used with permission. © 2017 Hasbro. All Rights Reserved. MY LITTLE PONY: THE MOVIE © 2017 My Little Pony Productions, LLC. The IDW logo is registered in the U.S. Patent and Trademark Office. IDW Publishing, a division of Idea and Design Works, LLC. Editorial offices: 2765 Truxtun Road, San Diego, CA 92106. Any similarities to persons living or dead are purely coincidental. With the exception of artwork used for review purposes, none of the contents of this publication may be reprinted without the permission of Idea and Design Works, LLC. Printed in Canada. IDW Publishing does not read or accept unsolicited submissions of ideas, stories, or artwork.

Originally published as MY LITTLE PONY: THE MOVIE PREQUEL issues #1–4.

Written by
JEREMY WHITLEY

Art by
ANDY PRICE

Colors by
HEATHER BRECKEL

Letters by
NEIL UYETAKE

Series Edits by
BOBBY CURNOW

Cover Art by
TONY FLEECS

Collection Edits by
JUSTIN EISINGER and ALONZO SIMON

Collection Design by
CLAUDIA CHONG

Publisher:
TED ADAMS

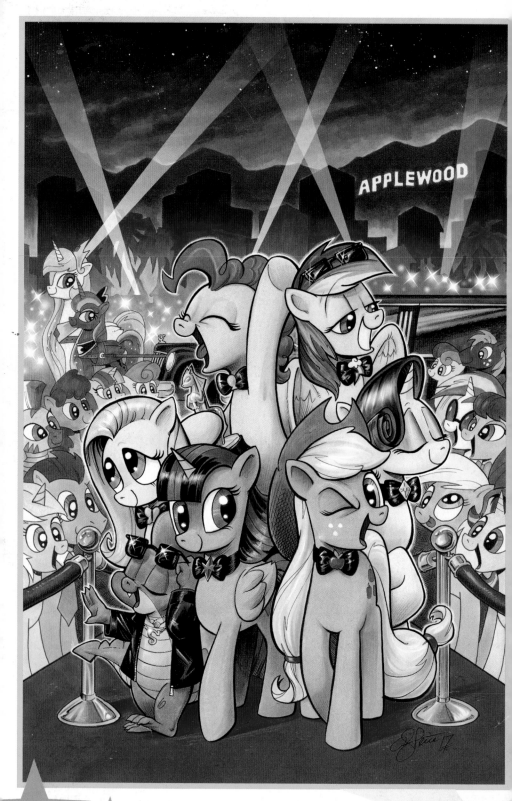

APPLEWOOD

Art by ANDY PRICE

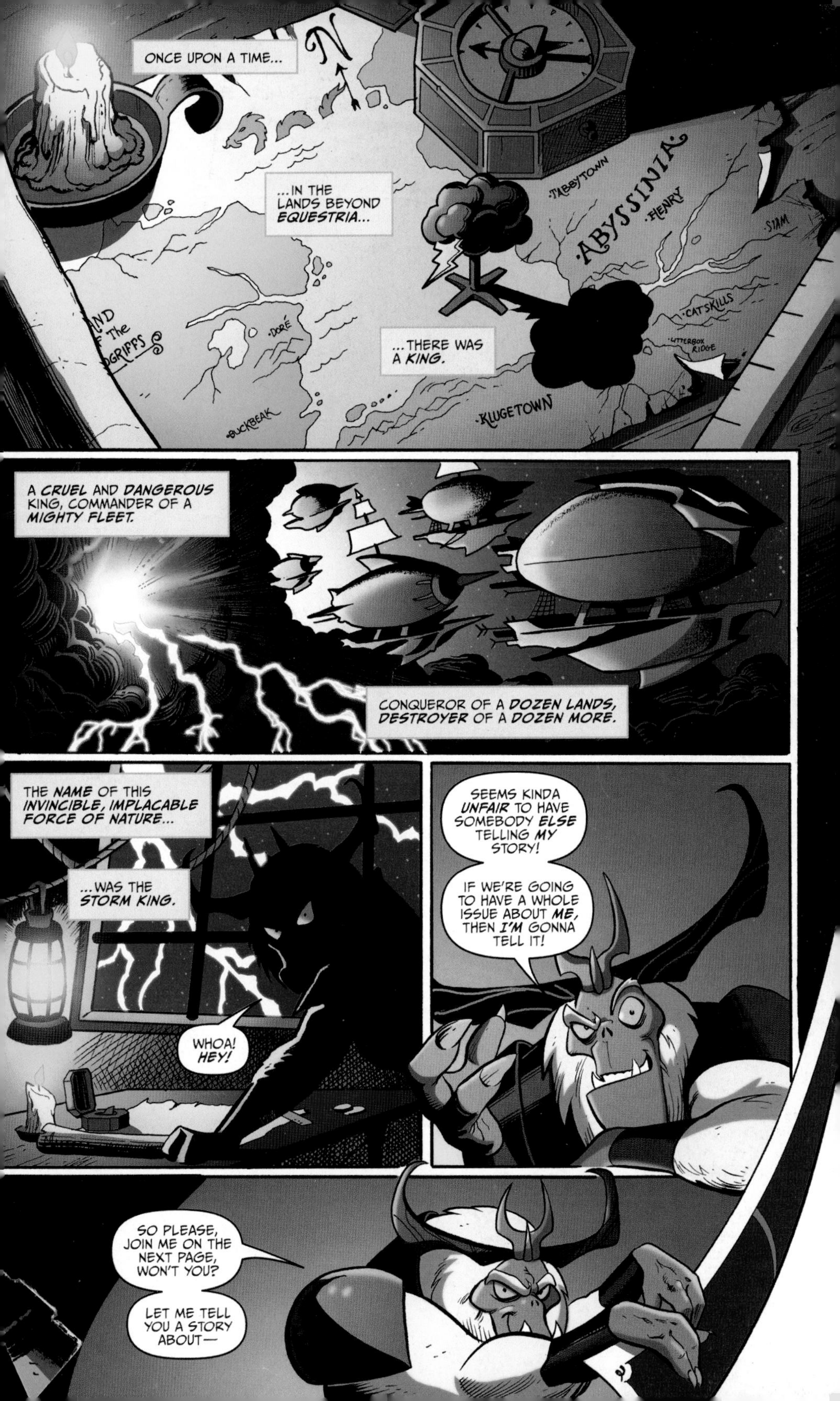

ONCE UPON A TIME...
N
...IN THE LANDS BEYOND EQUESTRIA...
TABBYTOWN
ABYSSINIA
HENRY
SIAM
CATSKILLS
DORÉ
...THERE WAS A KING.
KLUGETOWN
BUCKBEAK
A CRUEL AND DANGEROUS KING, COMMANDER OF A MIGHTY FLEET.
CONQUEROR OF A DOZEN LANDS, DESTROYER OF A DOZEN MORE.
THE NAME OF THIS INVINCIBLE, IMPLACABLE FORCE OF NATURE...
...WAS THE STORM KING.
WHOA! HEY!
SEEMS KINDA UNFAIR TO HAVE SOMEBODY ELSE TELLING MY STORY!
IF WE'RE GOING TO HAVE A WHOLE ISSUE ABOUT ME, THEN I'M GONNA TELL IT!
SO PLEASE, JOIN ME ON THE NEXT PAGE, WON'T YOU?
LET ME TELL YOU A STORY ABOUT—

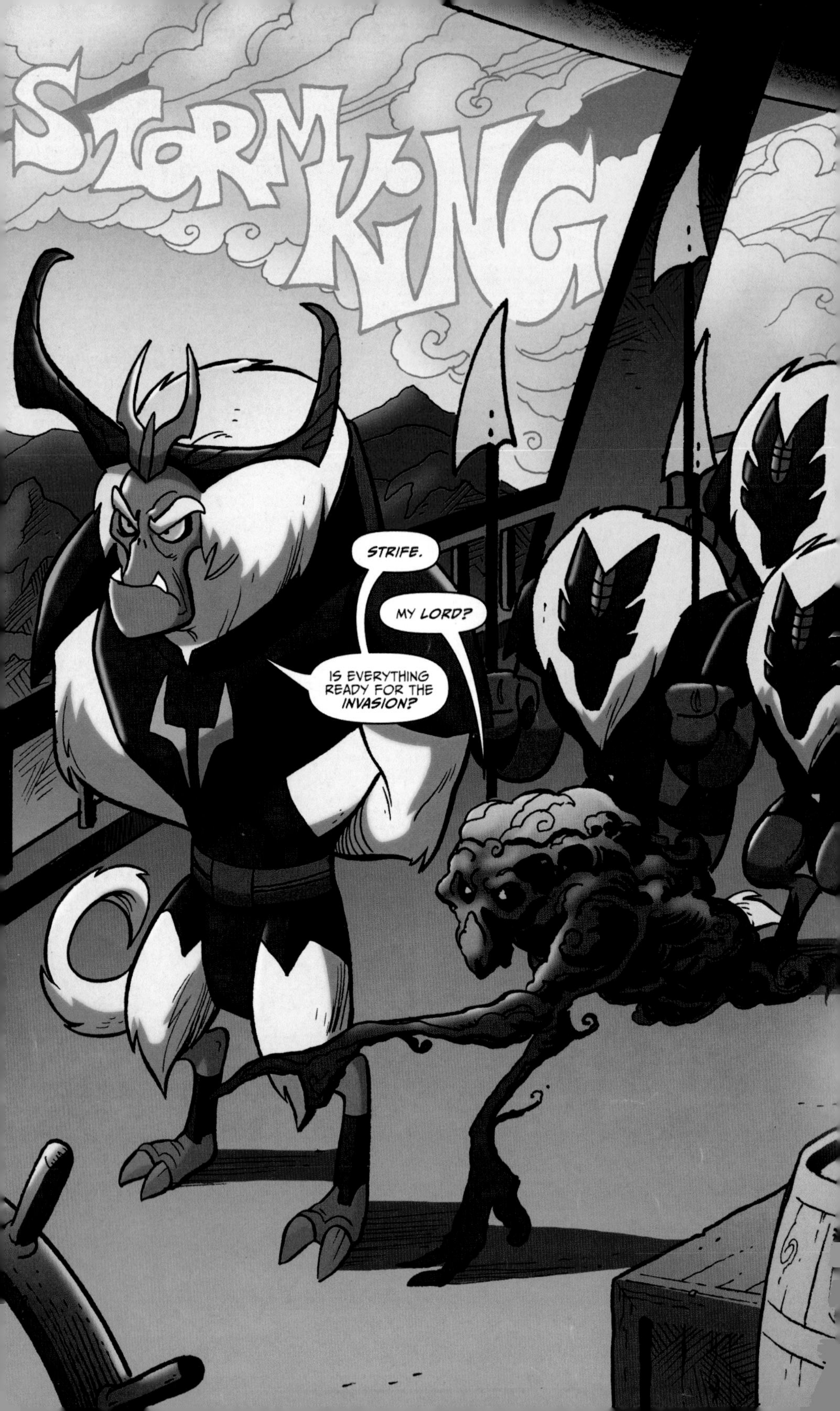
STORM KING
STRIFE.
MY LORD?
IS EVERYTHING READY FOR THE INVASION?

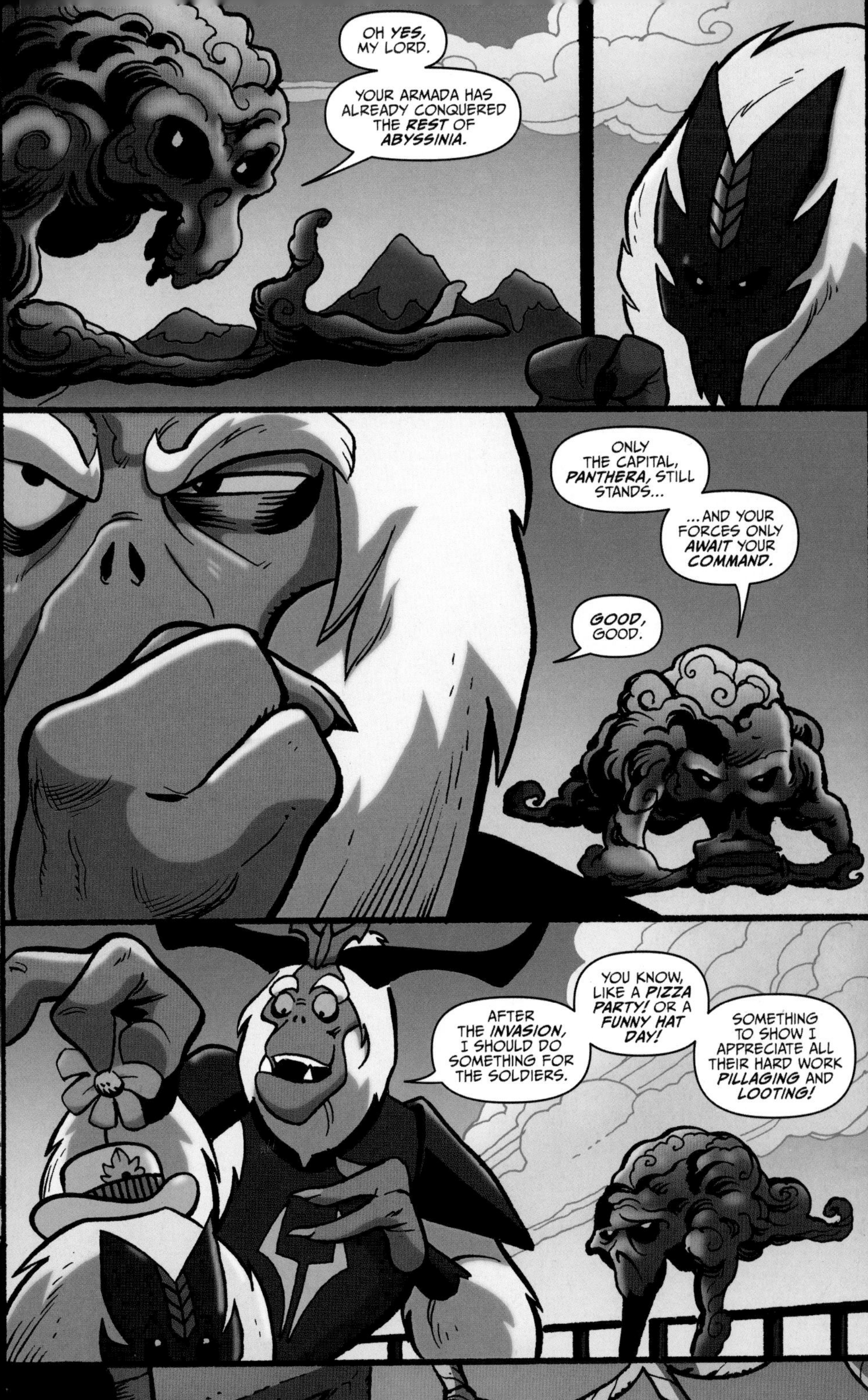
OH YES, MY LORD.
YOUR ARMADA HAS ALREADY CONQUERED THE REST OF ABYSSINIA.
ONLY THE CAPITAL, PANTHERA, STILL STANDS...
...AND YOUR FORCES ONLY AWAIT YOUR COMMAND.
GOOD, GOOD.
AFTER THE INVASION, I SHOULD DO SOMETHING FOR THE SOLDIERS.
YOU KNOW, LIKE A PIZZA PARTY! OR A FUNNY HAT DAY!
SOMETHING TO SHOW I APPRECIATE ALL THEIR HARD WORK PILLAGING AND LOOTING!

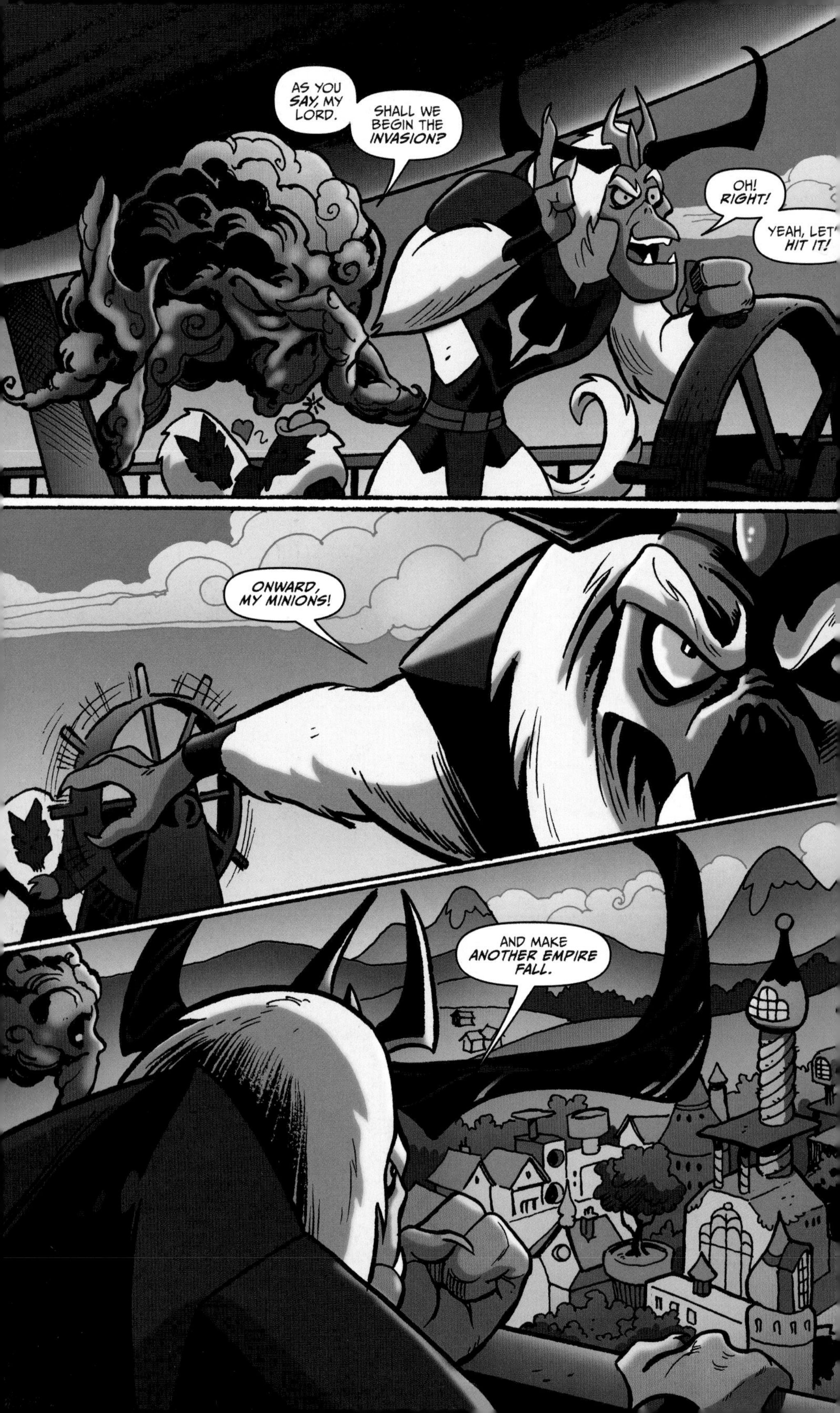
AS YOU SAY, MY LORD.
SHALL WE BEGIN THE INVASION?
OH! RIGHT!
YEAH, LET' HIT IT!
ONWARD, MY MINIONS!
AND MAKE ANOTHER EMPIRE FALL.

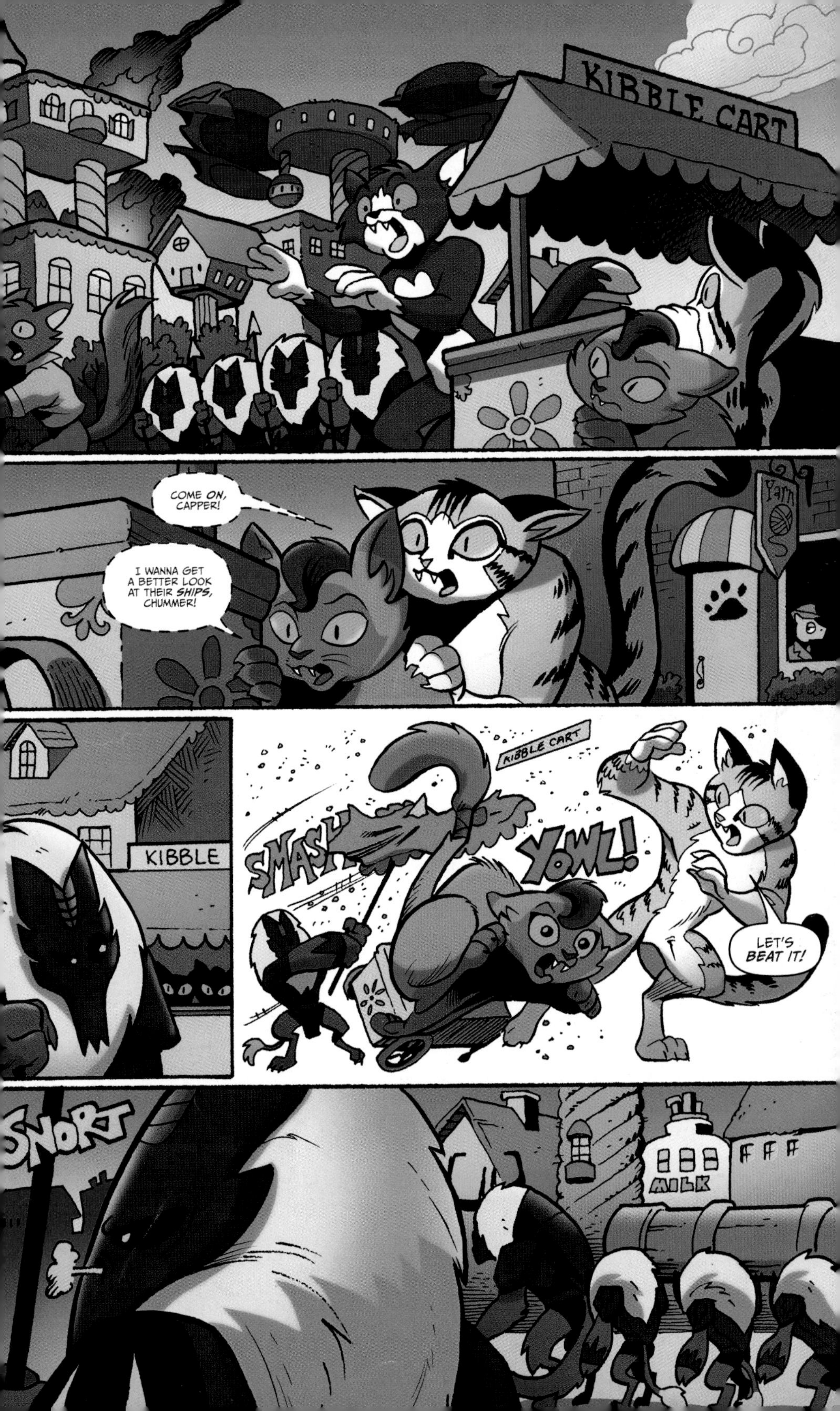
KIBBLE CART
COME ON, CAPPER!
I WANNA GET A BETTER LOOK AT THEIR SHIPS, CHUMMER!
Yarn
KIBBLE
KIBBLE CART
SMASH
YOWL!
LET'S BEAT IT!
SNORT
MILK

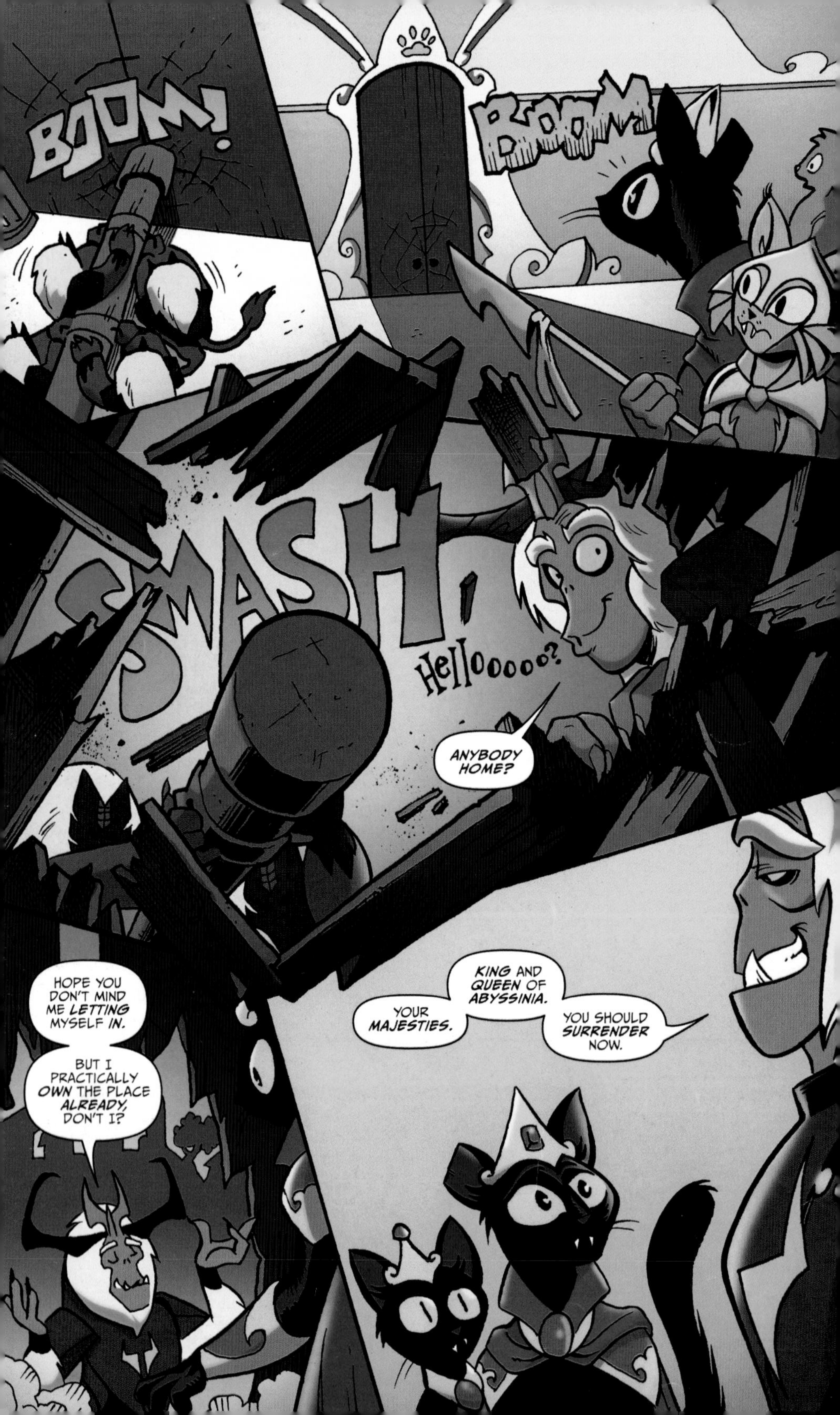
BOOM!
BOOM
SMASH!
Helloooooo?
ANYBODY HOME?
HOPE YOU DON'T MIND ME LETTING MYSELF IN.
BUT I PRACTICALLY OWN THE PLACE ALREADY, DON'T I?
YOUR MAJESTIES.
KING AND QUEEN OF ABYSSINIA.
YOU SHOULD SURRENDER NOW.

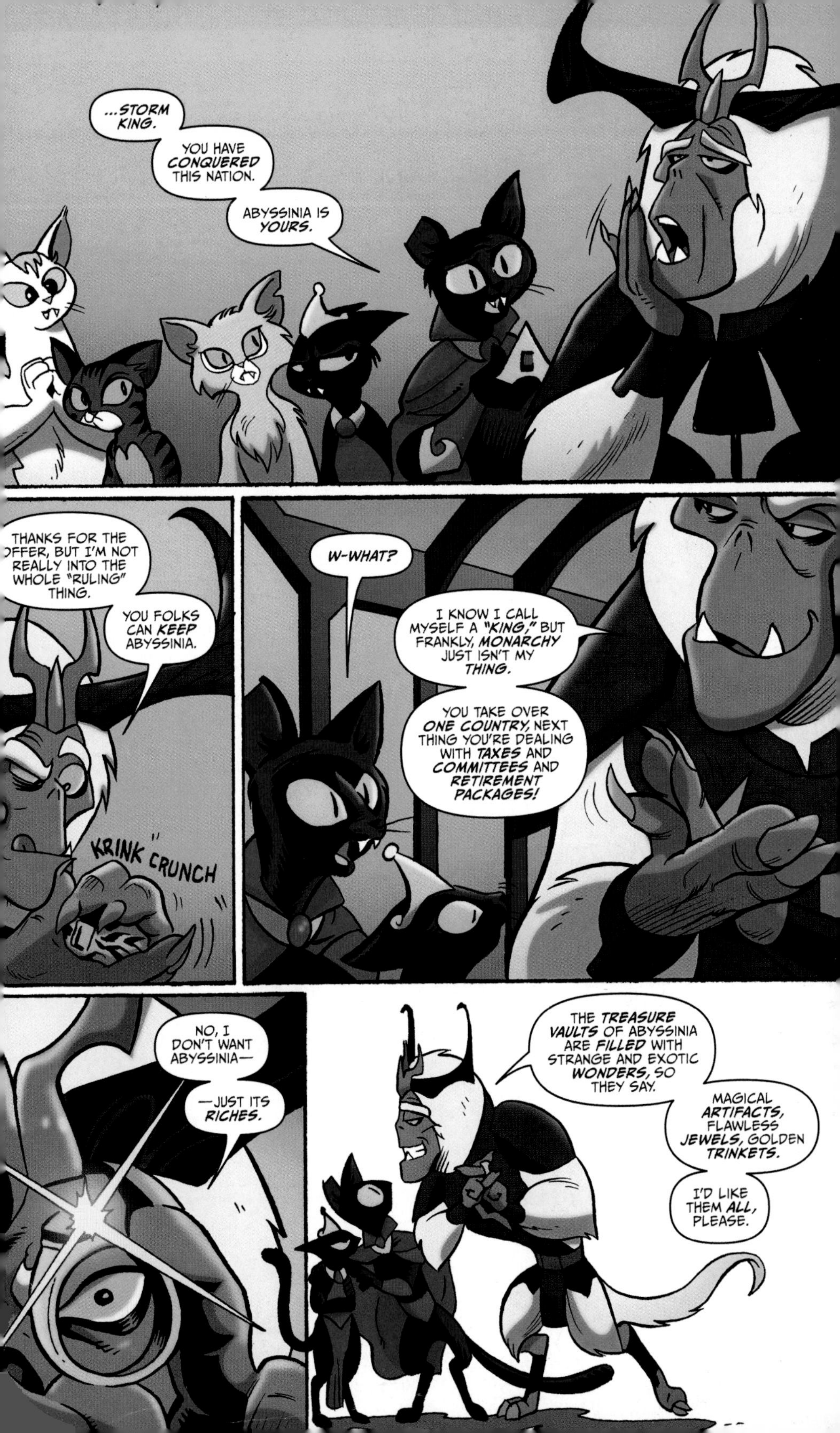
...STORM KING.
YOU HAVE CONQUERED THIS NATION.
ABYSSINIA IS YOURS.
THANKS FOR THE OFFER, BUT I'M NOT REALLY INTO THE WHOLE "RULING" THING.
YOU FOLKS CAN KEEP ABYSSINIA.
KRINK CRUNCH
W-WHAT?
I KNOW I CALL MYSELF A "KING," BUT FRANKLY, MONARCHY JUST ISN'T MY THING.
YOU TAKE OVER ONE COUNTRY, NEXT THING YOU'RE DEALING WITH TAXES AND COMMITTEES AND RETIREMENT PACKAGES!
NO, I DON'T WANT ABYSSINIA—
—JUST ITS RICHES.
THE TREASURE VAULTS OF ABYSSINIA ARE FILLED WITH STRANGE AND EXOTIC WONDERS, SO THEY SAY.
MAGICAL ARTIFACTS, FLAWLESS JEWELS, GOLDEN TRINKETS.
I'D LIKE THEM ALL, PLEASE.

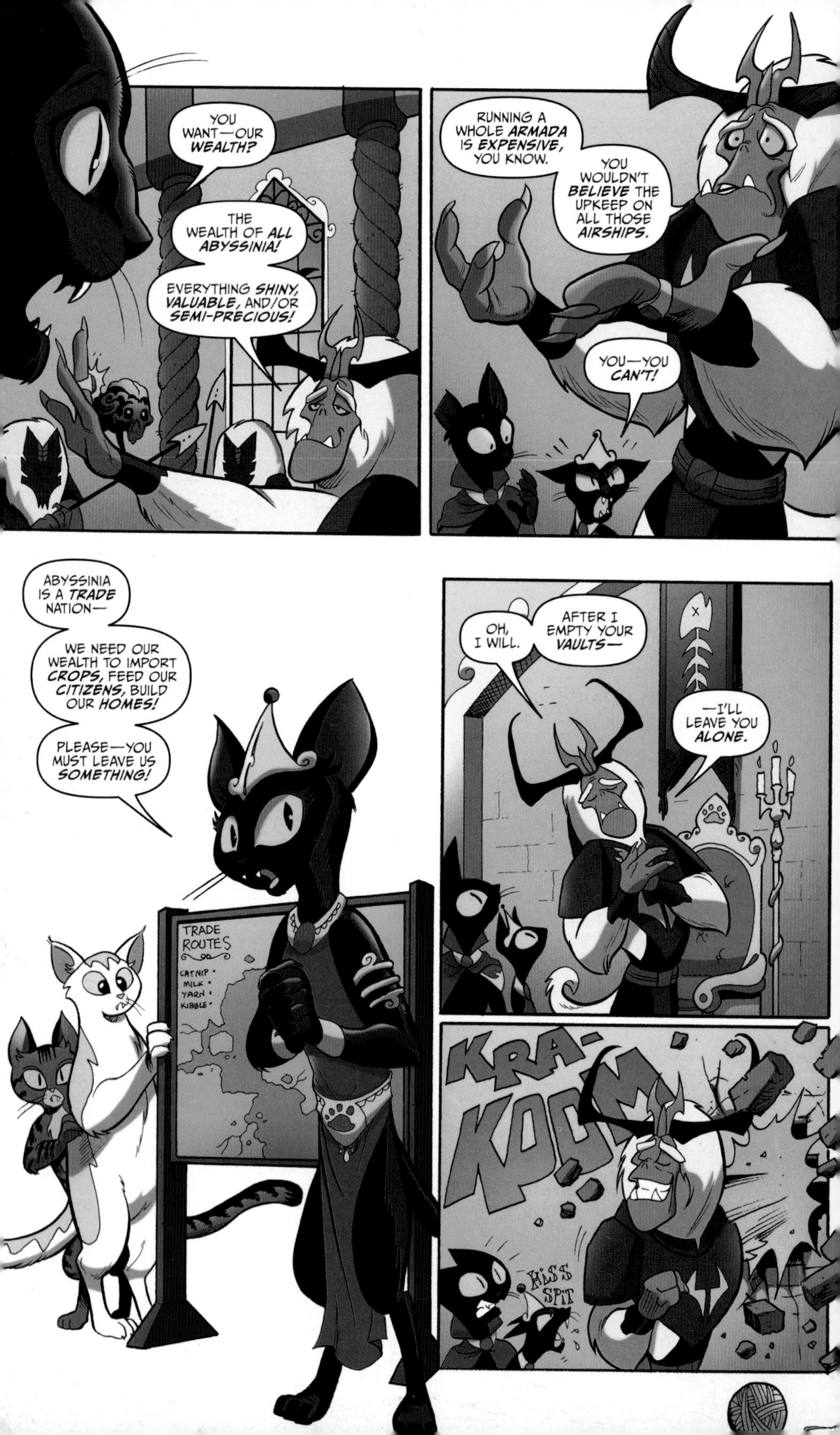
YOU WANT—OUR *WEALTH?*
THE WEALTH OF *ALL ABYSSINIA!*
EVERYTHING *SHINY, VALUABLE,* AND/OR *SEMI-PRECIOUS!*
RUNNING A WHOLE *ARMADA* IS *EXPENSIVE,* YOU KNOW.
YOU WOULDN'T *BELIEVE* THE UPKEEP ON ALL THOSE *AIRSHIPS.*
YOU—YOU *CAN'T!*
ABYSSINIA IS A *TRADE* NATION—
WE NEED OUR WEALTH TO IMPORT *CROPS,* FEED OUR *CITIZENS,* BUILD OUR *HOMES!*
PLEASE—YOU MUST LEAVE US *SOMETHING!*
TRADE ROUTES
CATNIP
MILK
YARN
KIBBLE
OH, I WILL.
AFTER I EMPTY YOUR *VAULTS*—
—I'LL LEAVE YOU *ALONE.*
KRA-KOOM
HISS
SPIT

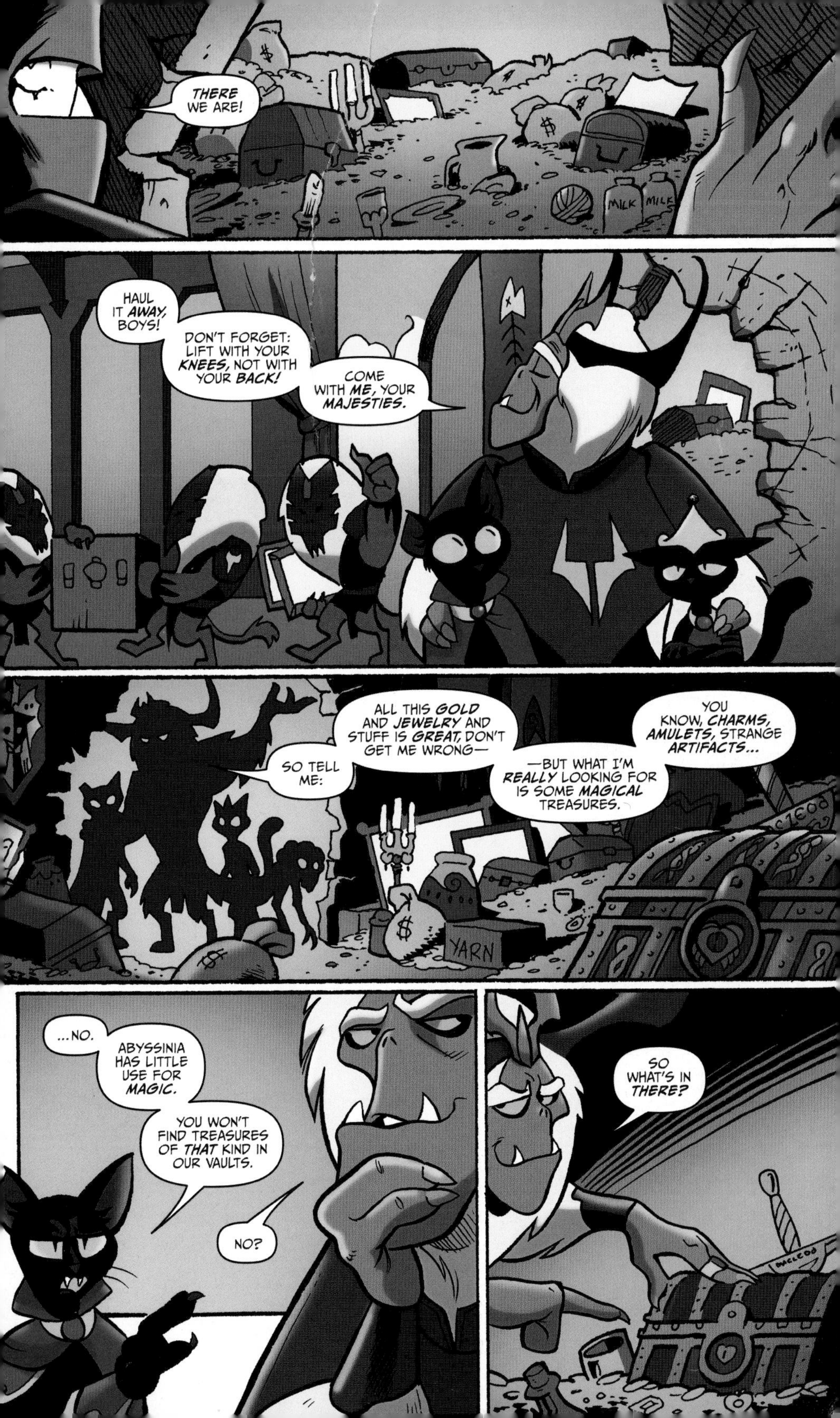
THERE WE ARE!
HAUL IT AWAY, BOYS!
DON'T FORGET: LIFT WITH YOUR KNEES, NOT WITH YOUR BACK!
COME WITH ME, YOUR MAJESTIES.
SO TELL ME:
ALL THIS GOLD AND JEWELRY AND STUFF IS GREAT, DON'T GET ME WRONG—
—BUT WHAT I'M REALLY LOOKING FOR IS SOME MAGICAL TREASURES.
YOU KNOW, CHARMS, AMULETS, STRANGE ARTIFACTS...
YARN
...NO.
ABYSSINIA HAS LITTLE USE FOR MAGIC.
YOU WON'T FIND TREASURES OF THAT KIND IN OUR VAULTS.
NO?
SO WHAT'S IN THERE?

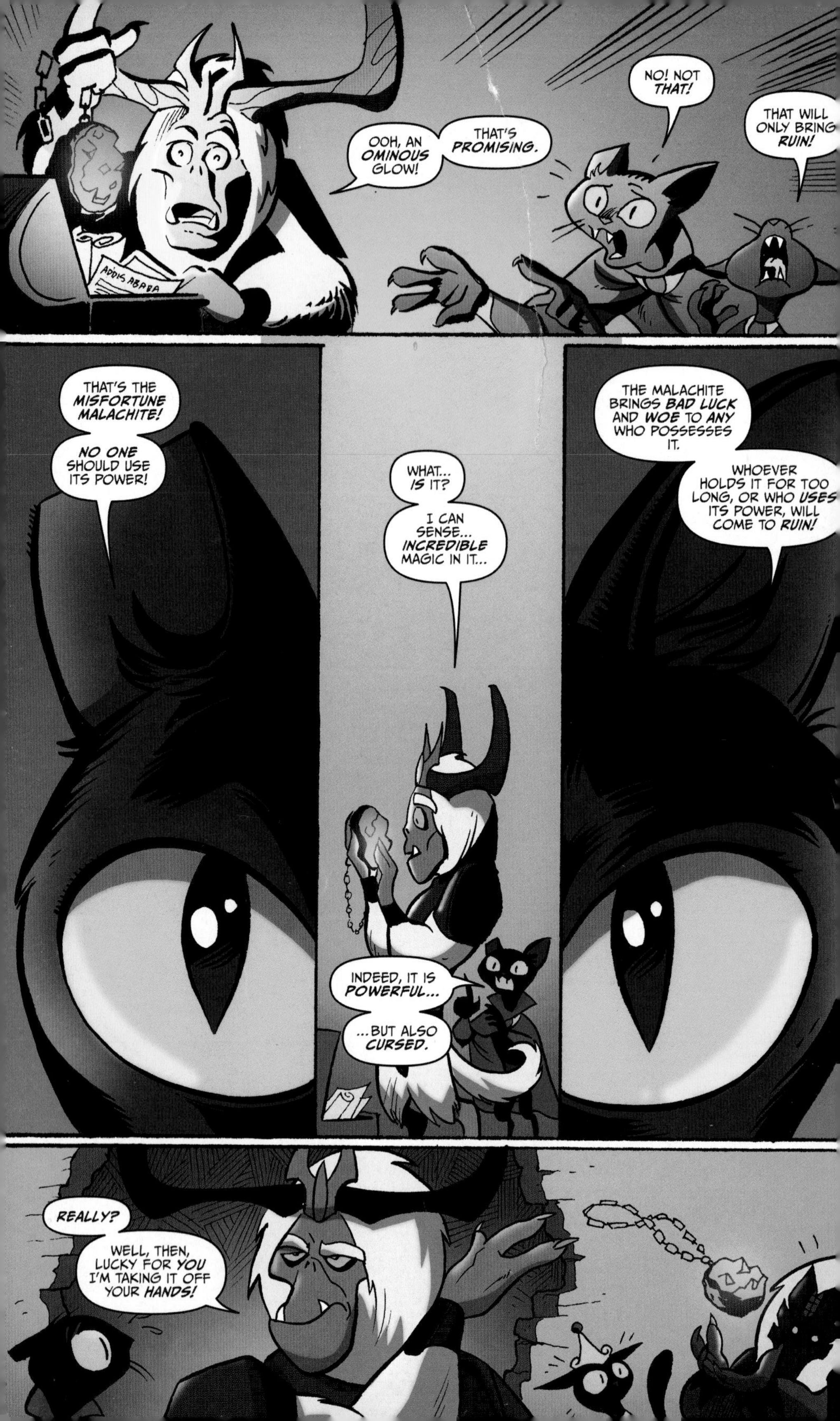

ADDIS ABABA
OOH, AN OMINOUS GLOW!
THAT'S PROMISING.
NO! NOT THAT!
THAT WILL ONLY BRING RUIN!
THAT'S THE MISFORTUNE MALACHITE!
NO ONE SHOULD USE ITS POWER!
WHAT... IS IT?
I CAN SENSE... INCREDIBLE MAGIC IN IT...
INDEED, IT IS POWERFUL...
...BUT ALSO CURSED.
THE MALACHITE BRINGS BAD LUCK AND WOE TO ANY WHO POSSESSES IT.
WHOEVER HOLDS IT FOR TOO LONG, OR WHO USES ITS POWER, WILL COME TO RUIN!
REALLY?
WELL, THEN, LUCKY FOR YOU I'M TAKING IT OFF YOUR HANDS!

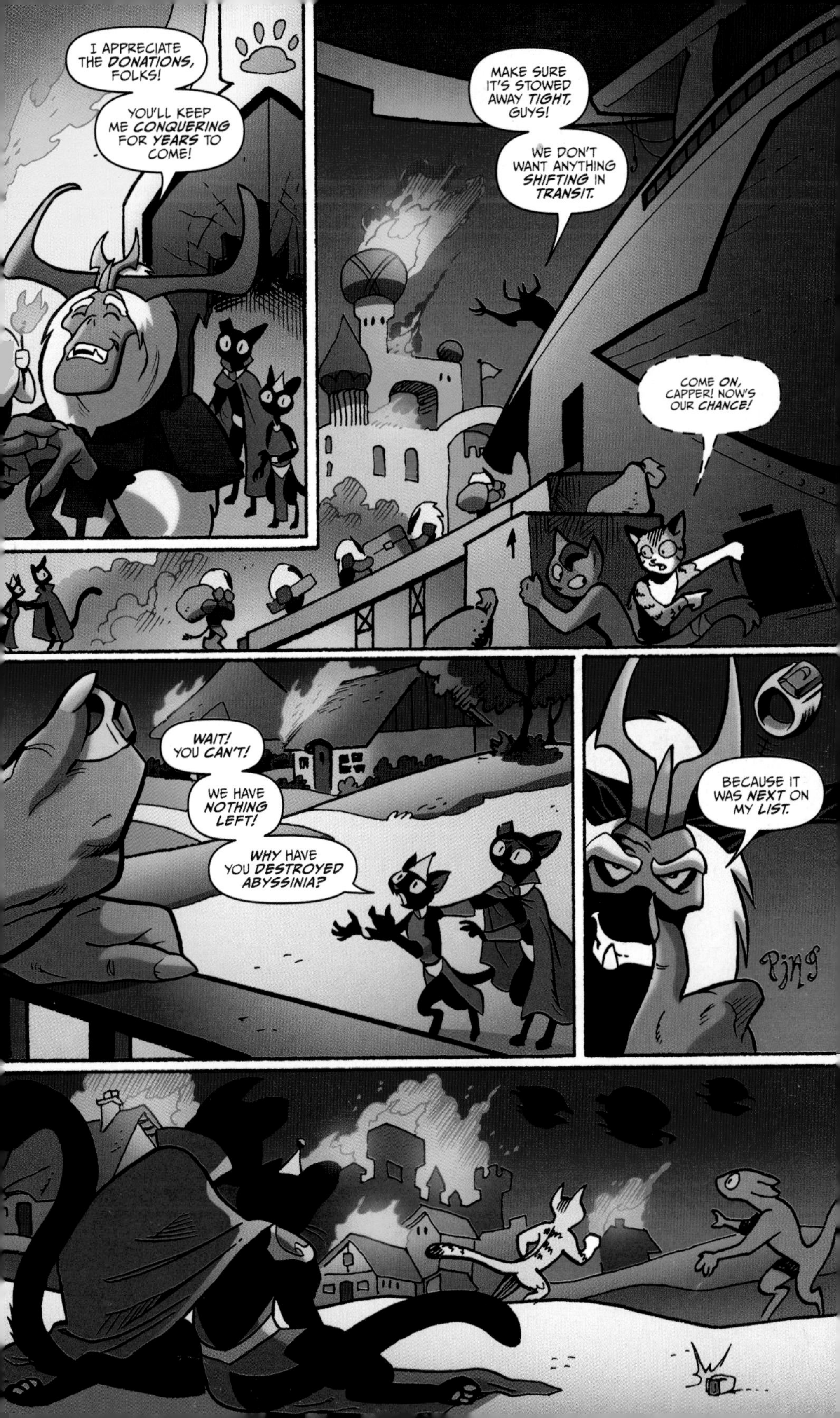
I APPRECIATE THE DONATIONS, FOLKS!
YOU'LL KEEP ME CONQUERING FOR YEARS TO COME!
MAKE SURE IT'S STOWED AWAY TIGHT, GUYS!
WE DON'T WANT ANYTHING SHIFTING IN TRANSIT.
COME ON, CAPPER! NOW'S OUR CHANCE!
WAIT! YOU CAN'T!
WE HAVE NOTHING LEFT!
WHY HAVE YOU DESTROYED ABYSSINIA?
BECAUSE IT WAS NEXT ON MY LIST.
PING

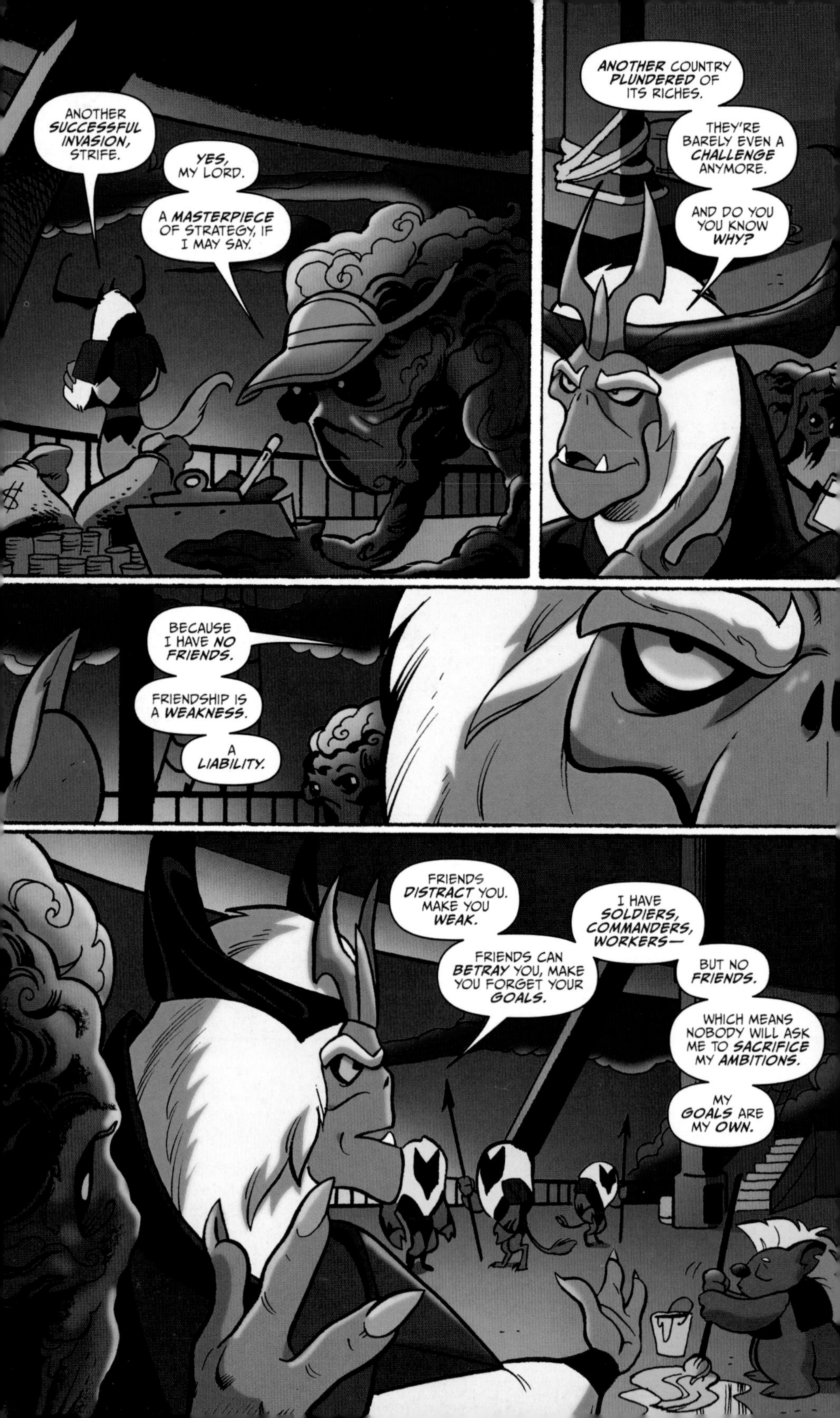
ANOTHER SUCCESSFUL INVASION, STRIFE.
YES, MY LORD.
A MASTERPIECE OF STRATEGY, IF I MAY SAY.
ANOTHER COUNTRY PLUNDERED OF ITS RICHES.
THEY'RE BARELY EVEN A CHALLENGE ANYMORE.
AND DO YOU YOU KNOW WHY?
BECAUSE I HAVE NO FRIENDS.
FRIENDSHIP IS A WEAKNESS.
A LIABILITY.
FRIENDS DISTRACT YOU. MAKE YOU WEAK.
FRIENDS CAN BETRAY YOU, MAKE YOU FORGET YOUR GOALS.
I HAVE SOLDIERS, COMMANDERS, WORKERS—
BUT NO FRIENDS.
WHICH MEANS NOBODY WILL ASK ME TO SACRIFICE MY AMBITIONS.
MY GOALS ARE MY OWN.

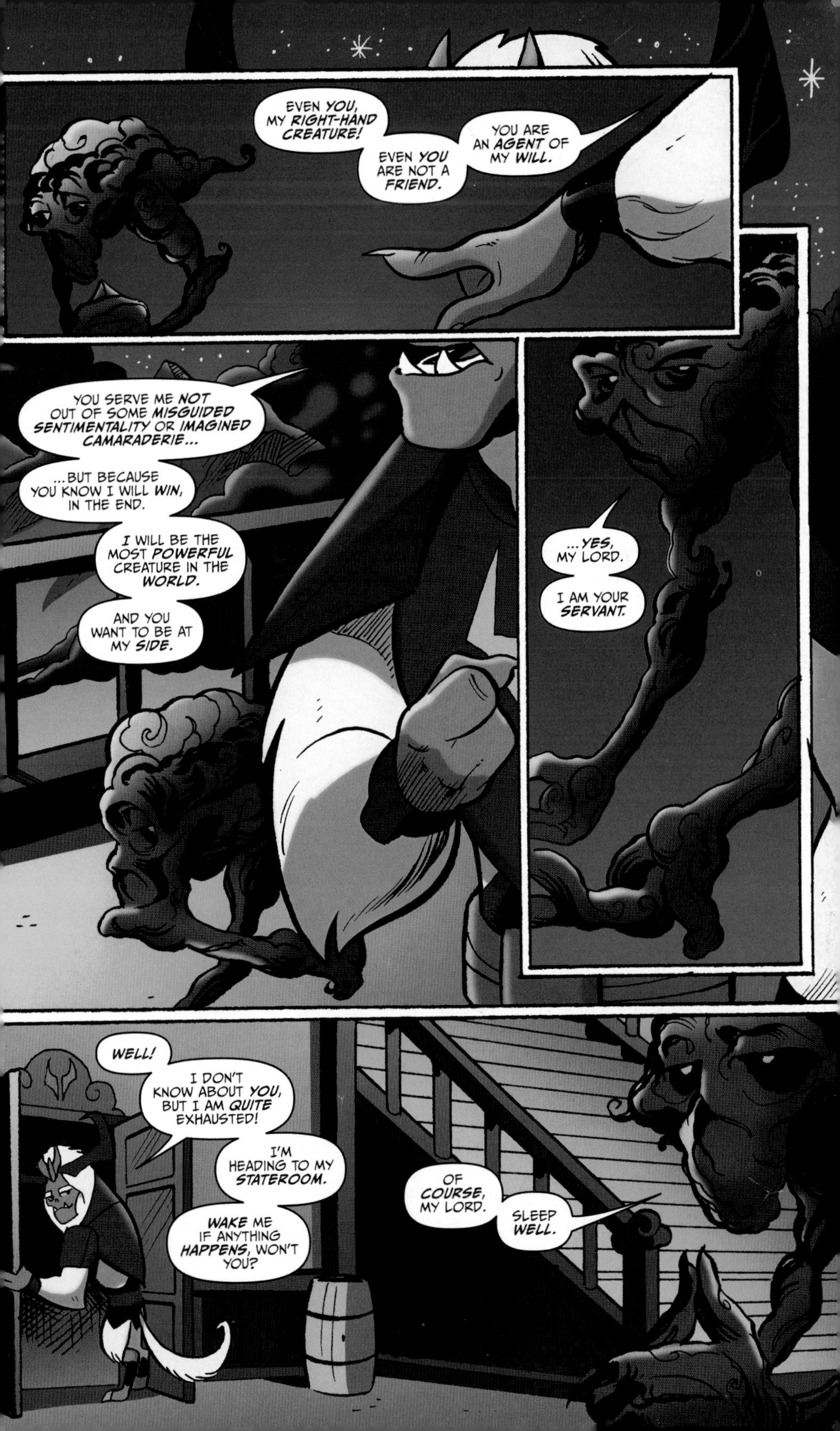
EVEN YOU, MY RIGHT-HAND CREATURE!
EVEN YOU ARE NOT A FRIEND.
YOU ARE AN AGENT OF MY WILL.
YOU SERVE ME NOT OUT OF SOME MISGUIDED SENTIMENTALITY OR IMAGINED CAMARADERIE...
...BUT BECAUSE YOU KNOW I WILL WIN, IN THE END.
I WILL BE THE MOST POWERFUL CREATURE IN THE WORLD.
AND YOU WANT TO BE AT MY SIDE.
...YES, MY LORD.
I AM YOUR SERVANT.
WELL!
I DON'T KNOW ABOUT YOU, BUT I AM QUITE EXHAUSTED!
I'M HEADING TO MY STATEROOM.
WAKE ME IF ANYTHING HAPPENS, WON'T YOU?
OF COURSE, MY LORD.
SLEEP WELL.

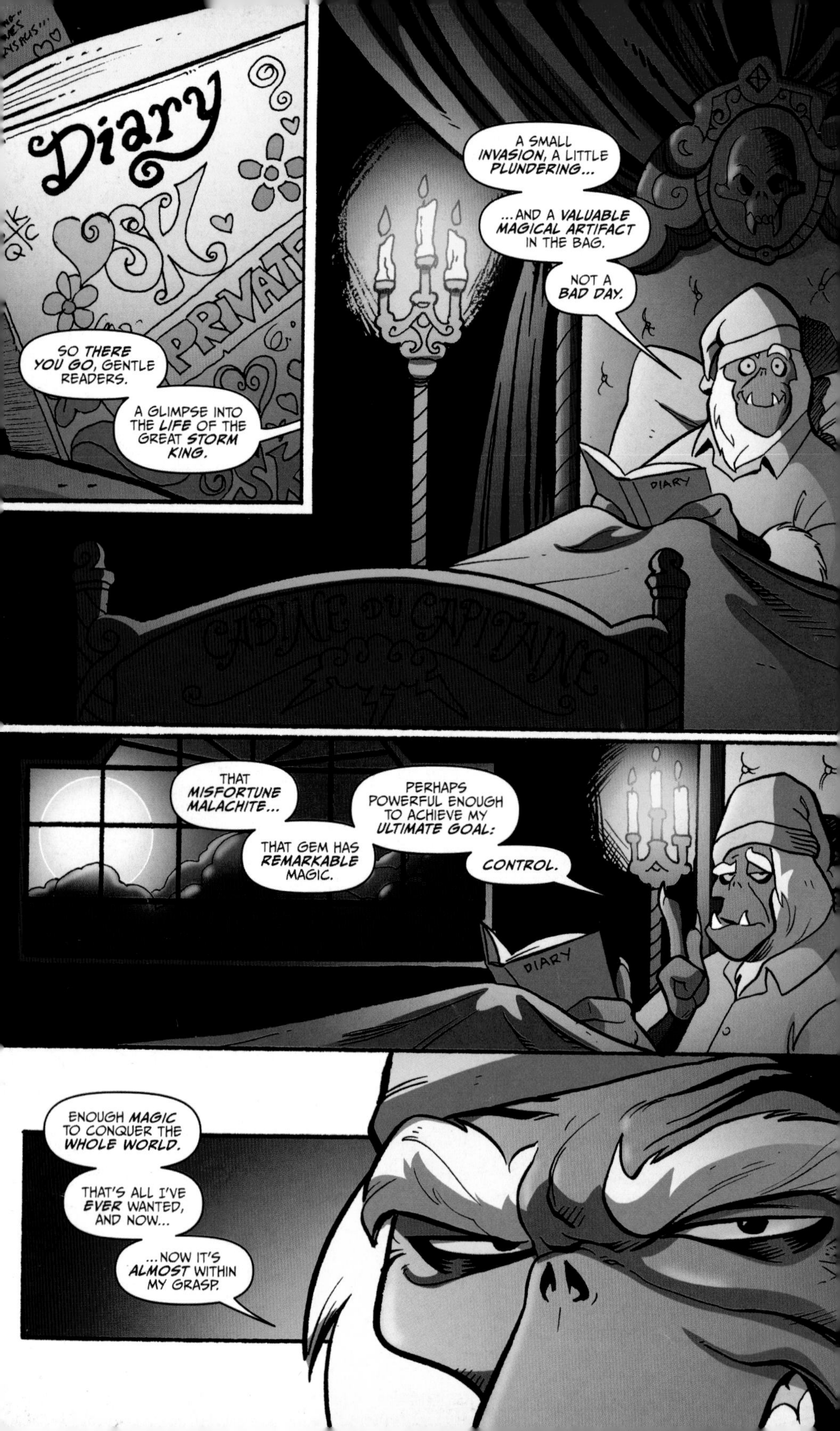

Diary
SK
PRIVATE
SO THERE YOU GO, GENTLE READERS.
A GLIMPSE INTO THE LIFE OF THE GREAT STORM KING.
A SMALL INVASION, A LITTLE PLUNDERING...
...AND A VALUABLE MAGICAL ARTIFACT IN THE BAG.
NOT A BAD DAY.
DIARY
CABINE DU CAPITAINE
THAT MISFORTUNE MALACHITE...
THAT GEM HAS REMARKABLE MAGIC.
PERHAPS POWERFUL ENOUGH TO ACHIEVE MY ULTIMATE GOAL:
CONTROL.
DIARY
ENOUGH MAGIC TO CONQUER THE WHOLE WORLD.
THAT'S ALL I'VE EVER WANTED, AND NOW...
...NOW IT'S ALMOST WITHIN MY GRASP.

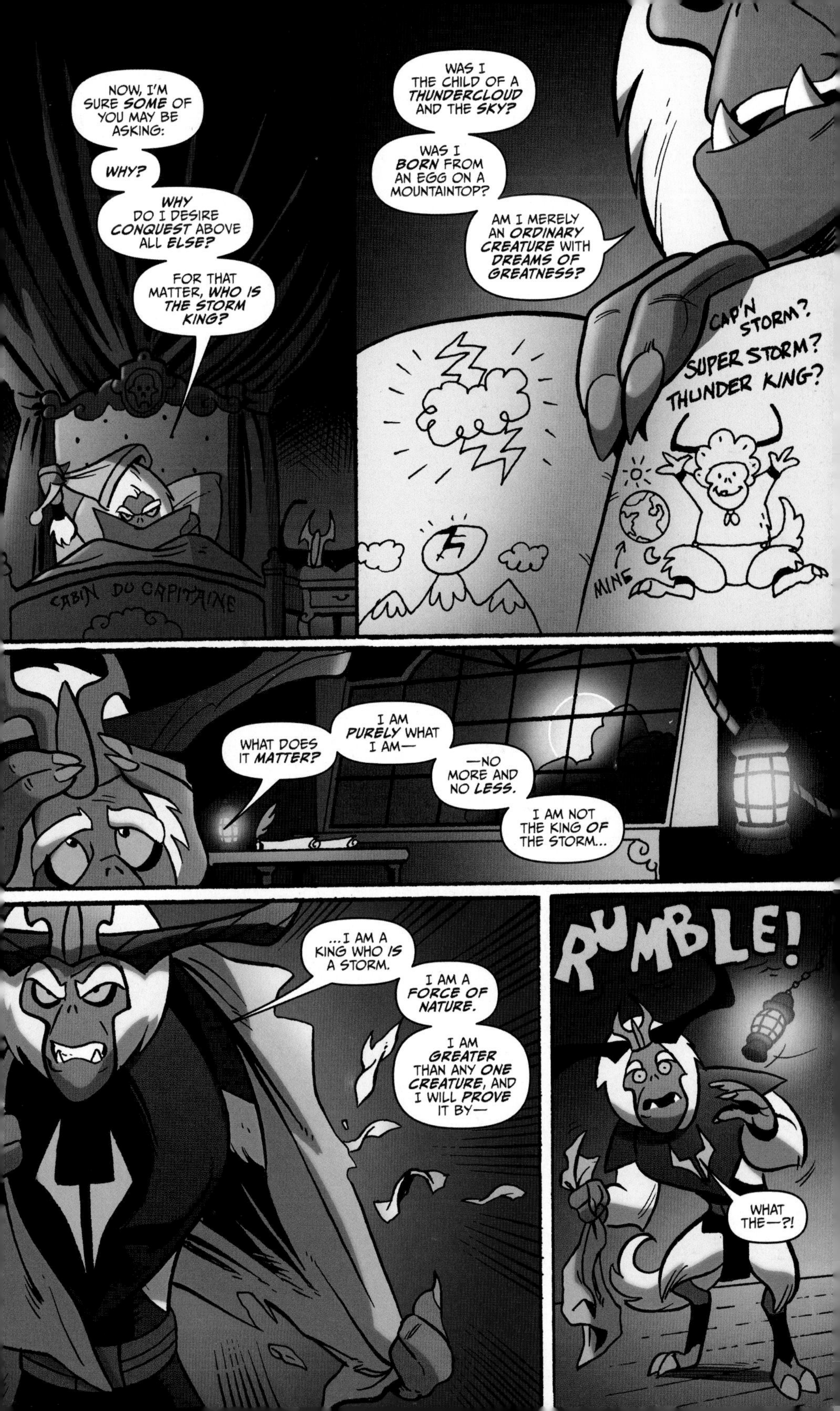
NOW, I'M SURE SOME OF YOU MAY BE ASKING:
WHY?
WHY DO I DESIRE CONQUEST ABOVE ALL ELSE?
FOR THAT MATTER, WHO IS THE STORM KING?
CABIN DU CAPITAINE
WAS I THE CHILD OF A THUNDERCLOUD AND THE SKY?
WAS I BORN FROM AN EGG ON A MOUNTAINTOP?
AM I MERELY AN ORDINARY CREATURE WITH DREAMS OF GREATNESS?
CAP'N STORM?
SUPER STORM?
THUNDER KING?
MINE
WHAT DOES IT MATTER?
I AM PURELY WHAT I AM—
—NO MORE AND NO LESS.
I AM NOT THE KING OF THE STORM...
...I AM A KING WHO IS A STORM.
I AM A FORCE OF NATURE.
I AM GREATER THAN ANY ONE CREATURE, AND I WILL PROVE IT BY—
RUMBLE!
WHAT THE—?!

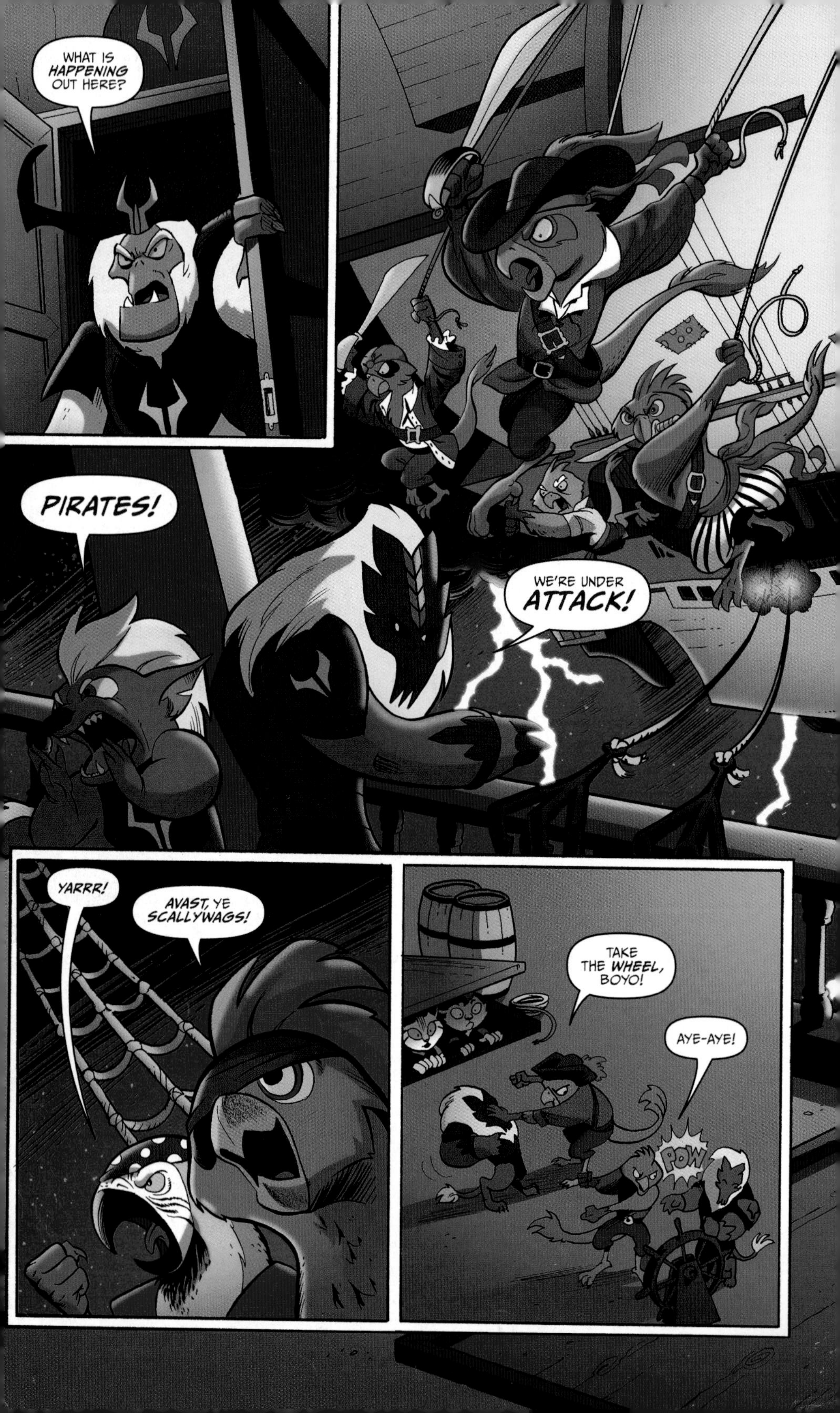
WHAT IS HAPPENING OUT HERE?
PIRATES!
WE'RE UNDER ATTACK!
YARRR!
AVAST, YE SCALLYWAGS!
TAKE THE WHEEL, BOYO!
AYE-AYE!
POW

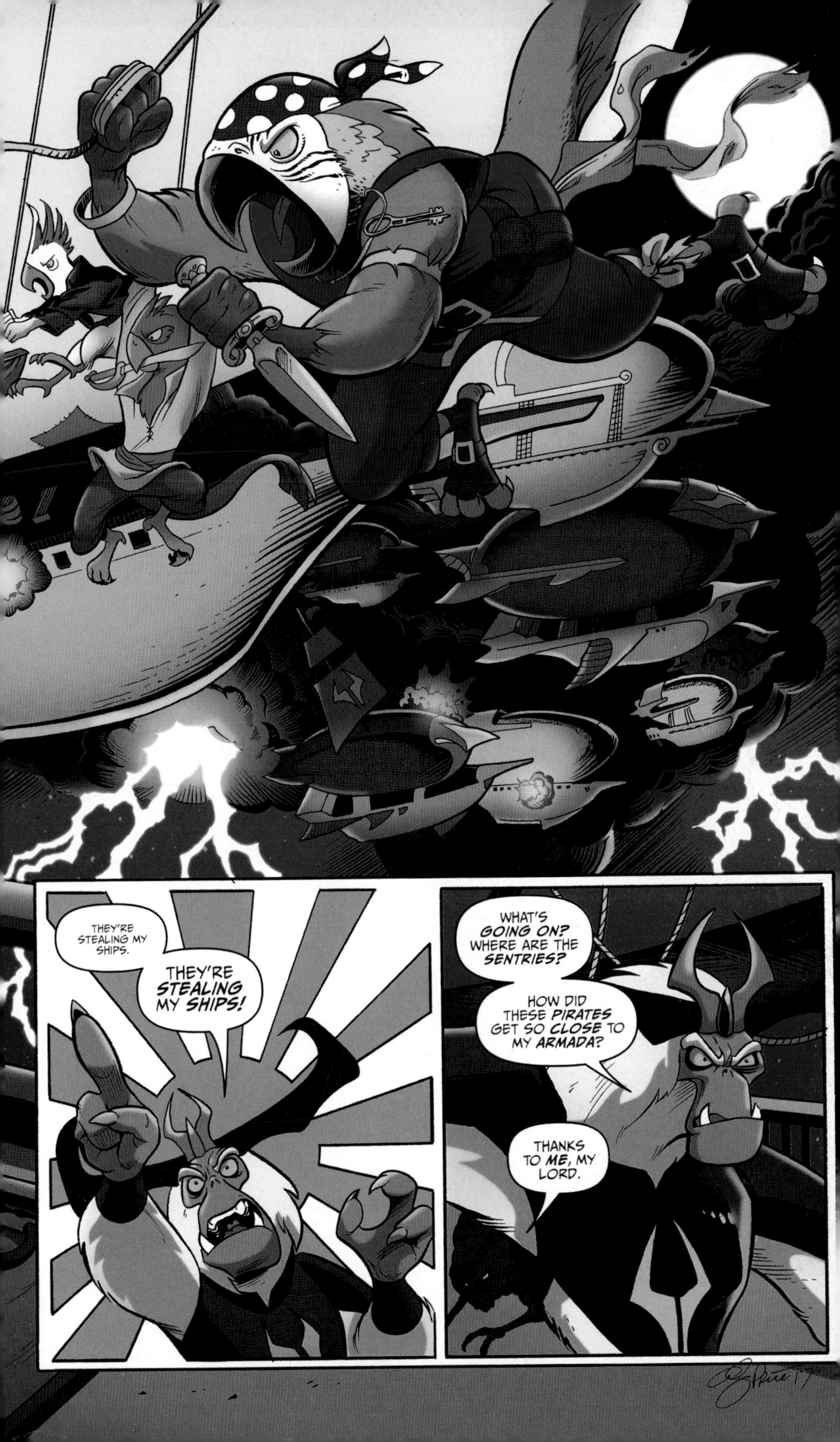

THEY'RE STEALING MY SHIPS.
THEY'RE STEALING MY SHIPS!
WHAT'S GOING ON? WHERE ARE THE SENTRIES?
HOW DID THESE PIRATES GET SO CLOSE TO MY ARMADA?
THANKS TO ME, MY LORD.

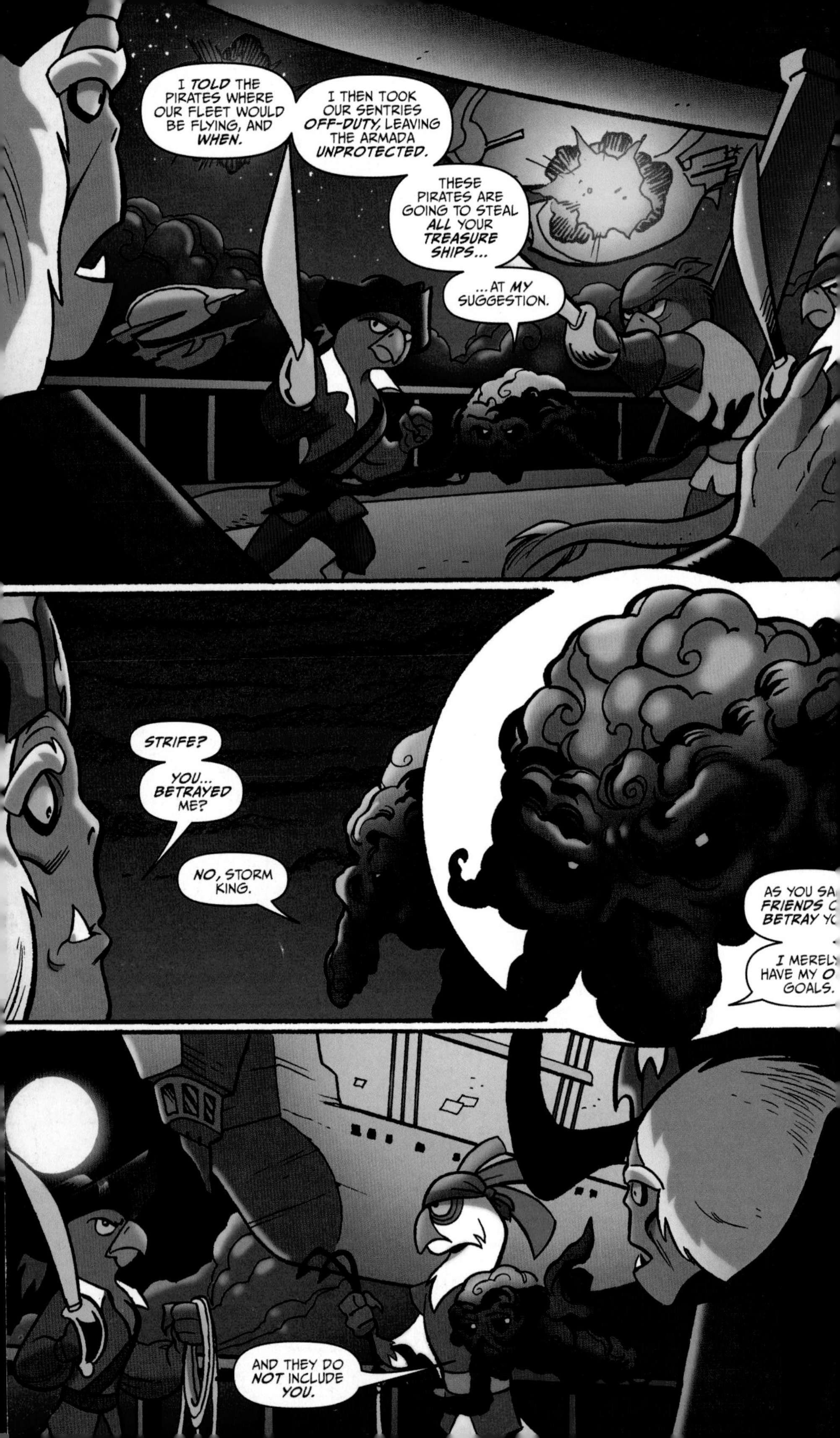
I TOLD THE PIRATES WHERE OUR FLEET WOULD BE FLYING, AND WHEN.
I THEN TOOK OUR SENTRIES OFF-DUTY, LEAVING THE ARMADA UNPROTECTED.
THESE PIRATES ARE GOING TO STEAL ALL YOUR TREASURE SHIPS...
...AT MY SUGGESTION.
STRIFE?
YOU... BETRAYED ME?
NO, STORM KING.
AS YOU SA FRIENDS C BETRAY YO
I MEREL HAVE MY O GOALS.
AND THEY DO NOT INCLUDE YOU.

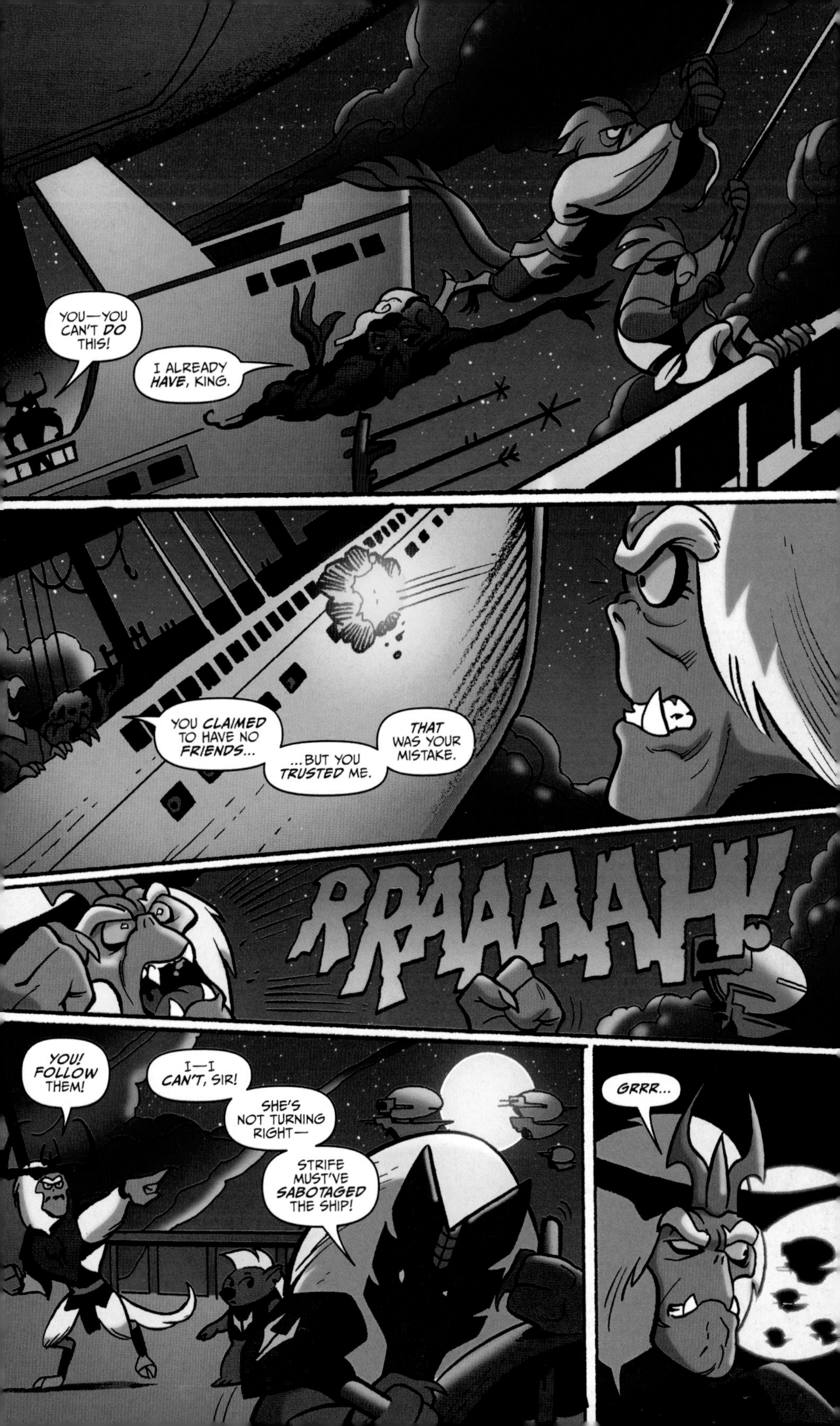
YOU—YOU CAN'T DO THIS!
I ALREADY HAVE, KING.
YOU CLAIMED TO HAVE NO FRIENDS...
...BUT YOU TRUSTED ME.
THAT WAS YOUR MISTAKE.
RRAAAAH!
YOU! FOLLOW THEM!
I—I CAN'T, SIR!
SHE'S NOT TURNING RIGHT—
STRIFE MUST'VE SABOTAGED THE SHIP!
GRRR...

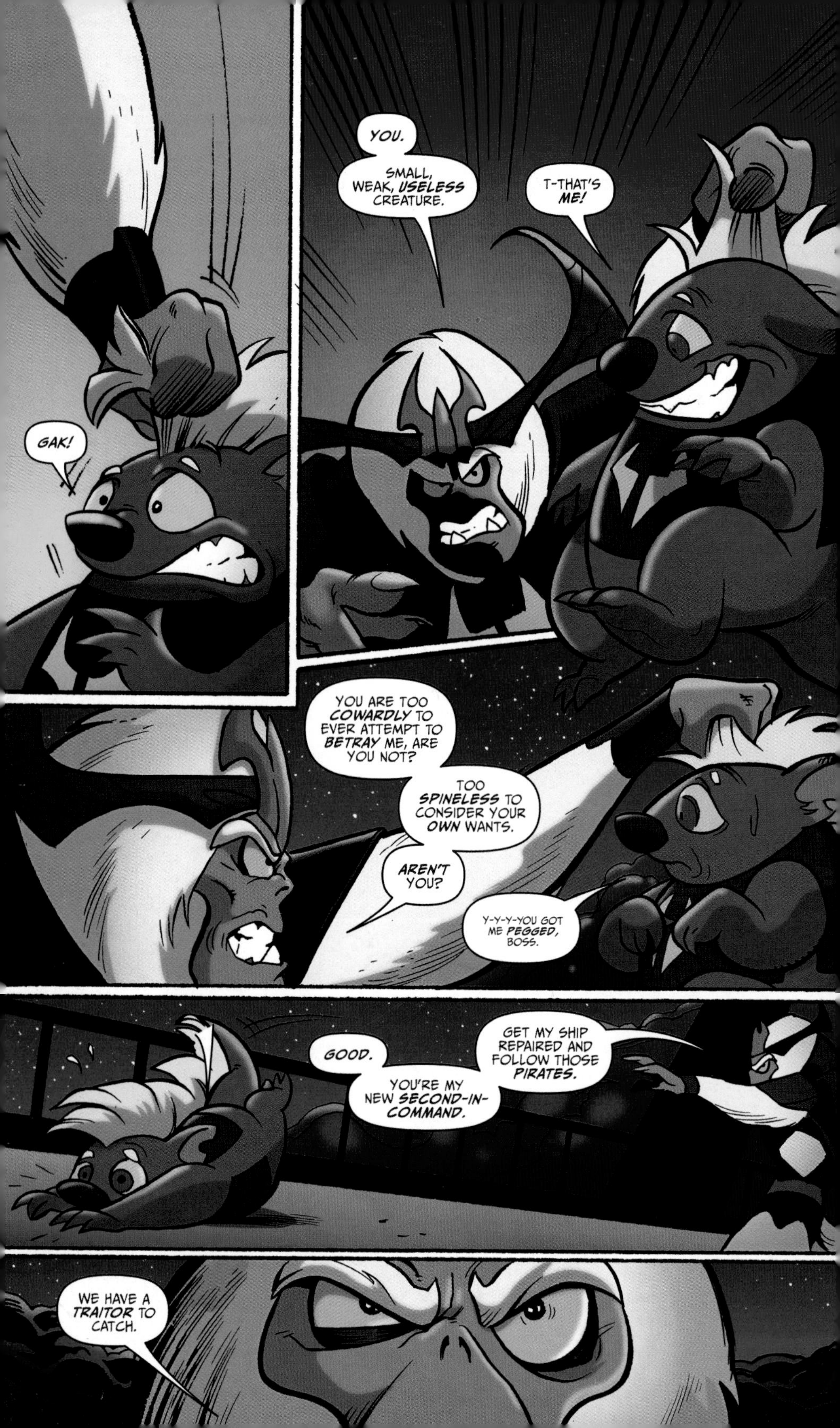
GAK!
YOU.
SMALL, WEAK, USELESS CREATURE.
T-THAT'S ME!
YOU ARE TOO COWARDLY TO EVER ATTEMPT TO BETRAY ME, ARE YOU NOT?
TOO SPINELESS TO CONSIDER YOUR OWN WANTS.
AREN'T YOU?
Y-Y-Y-YOU GOT ME PEGGED, BOSS.
GOOD.
YOU'RE MY NEW SECOND-IN-COMMAND.
GET MY SHIP REPAIRED AND FOLLOW THOSE PIRATES.
WE HAVE A TRAITOR TO CATCH.

Art by TONY FLEECS

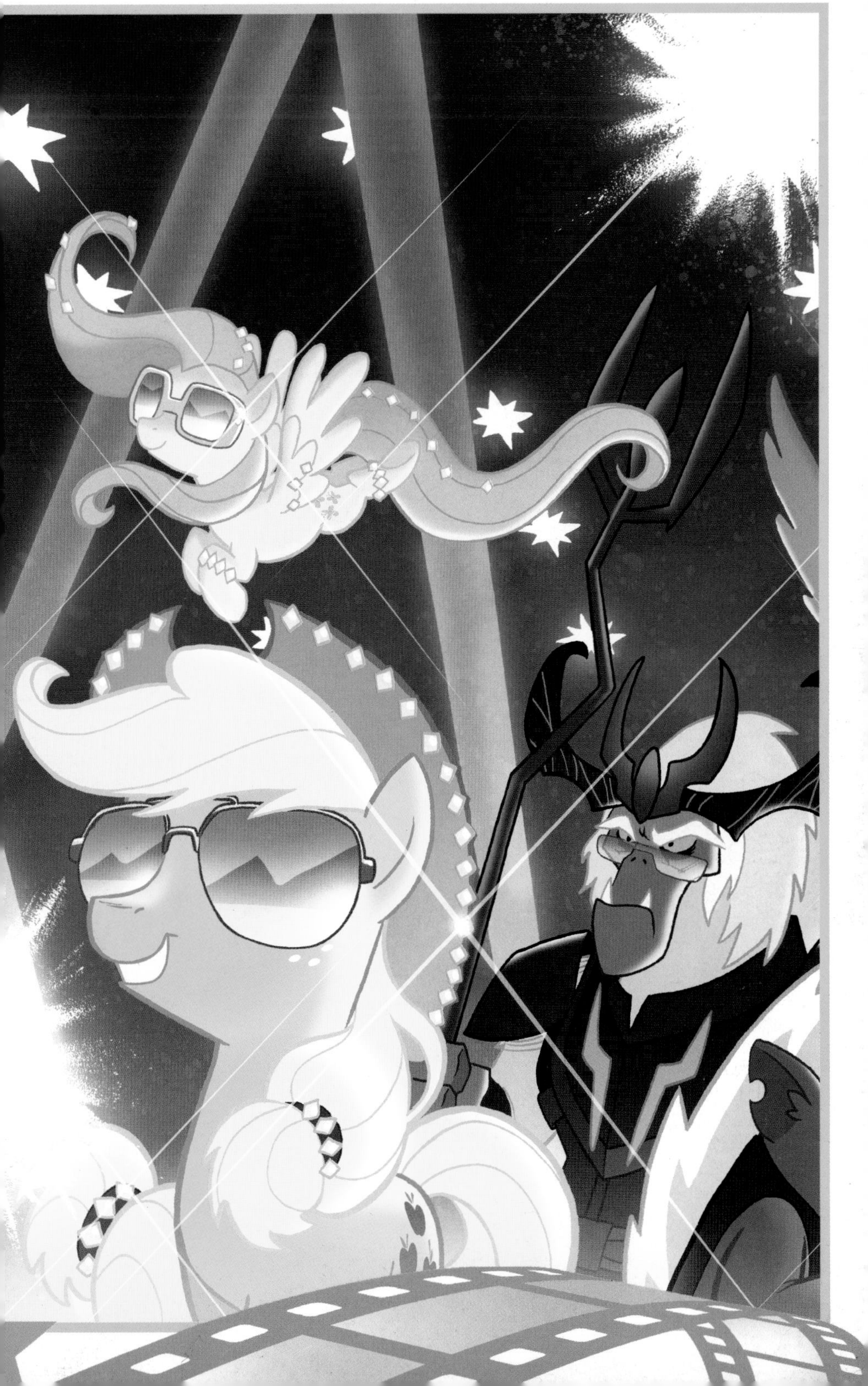

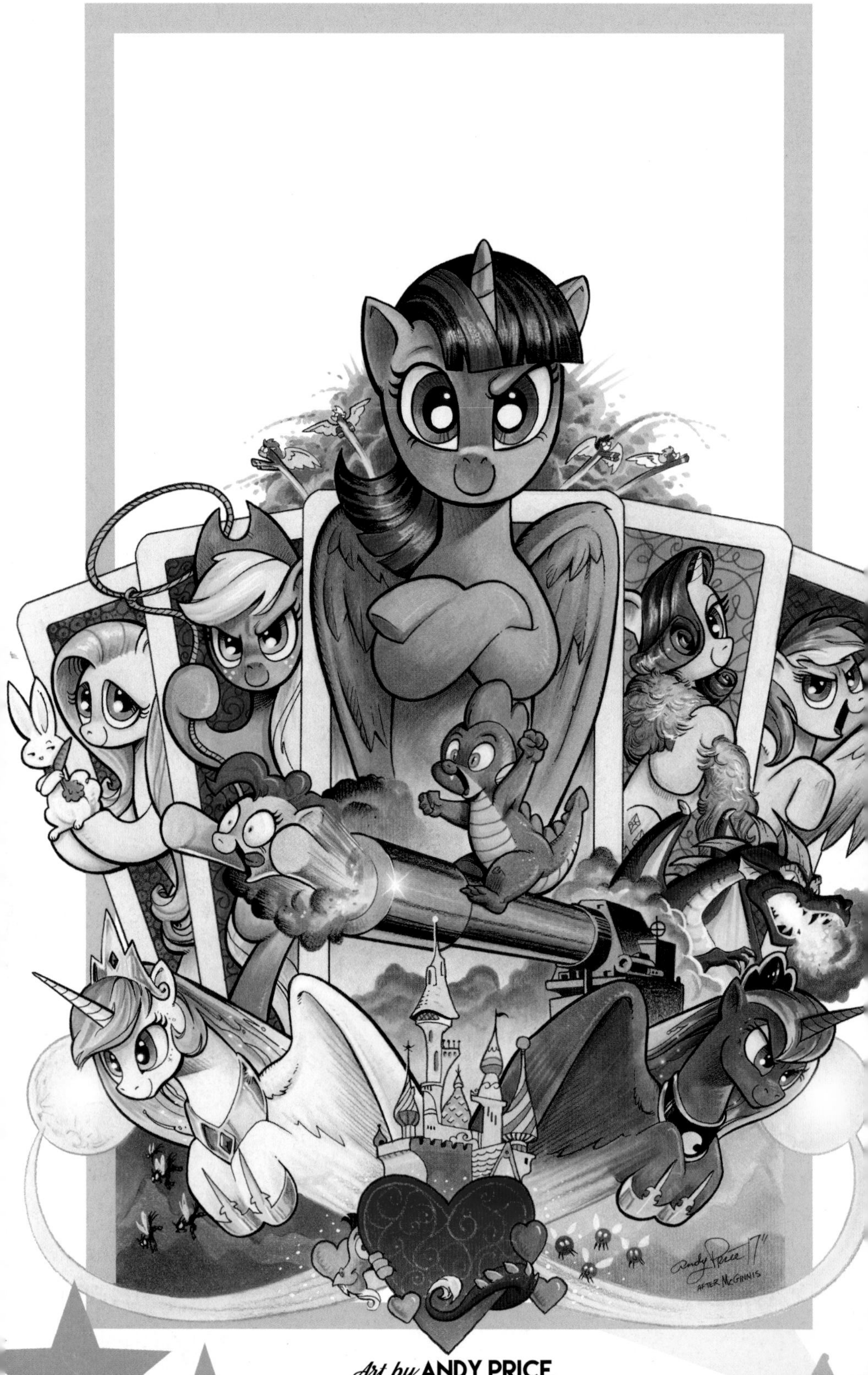
Andy Price '17
AFTER McGINNIS

Art by **ANDY PRICE**

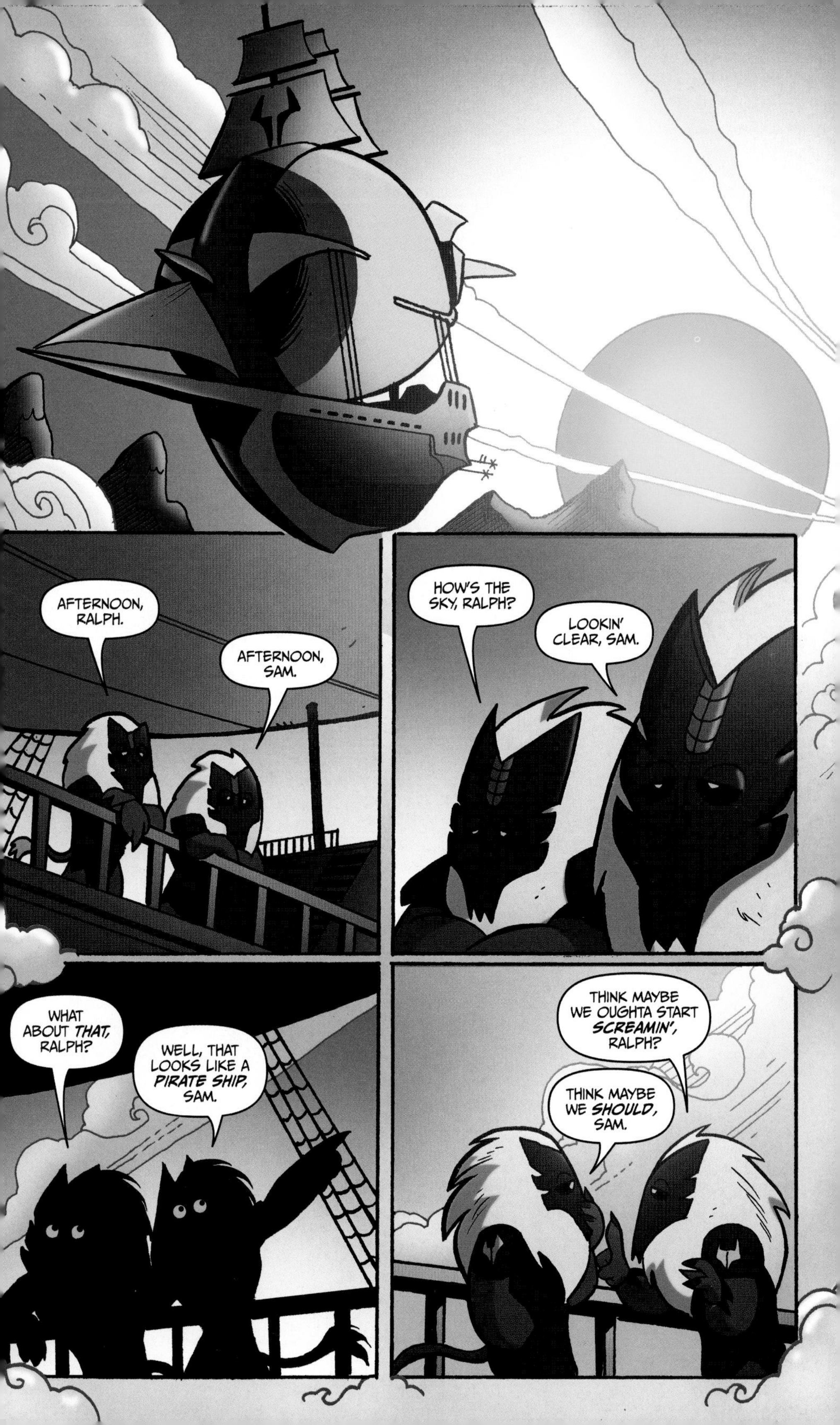
AFTERNOON, RALPH.
AFTERNOON, SAM.
HOW'S THE SKY, RALPH?
LOOKIN' CLEAR, SAM.
WHAT ABOUT *THAT,* RALPH?
WELL, THAT LOOKS LIKE A *PIRATE SHIP,* SAM.
THINK MAYBE WE OUGHTA START *SCREAMIN',* RALPH?
THINK MAYBE WE *SHOULD,* SAM.

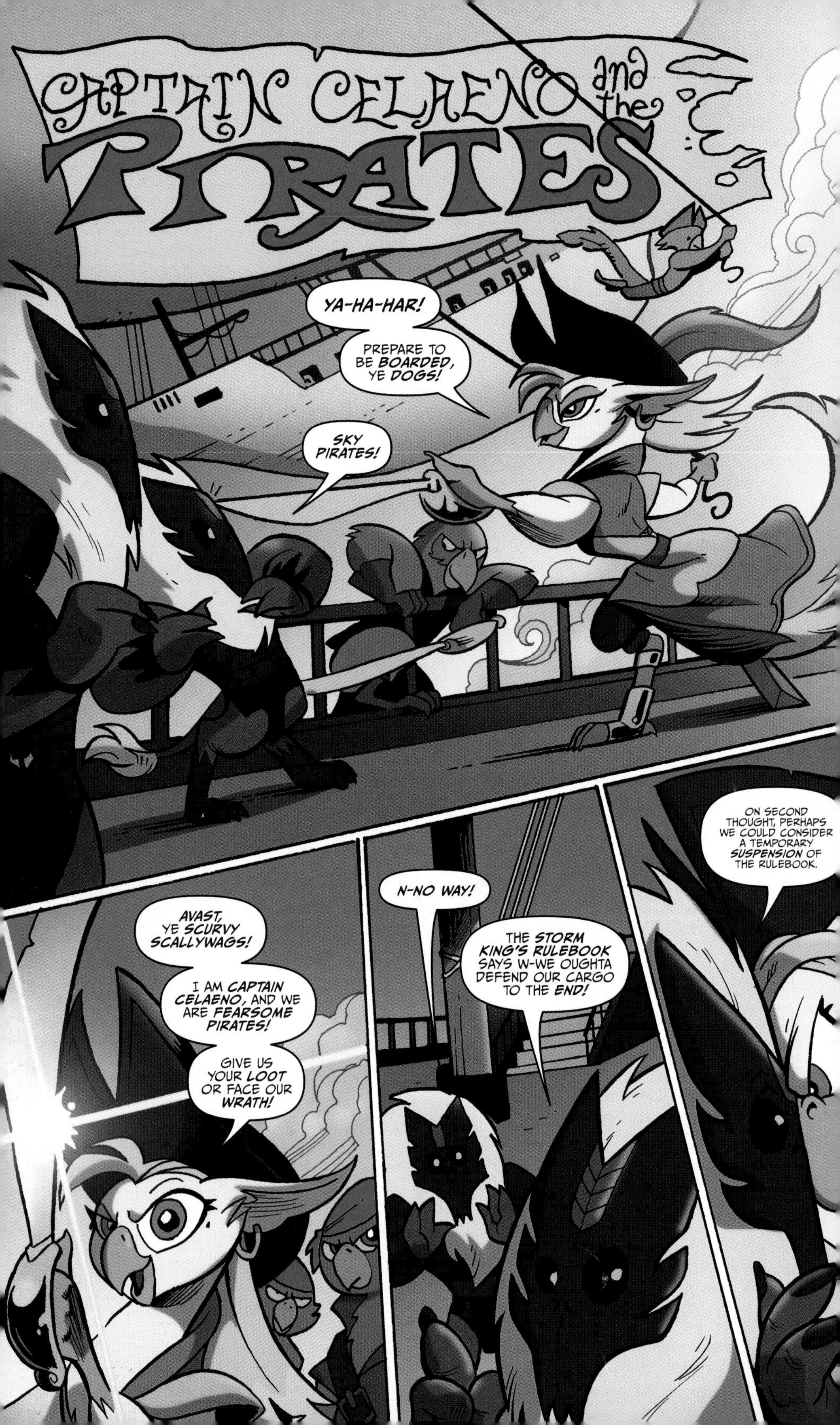
CAPTAIN CELAENO and the PIRATES
YA-HA-HAR!
PREPARE TO BE BOARDED, YE DOGS!
SKY PIRATES!
AVAST, YE SCURVY SCALLYWAGS!
I AM CAPTAIN CELAENO, AND WE ARE FEARSOME PIRATES!
GIVE US YOUR LOOT OR FACE OUR WRATH!
N-NO WAY!
THE STORM KING'S RULEBOOK SAYS W-WE OUGHTA DEFEND OUR CARGO TO THE END!
ON SECOND THOUGHT, PERHAPS WE COULD CONSIDER A TEMPORARY SUSPENSION OF THE RULEBOOK.

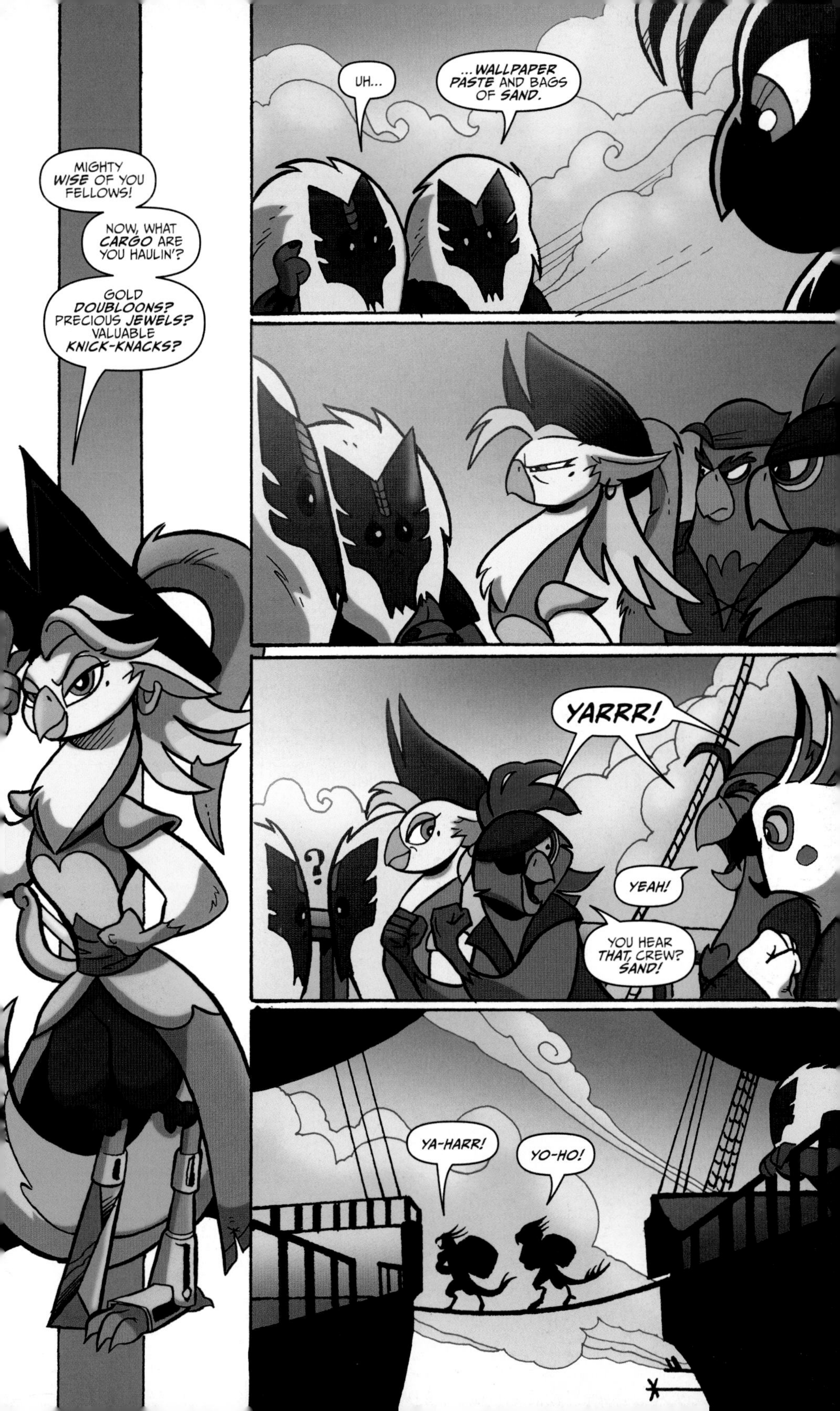
MIGHTY WISE OF YOU FELLOWS!
NOW, WHAT CARGO ARE YOU HAULIN'?
GOLD DOUBLOONS? PRECIOUS JEWELS? VALUABLE KNICK-KNACKS?
UH...
...WALLPAPER PASTE AND BAGS OF SAND.
YARRR!
YEAH!
YOU HEAR THAT, CREW? SAND!
YA-HARR!
YO-HO!

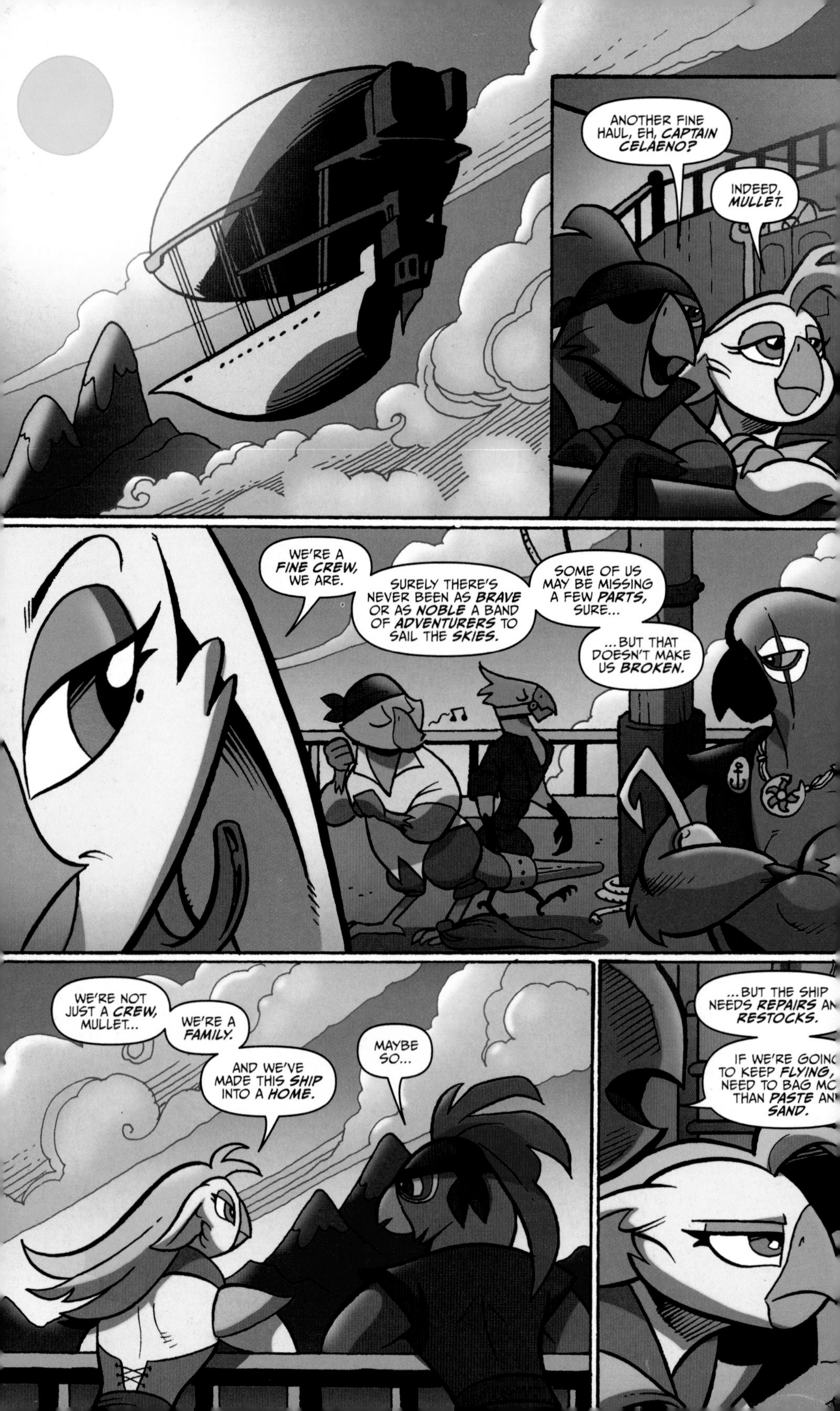

ANOTHER FINE HAUL, EH, CAPTAIN CELAENO?
INDEED, MULLET.
WE'RE A FINE CREW, WE ARE.
SURELY THERE'S NEVER BEEN AS BRAVE OR AS NOBLE A BAND OF ADVENTURERS TO SAIL THE SKIES.
SOME OF US MAY BE MISSING A FEW PARTS, SURE...
...BUT THAT DOESN'T MAKE US BROKEN.
WE'RE NOT JUST A CREW, MULLET...
WE'RE A FAMILY.
AND WE'VE MADE THIS SHIP INTO A HOME.
MAYBE SO...
...BUT THE SHIP NEEDS REPAIRS AN
RESTOCKS.
IF WE'RE GOIN
TO KEEP FLYING,
NEED TO BAG MO
THAN PASTE AN
SAND.

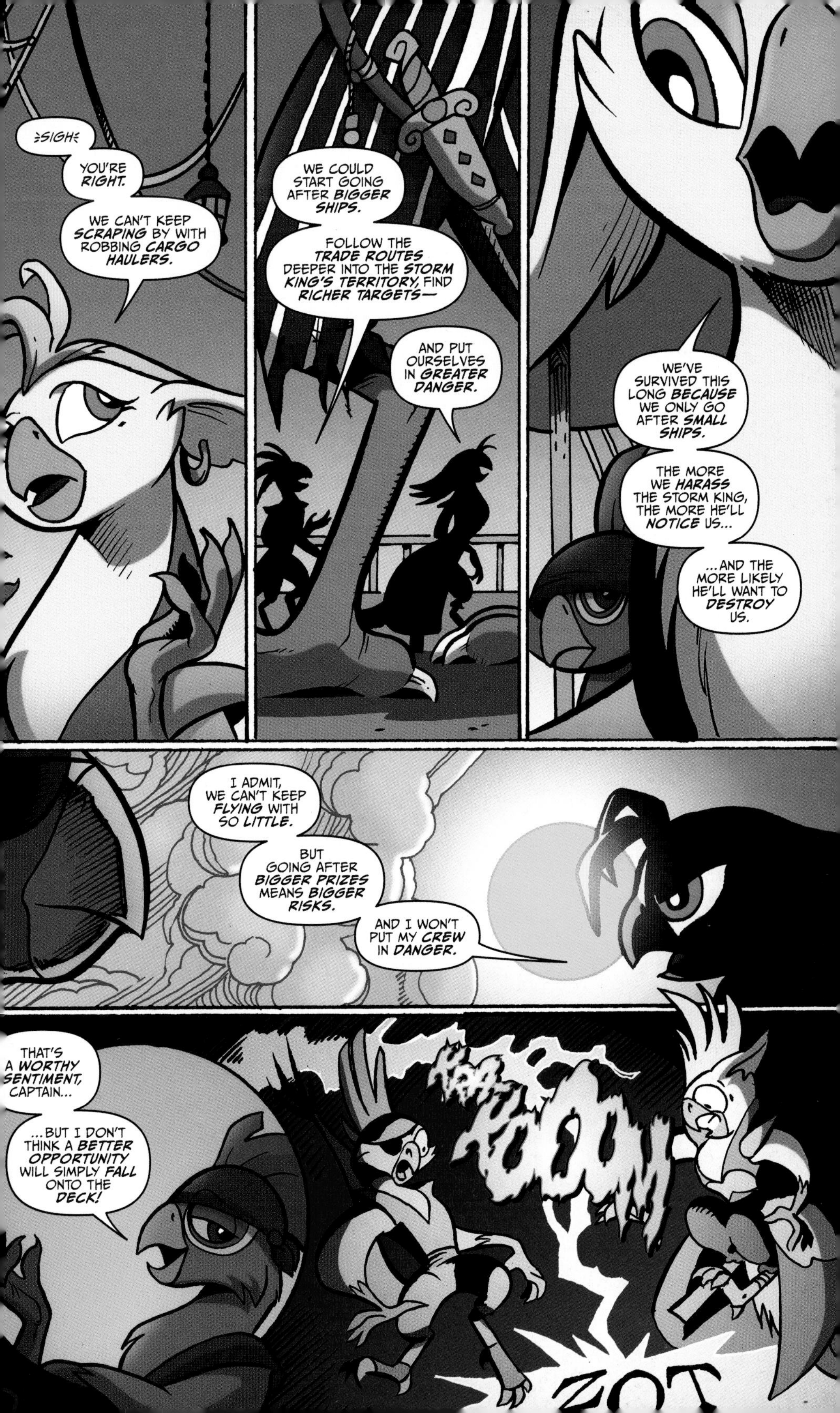

⋛SIGH⋚
YOU'RE RIGHT.
WE CAN'T KEEP SCRAPING BY WITH ROBBING CARGO HAULERS.
WE COULD START GOING AFTER BIGGER SHIPS.
FOLLOW THE TRADE ROUTES DEEPER INTO THE STORM KING'S TERRITORY, FIND RICHER TARGETS—
AND PUT OURSELVES IN GREATER DANGER.
WE'VE SURVIVED THIS LONG BECAUSE WE ONLY GO AFTER SMALL SHIPS.
THE MORE WE HARASS THE STORM KING, THE MORE HE'LL NOTICE US...
...AND THE MORE LIKELY HE'LL WANT TO DESTROY US.
I ADMIT, WE CAN'T KEEP FLYING WITH SO LITTLE.
BUT GOING AFTER BIGGER PRIZES MEANS BIGGER RISKS.
AND I WON'T PUT MY CREW IN DANGER.
THAT'S A WORTHY SENTIMENT, CAPTAIN...
...BUT I DON'T THINK A BETTER OPPORTUNITY WILL SIMPLY FALL ONTO THE DECK!
KRA-TOOOOM
ZOT

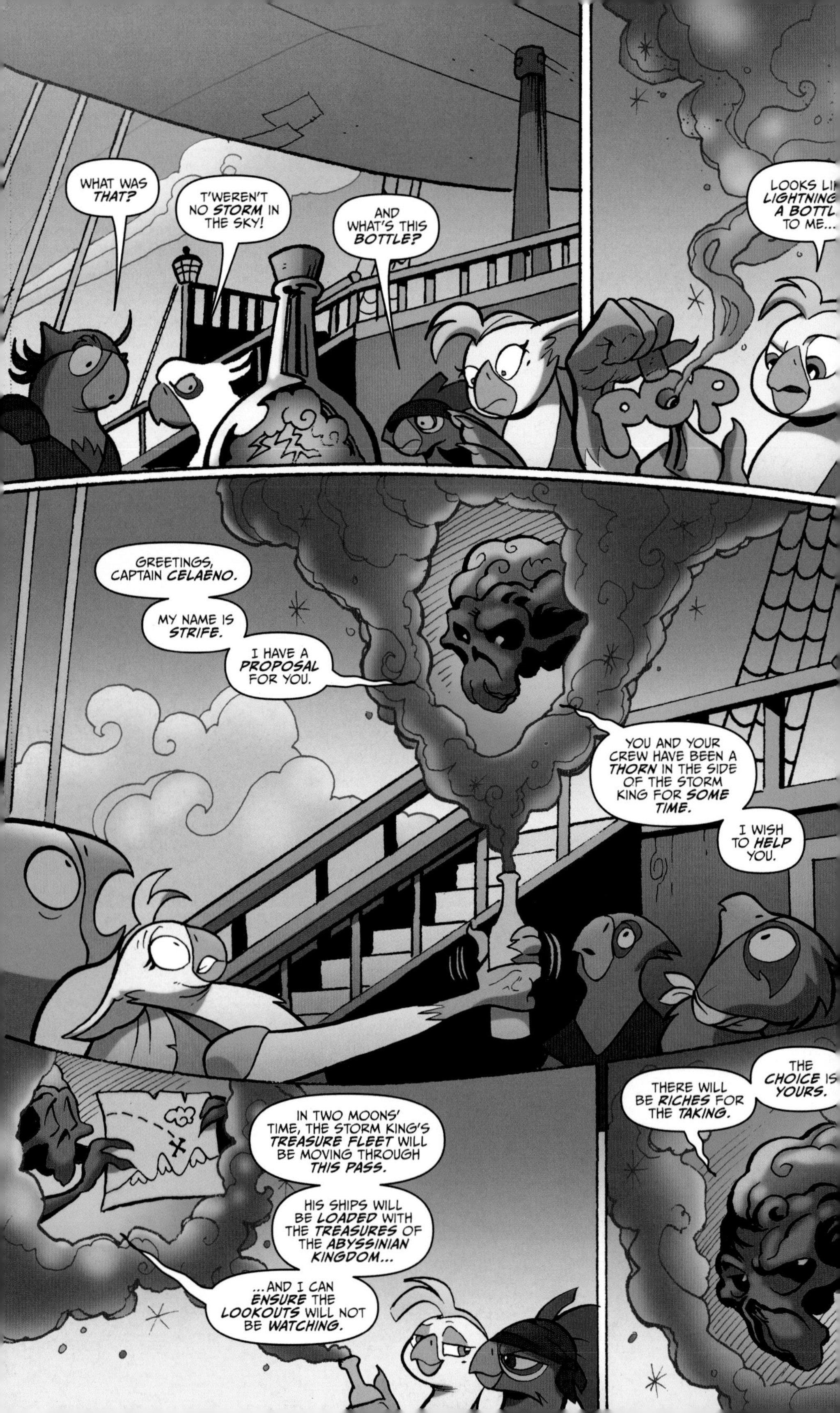
WHAT WAS THAT?
T'WEREN'T NO STORM IN THE SKY!
AND WHAT'S THIS BOTTLE?
LOOKS LI LIGHTNING A BOTTL TO ME...
POP
GREETINGS, CAPTAIN CELAENO.
MY NAME IS STRIFE.
I HAVE A PROPOSAL FOR YOU.
YOU AND YOUR CREW HAVE BEEN A THORN IN THE SIDE OF THE STORM KING FOR SOME TIME.
I WISH TO HELP YOU.
IN TWO MOONS' TIME, THE STORM KING'S TREASURE FLEET WILL BE MOVING THROUGH THIS PASS.
HIS SHIPS WILL BE LOADED WITH THE TREASURES OF THE ABYSSINIAN KINGDOM...
...AND I CAN ENSURE THE LOOKOUTS WILL NOT BE WATCHING.
THERE WILL BE RICHES FOR THE TAKING.
THE CHOICE IS YOURS.

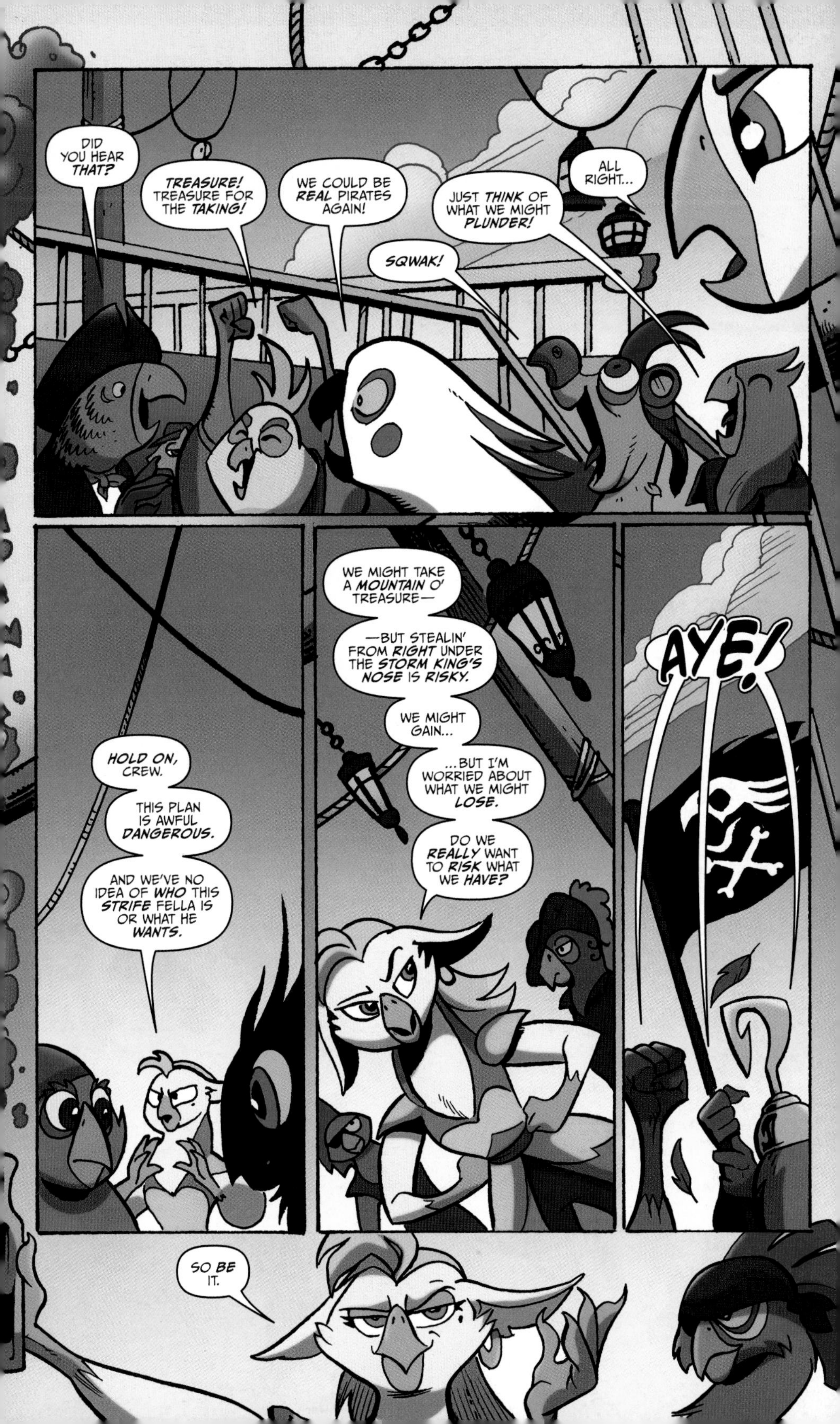

DID YOU HEAR THAT?
TREASURE! TREASURE FOR THE TAKING!
WE COULD BE REAL PIRATES AGAIN!
SQWAK!
JUST THINK OF WHAT WE MIGHT PLUNDER!
ALL RIGHT...
HOLD ON, CREW.
THIS PLAN IS AWFUL DANGEROUS.
AND WE'VE NO IDEA OF WHO THIS STRIFE FELLA IS OR WHAT HE WANTS.
WE MIGHT TAKE A MOUNTAIN O' TREASURE—
—BUT STEALIN' FROM RIGHT UNDER THE STORM KING'S NOSE IS RISKY.
WE MIGHT GAIN...
...BUT I'M WORRIED ABOUT WHAT WE MIGHT LOSE.
DO WE REALLY WANT TO RISK WHAT WE HAVE?
AYE!
SO BE IT.

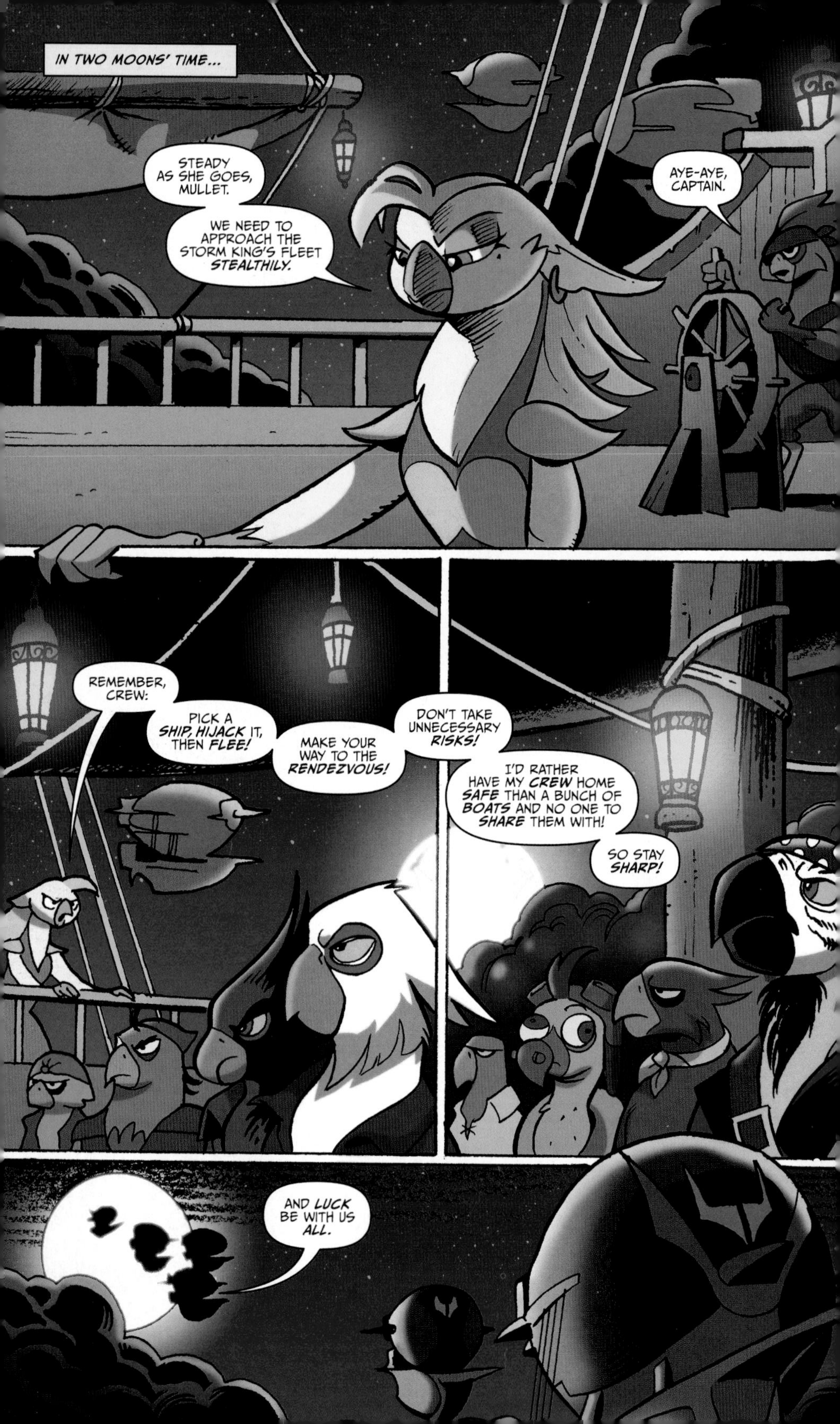

IN TWO MOONS' TIME...
STEADY AS SHE GOES, MULLET.
WE NEED TO APPROACH THE STORM KING'S FLEET *STEALTHILY.*
AYE-AYE, CAPTAIN.
REMEMBER, CREW:
PICK A *SHIP, HIJACK* IT, THEN *FLEE!*
MAKE YOUR WAY TO THE *RENDEZVOUS!*
DON'T TAKE UNNECESSARY *RISKS!*
I'D RATHER HAVE MY *CREW* HOME *SAFE* THAN A BUNCH OF *BOATS* AND NO ONE TO *SHARE* THEM WITH!
SO STAY *SHARP!*
AND *LUCK* BE WITH US *ALL.*

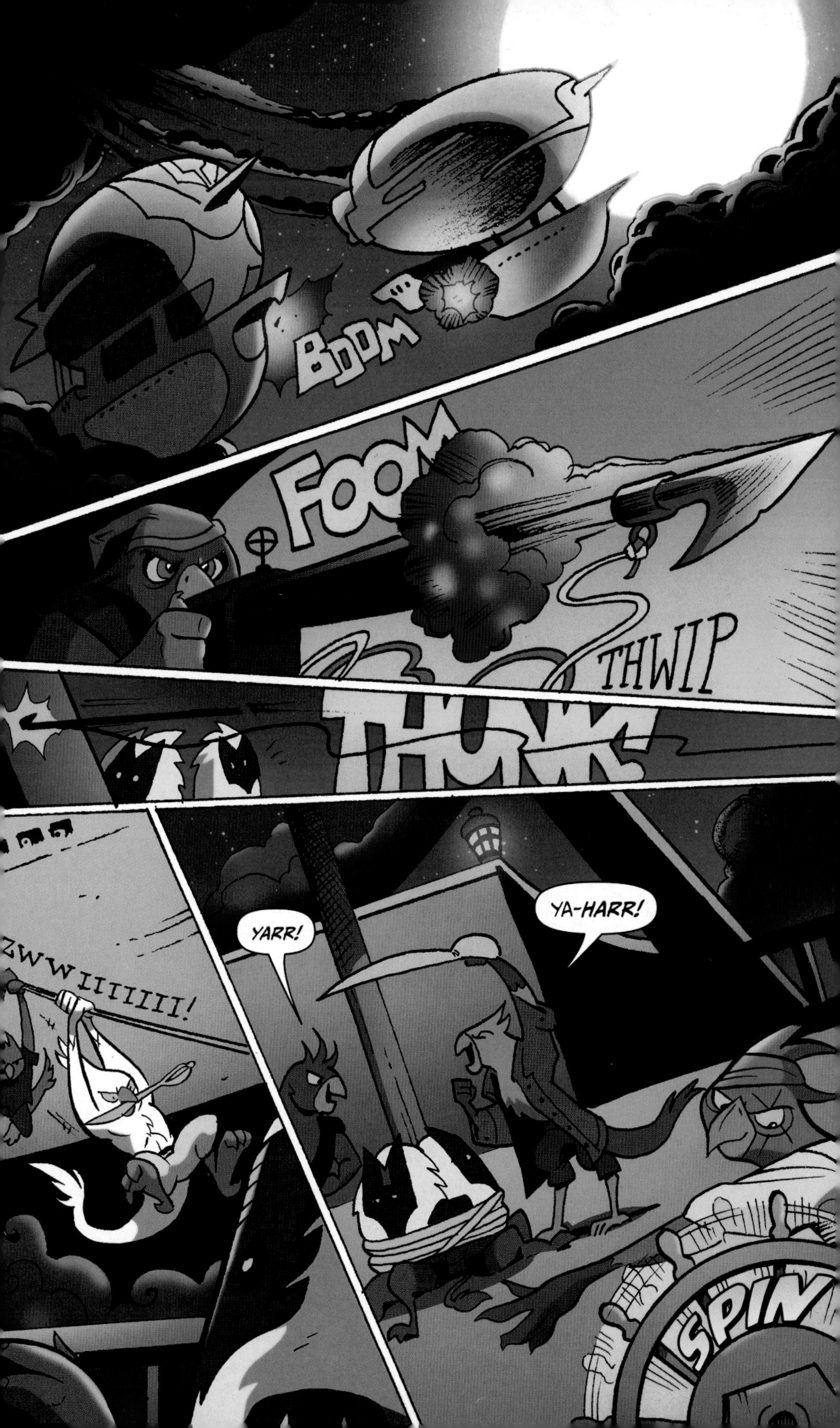
BOOM
FOOM
THWIP
THUNK
ZWWIIIIIII!
YARR!
YA-HARR!
SPIN

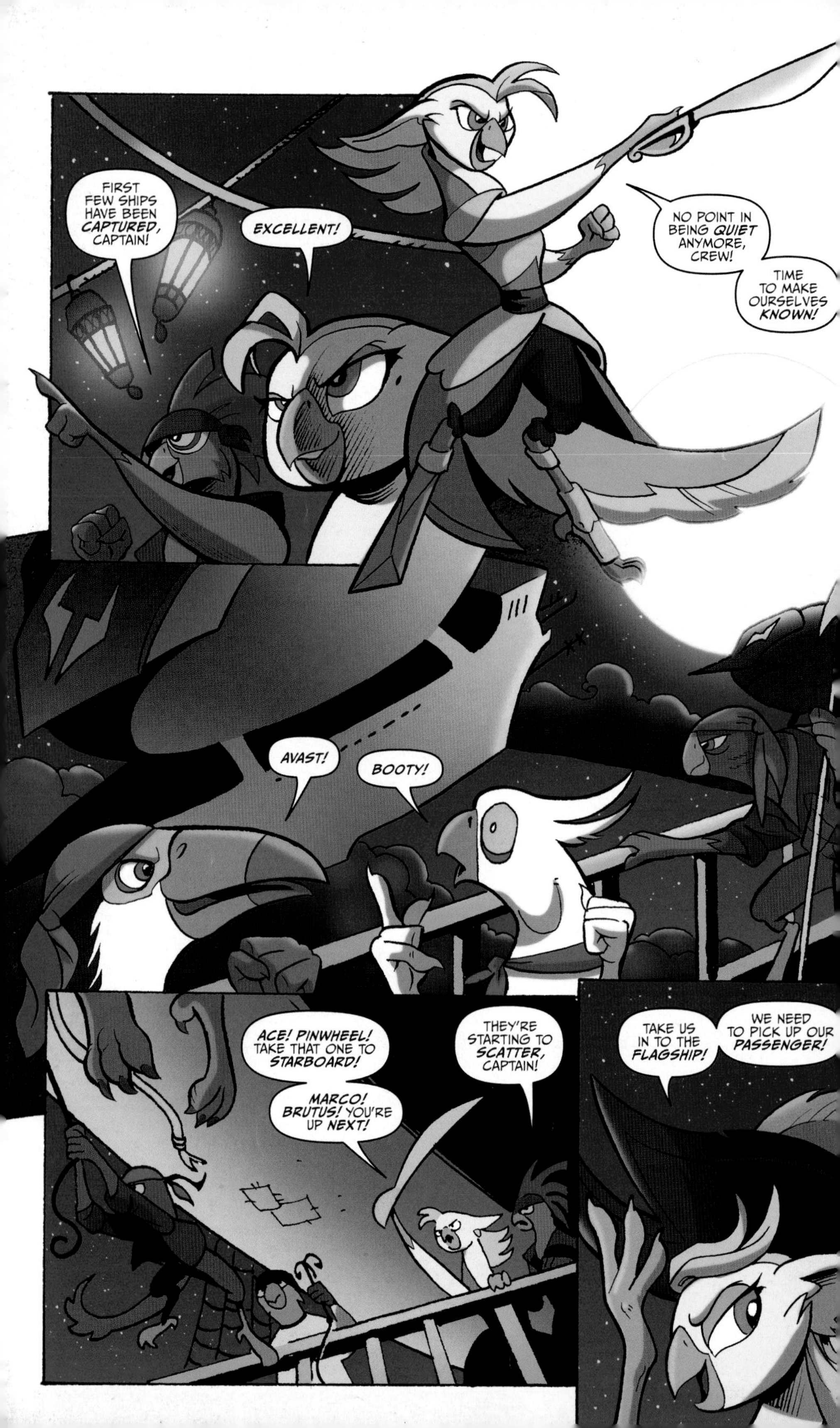
FIRST FEW SHIPS HAVE BEEN CAPTURED, CAPTAIN!
EXCELLENT!
NO POINT IN BEING QUIET ANYMORE, CREW!
TIME TO MAKE OURSELVES KNOWN!
AVAST!
BOOTY!
ACE! PINWHEEL! TAKE THAT ONE TO STARBOARD!
MARCO! BRUTUS! YOU'RE UP NEXT!
THEY'RE STARTING TO SCATTER, CAPTAIN!
TAKE US IN TO THE FLAGSHIP!
WE NEED TO PICK UP OUR PASSENGER!

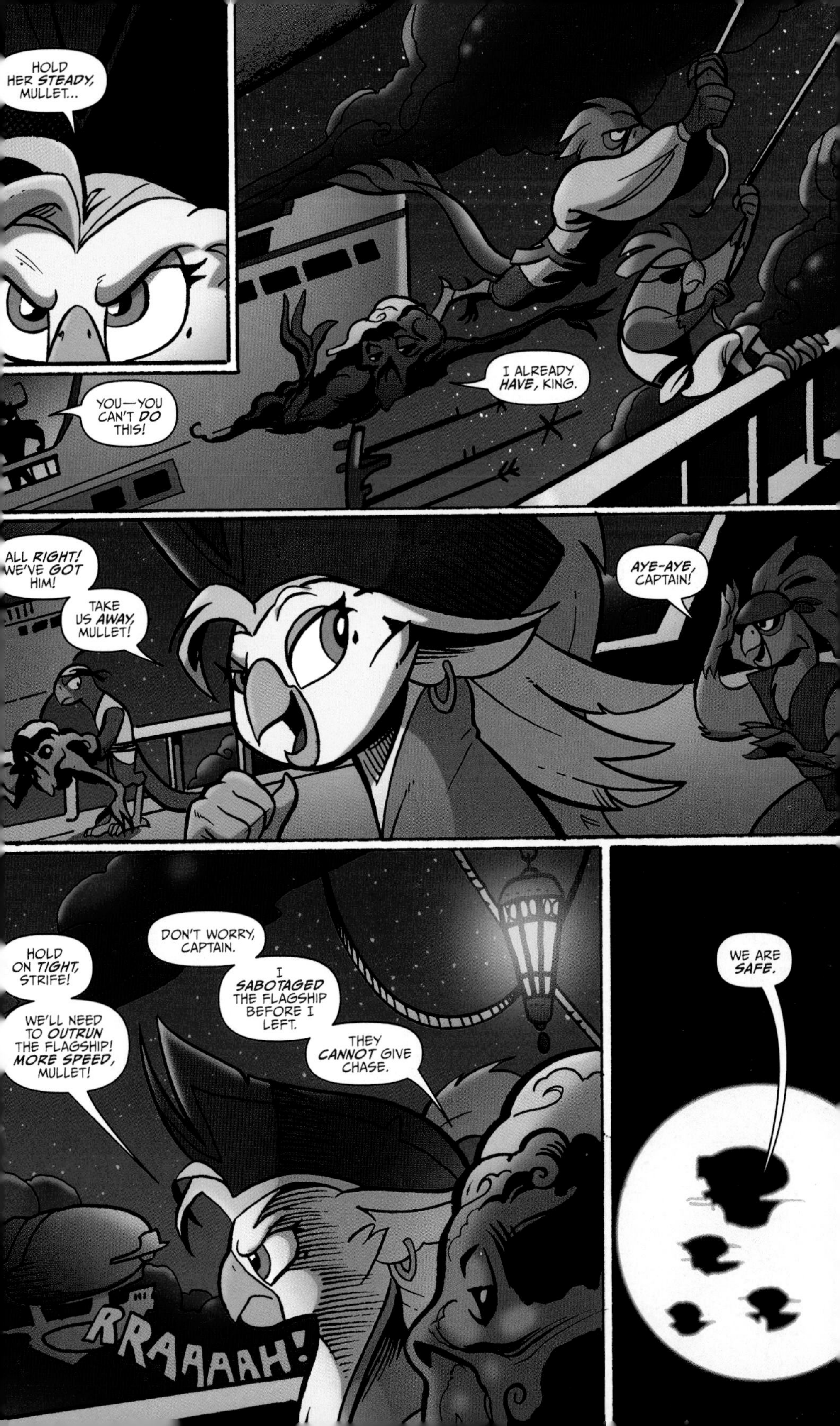
HOLD HER STEADY, MULLET...
YOU—YOU CAN'T DO THIS!
I ALREADY HAVE, KING.
ALL RIGHT! WE'VE GOT HIM!
TAKE US AWAY, MULLET!
AYE-AYE, CAPTAIN!
HOLD ON TIGHT, STRIFE!
WE'LL NEED TO OUTRUN THE FLAGSHIP! MORE SPEED, MULLET!
DON'T WORRY, CAPTAIN.
I SABOTAGED THE FLAGSHIP BEFORE I LEFT.
THEY CANNOT GIVE CHASE.
RRAAAAH!
WE ARE SAFE.

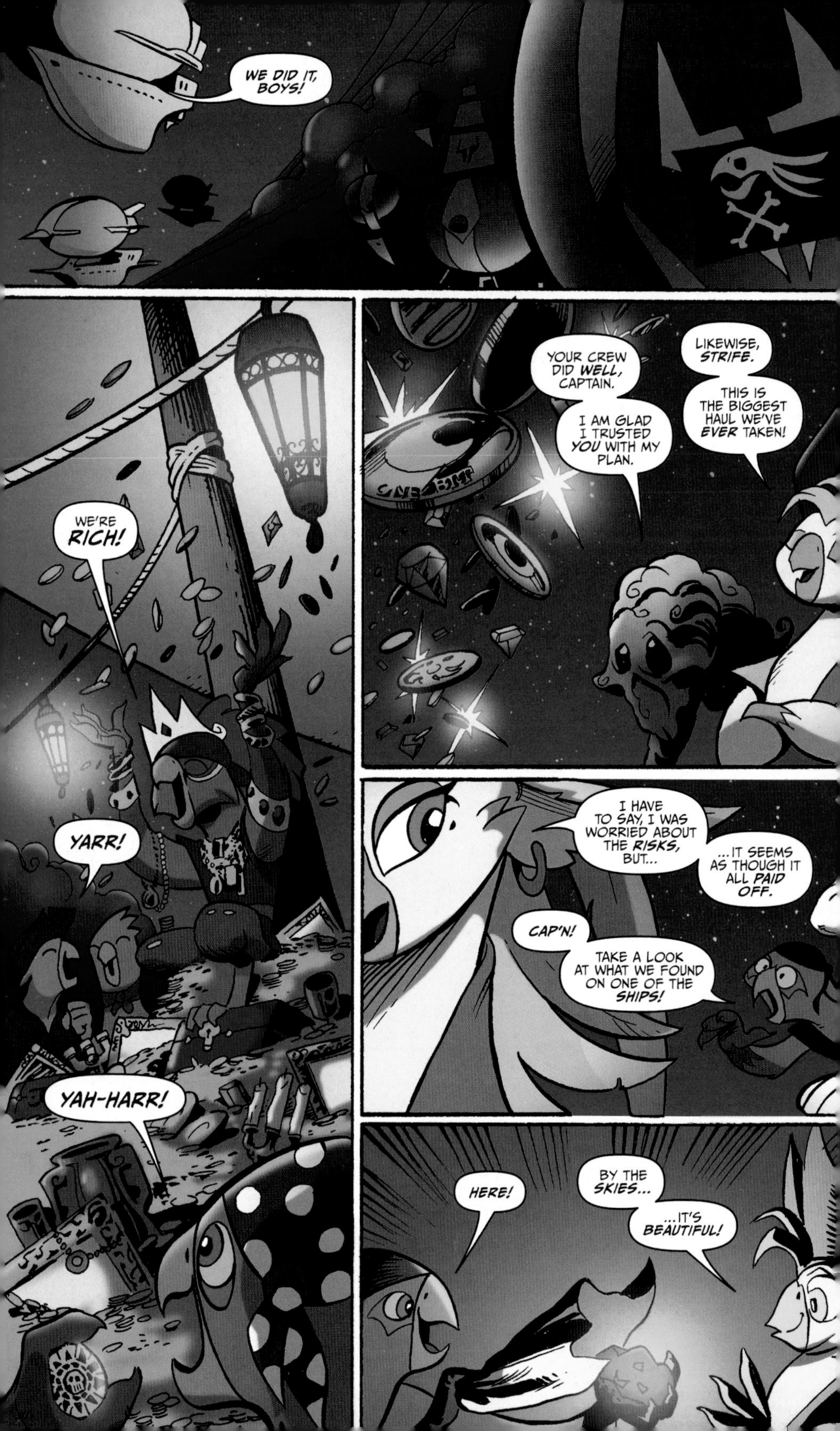
WE DID IT, BOYS!
WE'RE RICH!
YARR!
YAH-HARR!
YOUR CREW DID WELL, CAPTAIN.
I AM GLAD I TRUSTED YOU WITH MY PLAN.
LIKEWISE, STRIFE.
THIS IS THE BIGGEST HAUL WE'VE EVER TAKEN!
I HAVE TO SAY, I WAS WORRIED ABOUT THE RISKS, BUT...
...IT SEEMS AS THOUGH IT ALL PAID OFF.
CAP'N!
TAKE A LOOK AT WHAT WE FOUND ON ONE OF THE SHIPS!
HERE!
BY THE SKIES...
...IT'S BEAUTIFUL!

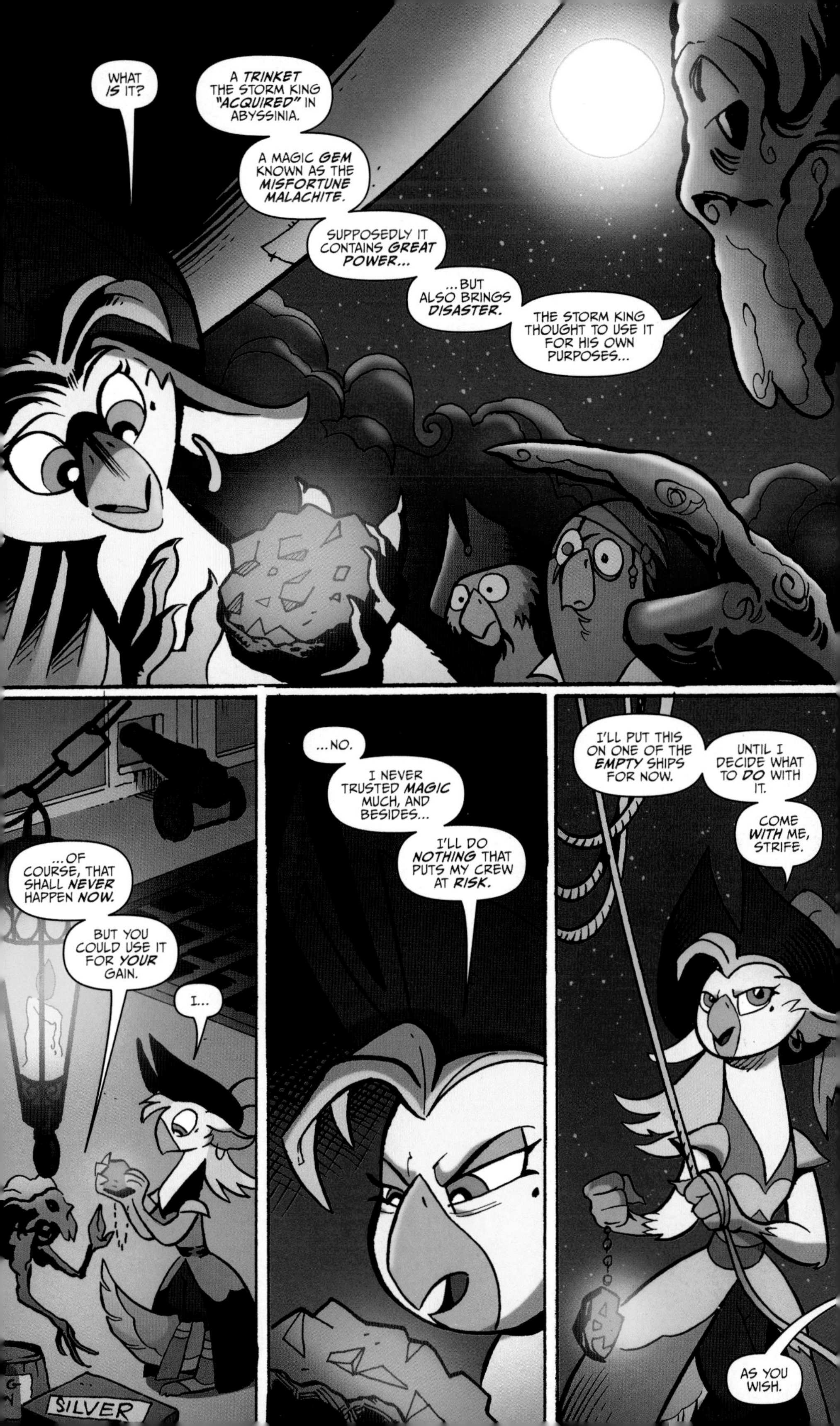
WHAT *IS* IT?
A *TRINKET* THE STORM KING *"ACQUIRED"* IN ABYSSINIA.
A MAGIC *GEM* KNOWN AS THE *MISFORTUNE MALACHITE.*
SUPPOSEDLY IT CONTAINS *GREAT POWER...*
...BUT ALSO BRINGS *DISASTER.*
THE STORM KING THOUGHT TO USE IT FOR HIS OWN PURPOSES...
...OF COURSE, THAT SHALL *NEVER* HAPPEN *NOW.*
BUT YOU COULD USE IT FOR *YOUR* GAIN.
I...
SILVER
...NO.
I NEVER TRUSTED *MAGIC* MUCH, AND BESIDES...
I'LL DO *NOTHING* THAT PUTS MY CREW AT *RISK.*
I'LL PUT THIS ON ONE OF THE *EMPTY* SHIPS FOR NOW.
UNTIL I DECIDE WHAT TO *DO* WITH IT.
COME *WITH* ME, STRIFE.
AS YOU WISH.

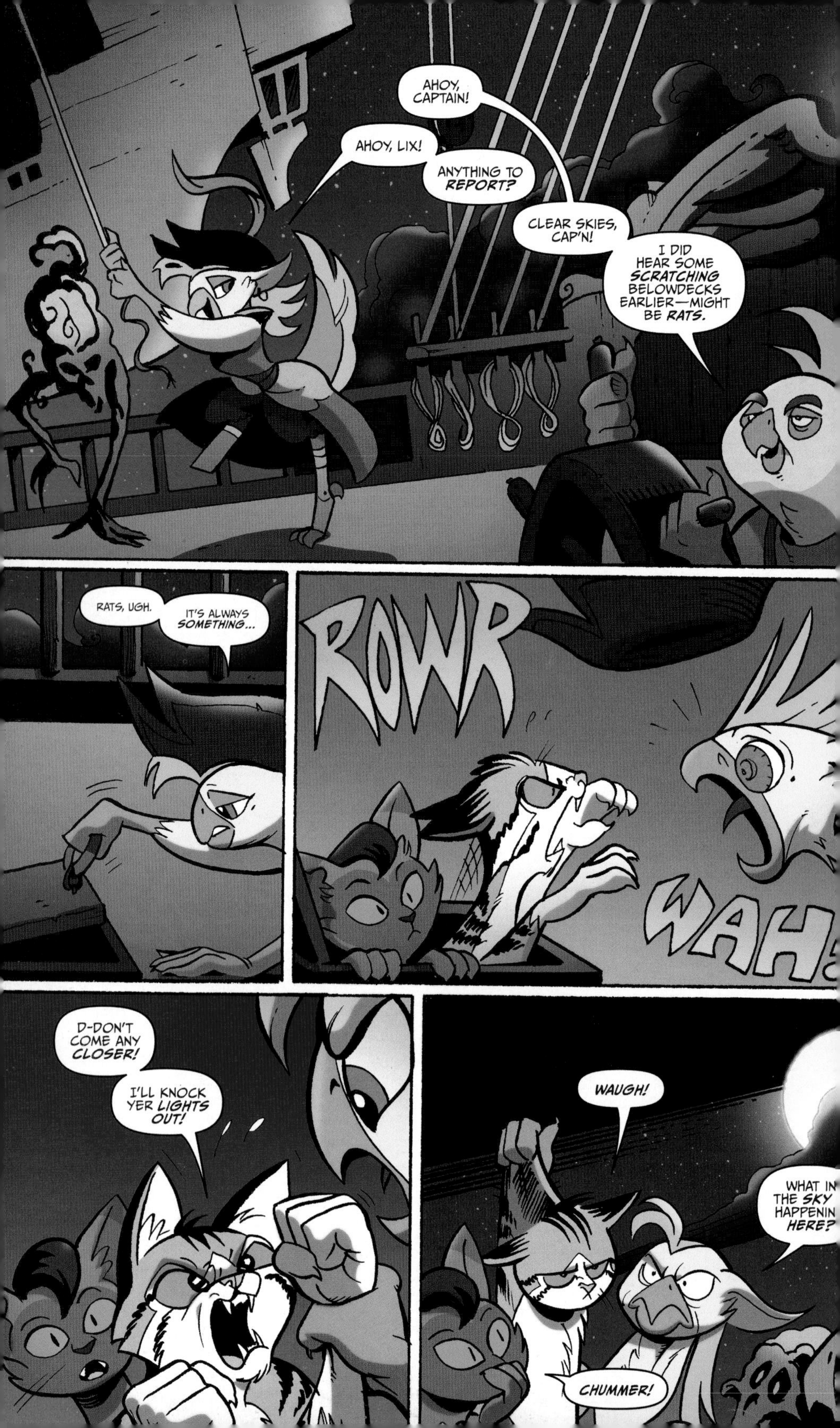
AHOY, CAPTAIN!
AHOY, LIX!
ANYTHING TO REPORT?
CLEAR SKIES, CAP'N!
I DID HEAR SOME SCRATCHING BELOWDECKS EARLIER—MIGHT BE RATS.
RATS, UGH.
IT'S ALWAYS SOMETHING...
ROWR
WAH!
D-DON'T COME ANY CLOSER!
I'LL KNOCK YER LIGHTS OUT!
WAUGH!
WHAT IN THE SKY HAPPENIN HERE?
CHUMMER!

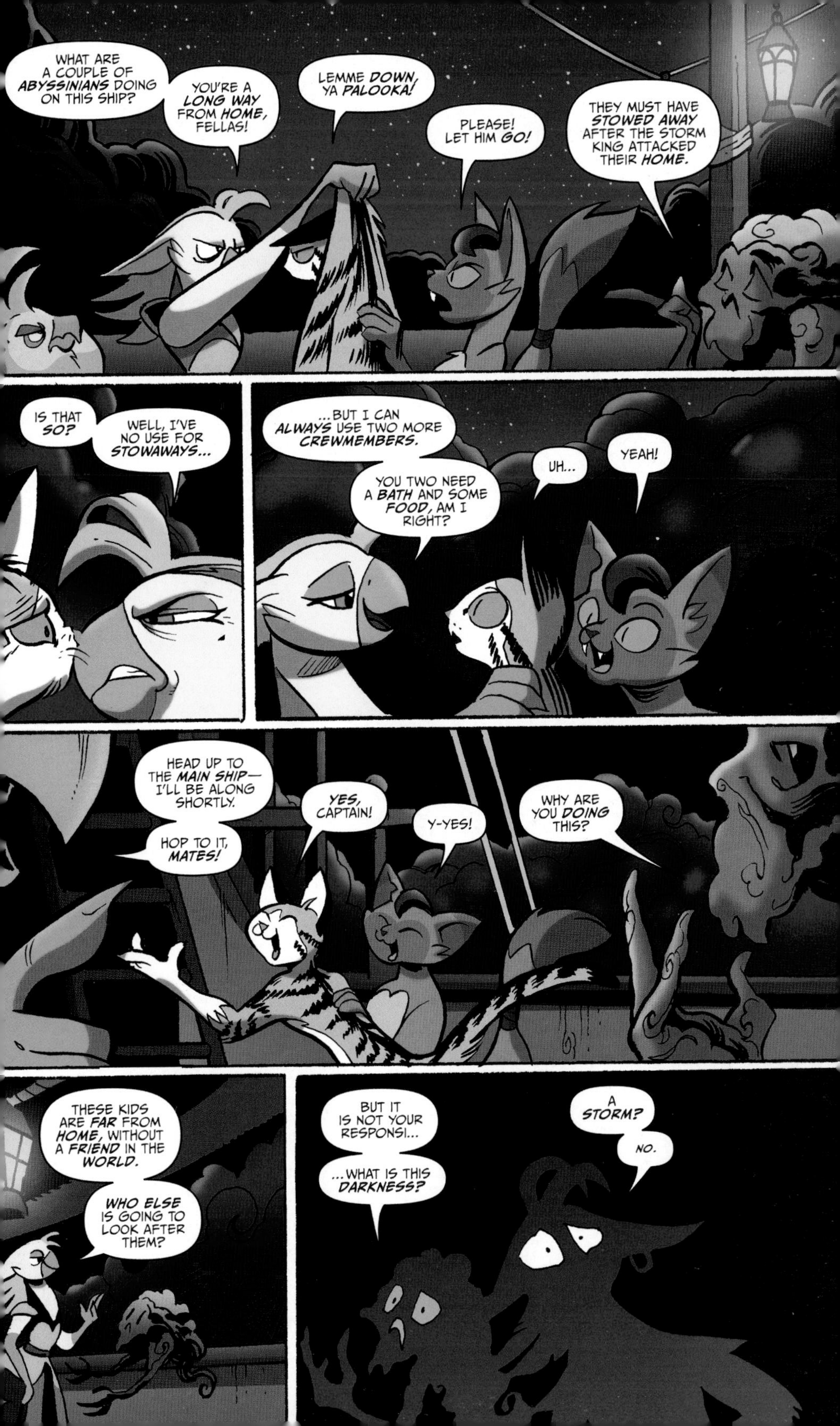
WHAT ARE A COUPLE OF ABYSSINIANS DOING ON THIS SHIP?
YOU'RE A LONG WAY FROM HOME, FELLAS!
LEMME DOWN, YA PALOOKA!
PLEASE! LET HIM GO!
THEY MUST HAVE STOWED AWAY AFTER THE STORM KING ATTACKED THEIR HOME.
IS THAT SO?
WELL, I'VE NO USE FOR STOWAWAYS...
...BUT I CAN ALWAYS USE TWO MORE CREWMEMBERS.
YOU TWO NEED A BATH AND SOME FOOD, AM I RIGHT?
UH...
YEAH!
HEAD UP TO THE MAIN SHIP— I'LL BE ALONG SHORTLY.
HOP TO IT, MATES!
YES, CAPTAIN!
Y-YES!
WHY ARE YOU DOING THIS?
THESE KIDS ARE FAR FROM HOME, WITHOUT A FRIEND IN THE WORLD.
WHO ELSE IS GOING TO LOOK AFTER THEM?
BUT IT IS NOT YOUR RESPONSI...
...WHAT IS THIS DARKNESS?
A STORM?
NO.

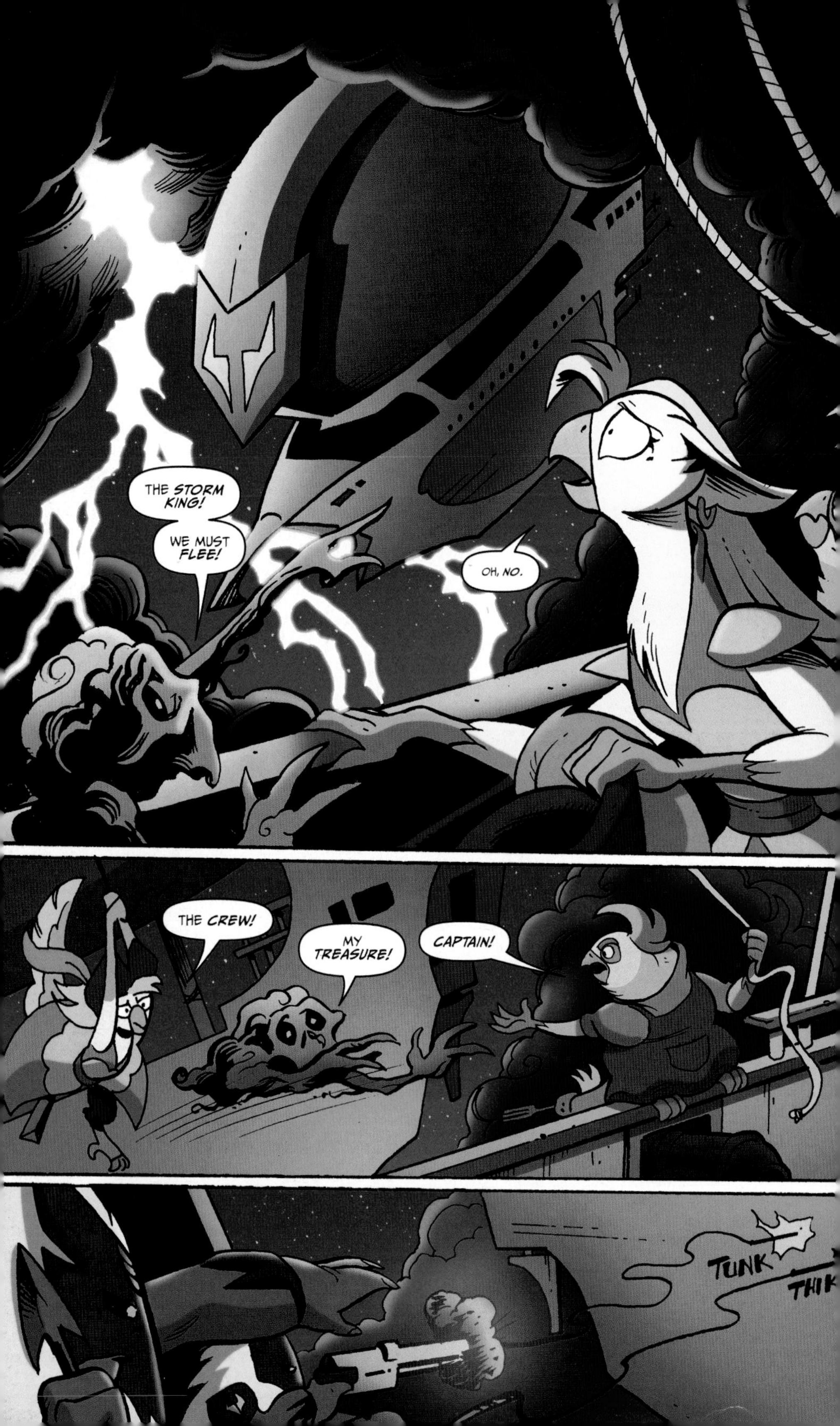
THE STORM KING!
WE MUST FLEE!
OH, NO.
THE CREW!
MY TREASURE!
CAPTAIN!
TUNK
THIK

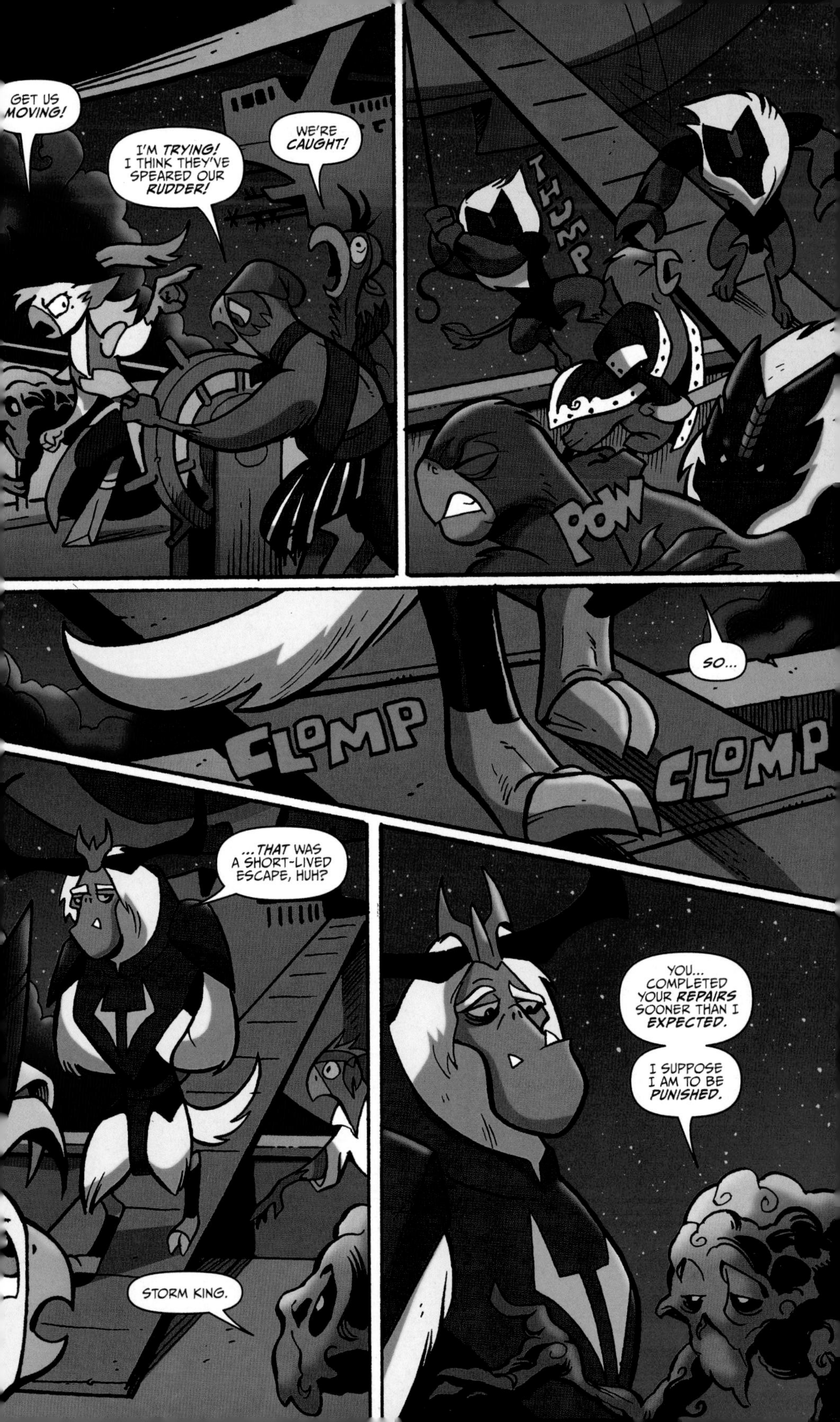
GET US MOVING!
I'M TRYING! I THINK THEY'VE SPEARED OUR RUDDER!
WE'RE CAUGHT!
THUMP
POW
SO...
CLOMP
CLOMP
...THAT WAS A SHORT-LIVED ESCAPE, HUH?
STORM KING.
YOU... COMPLETED YOUR REPAIRS SOONER THAN I EXPECTED.
I SUPPOSE I AM TO BE PUNISHED.

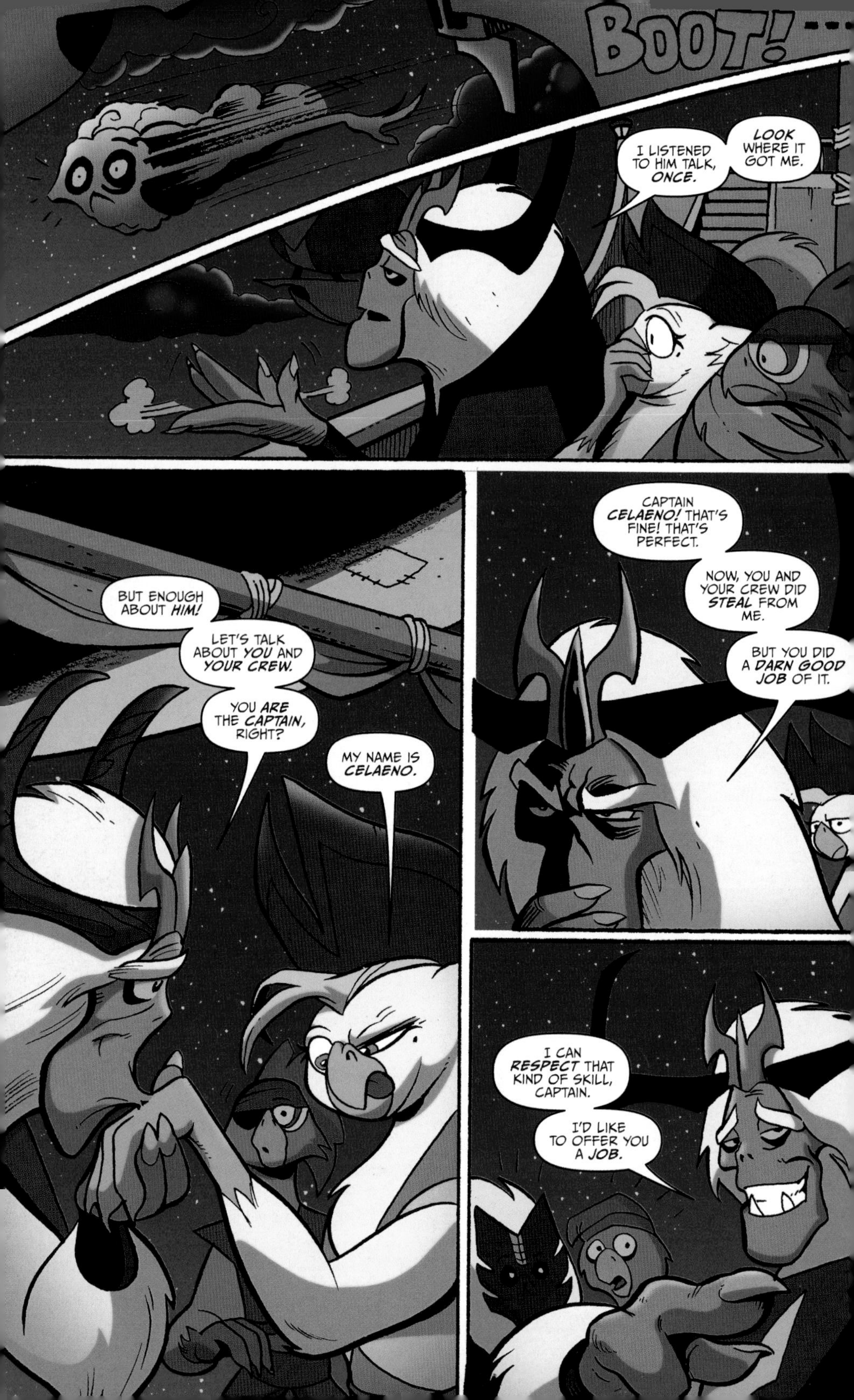
BOOT!---
I LISTENED TO HIM TALK, ONCE.
LOOK WHERE IT GOT ME.
BUT ENOUGH ABOUT HIM!
LET'S TALK ABOUT YOU AND YOUR CREW.
YOU ARE THE CAPTAIN, RIGHT?
MY NAME IS CELAENO.
CAPTAIN CELAENO! THAT'S FINE! THAT'S PERFECT.
NOW, YOU AND YOUR CREW DID STEAL FROM ME.
BUT YOU DID A DARN GOOD JOB OF IT.
I CAN RESPECT THAT KIND OF SKILL, CAPTAIN.
I'D LIKE TO OFFER YOU A JOB.

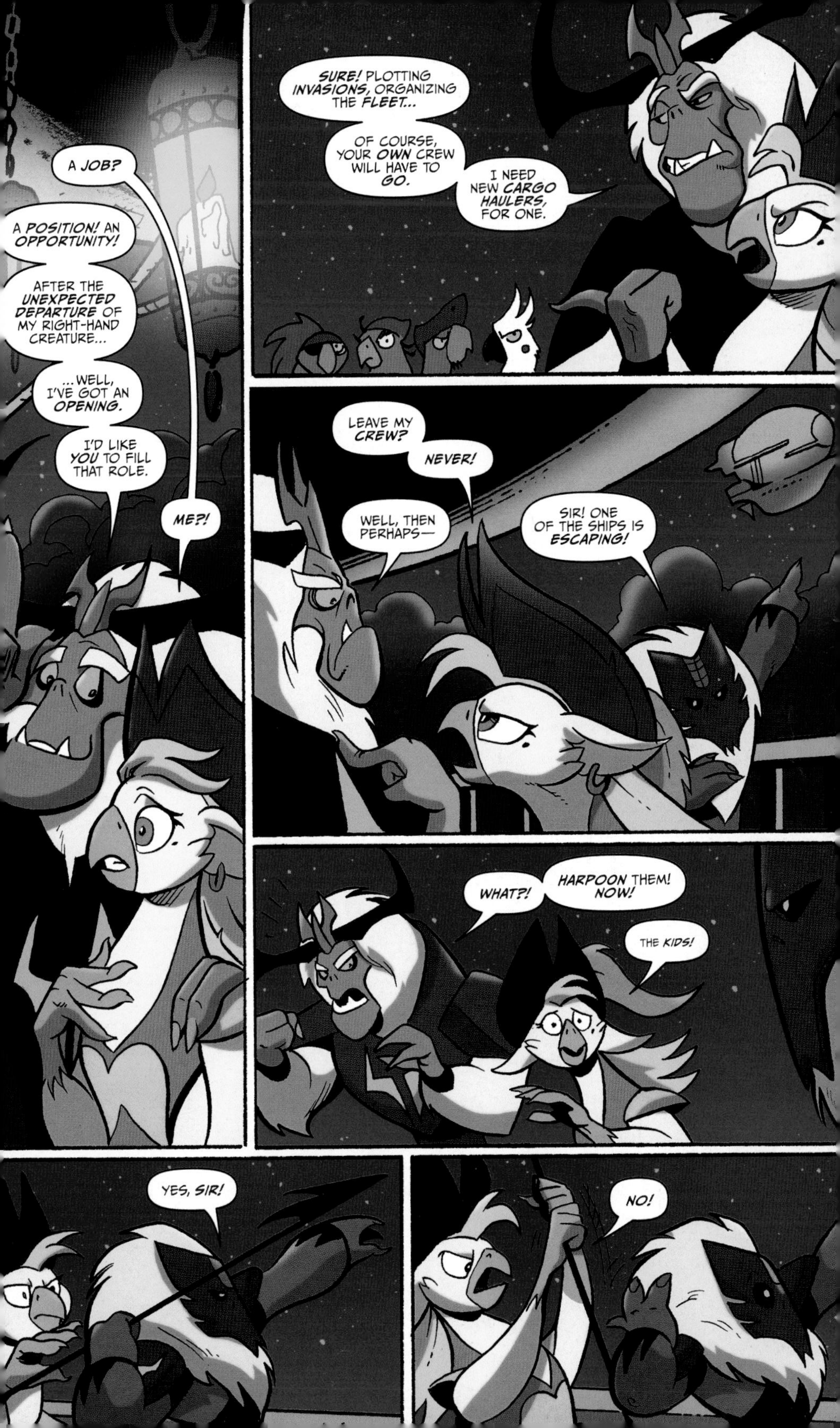
A JOB?
A POSITION! AN OPPORTUNITY!
AFTER THE UNEXPECTED DEPARTURE OF MY RIGHT-HAND CREATURE...
...WELL, I'VE GOT AN OPENING.
I'D LIKE YOU TO FILL THAT ROLE.
ME?!
SURE! PLOTTING INVASIONS, ORGANIZING THE FLEET...
OF COURSE, YOUR OWN CREW WILL HAVE TO GO.
I NEED NEW CARGO HAULERS, FOR ONE.
LEAVE MY CREW?
NEVER!
WELL, THEN PERHAPS—
SIR! ONE OF THE SHIPS IS ESCAPING!
WHAT?!
HARPOON THEM! NOW!
THE KIDS!
YES, SIR!
NO!

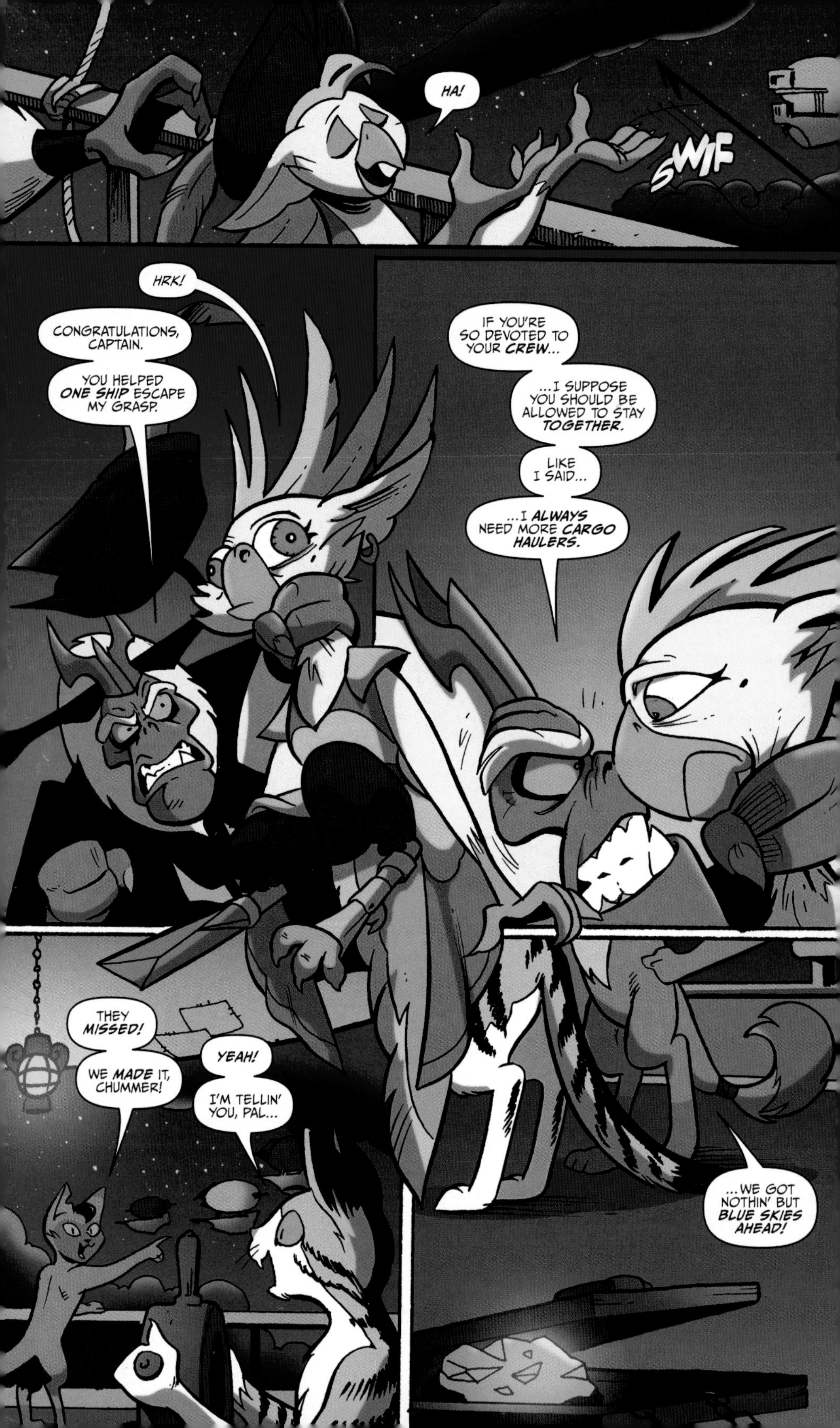
HA!
SWIF
HRK!
CONGRATULATIONS, CAPTAIN.
YOU HELPED ONE SHIP ESCAPE MY GRASP.
IF YOU'RE SO DEVOTED TO YOUR CREW...
...I SUPPOSE YOU SHOULD BE ALLOWED TO STAY TOGETHER.
LIKE I SAID...
...I ALWAYS NEED MORE CARGO HAULERS.
THEY MISSED!
WE MADE IT, CHUMMER!
YEAH!
I'M TELLIN' YOU, PAL...
...WE GOT NOTHIN' BUT BLUE SKIES AHEAD!

Art by TONY FLEECS

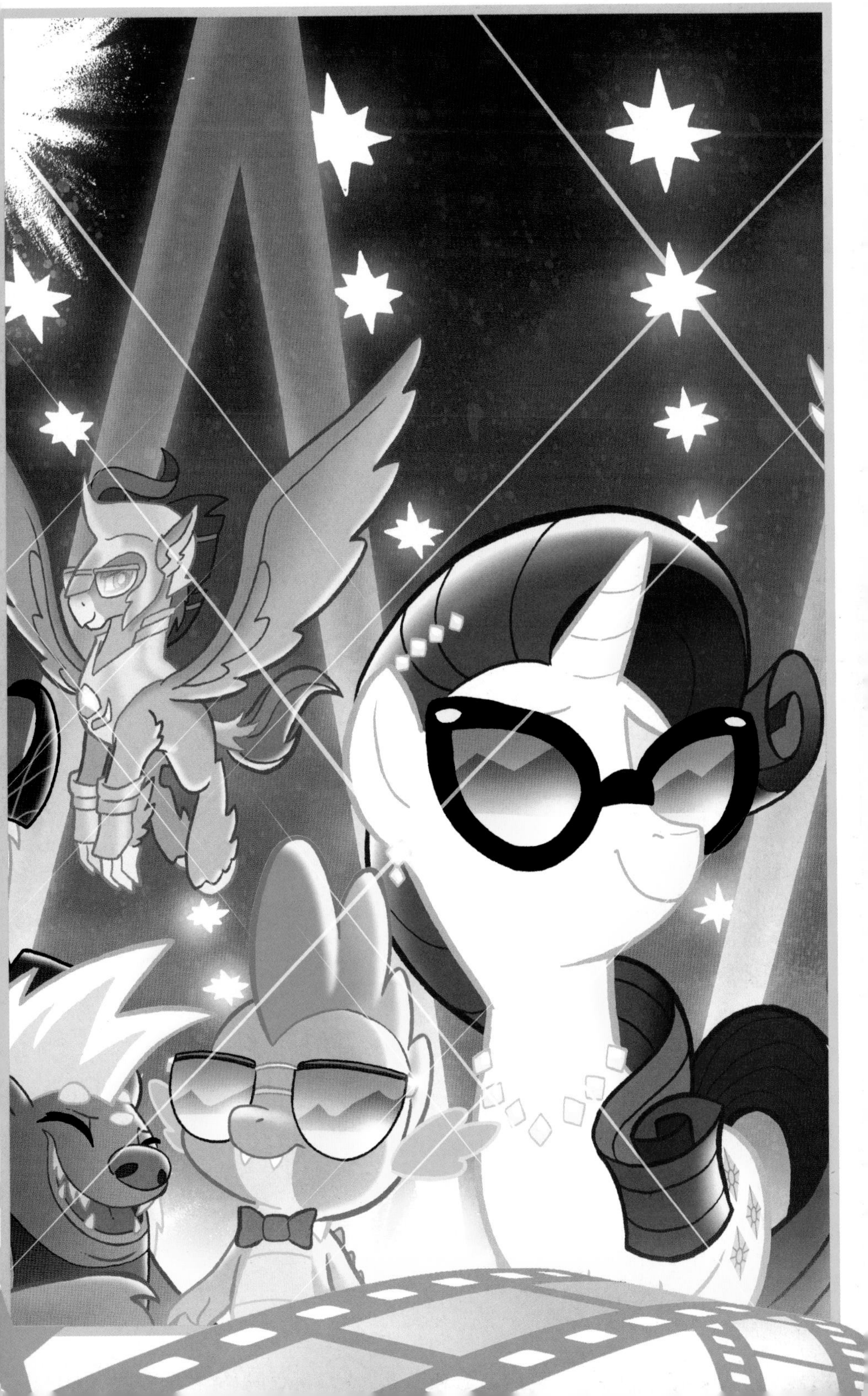

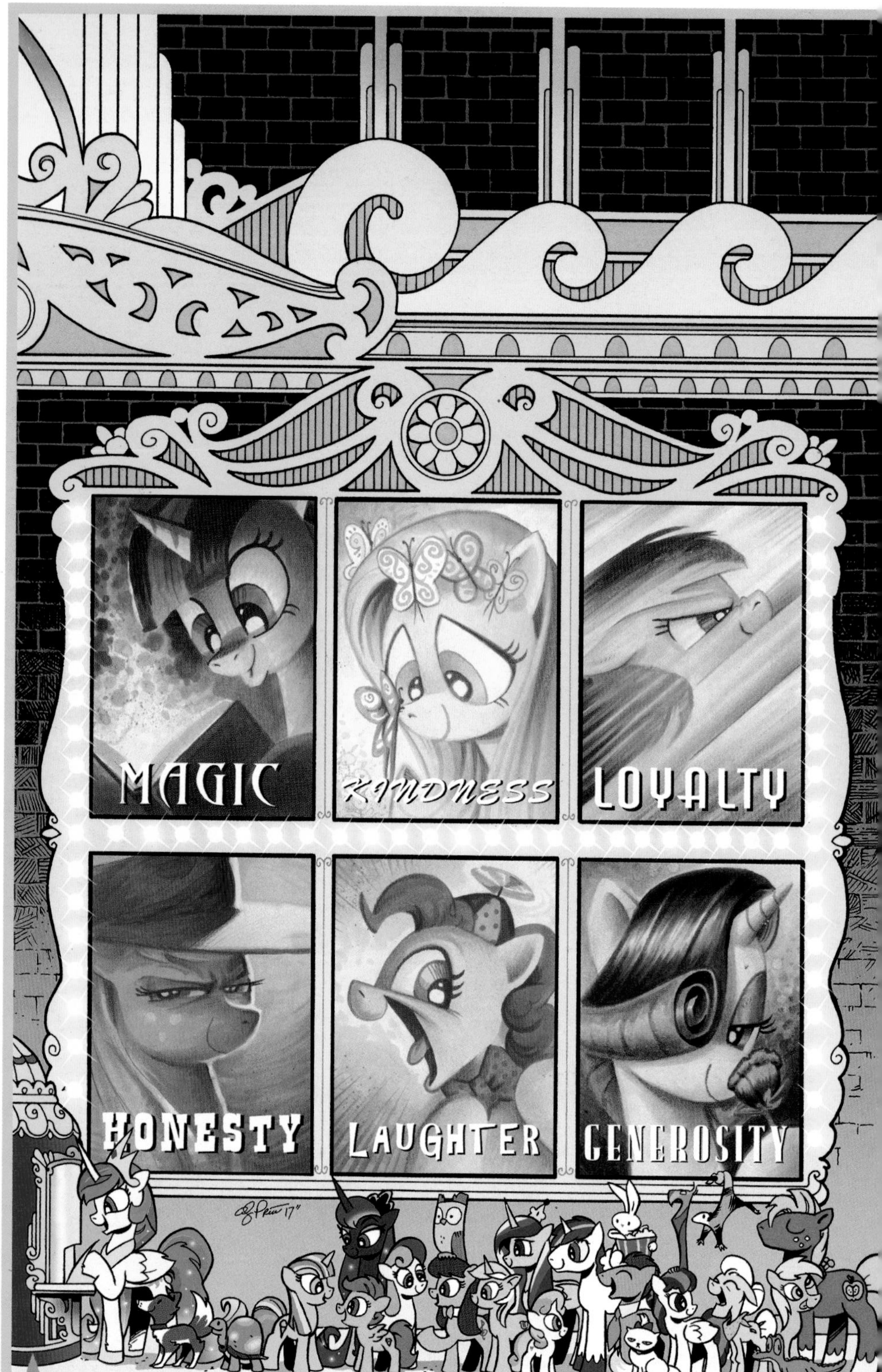
MAGIC
KINDNESS
LOYALTY
HONESTY
LAUGHTER
GENEROSITY

Art by **ANDY PRICE**

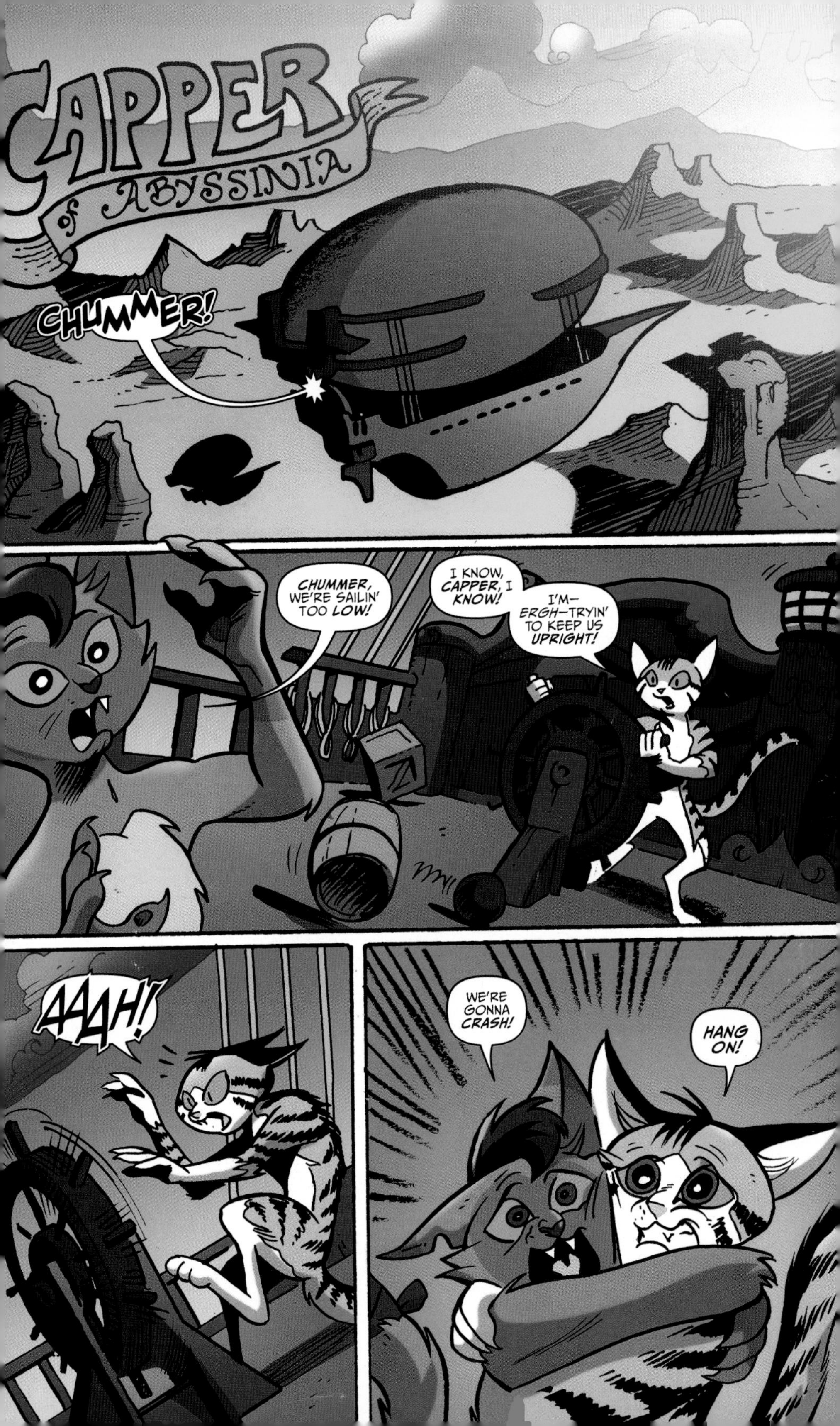

CAPPER of ABYSSINIA
CHUMMER!
CHUMMER, WE'RE SAILIN' TOO LOW!
I KNOW, CAPPER, I KNOW!
I'M—ERGH—TRYIN' TO KEEP US UPRIGHT!
AAAH!
WE'RE GONNA CRASH!
HANG ON!

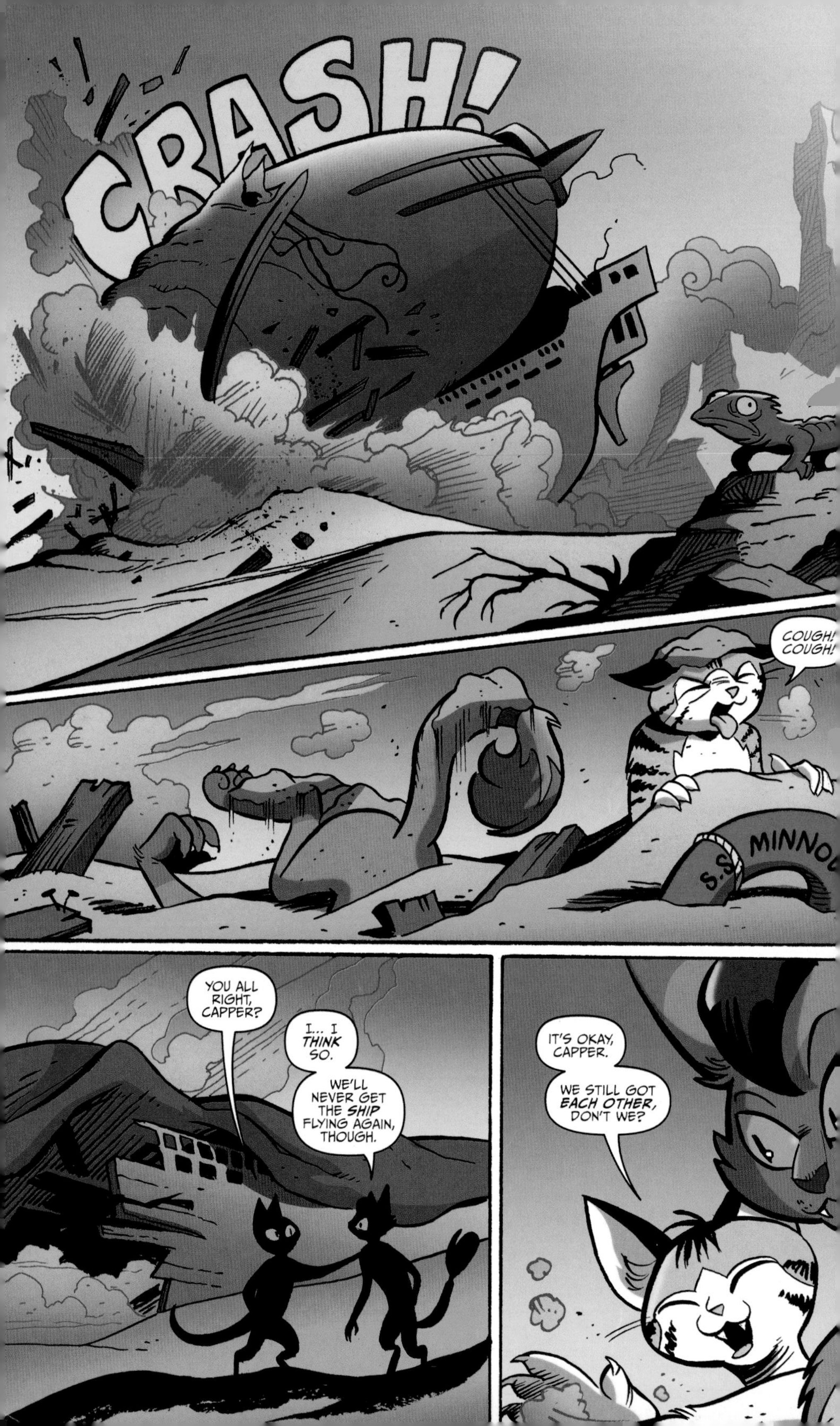
CRASH!
COUGH! COUGH!
S.S. MINNOW
YOU ALL RIGHT, CAPPER?
I... I THINK SO.
WE'LL NEVER GET THE SHIP FLYING AGAIN, THOUGH.
IT'S OKAY, CAPPER.
WE STILL GOT EACH OTHER, DON'T WE?

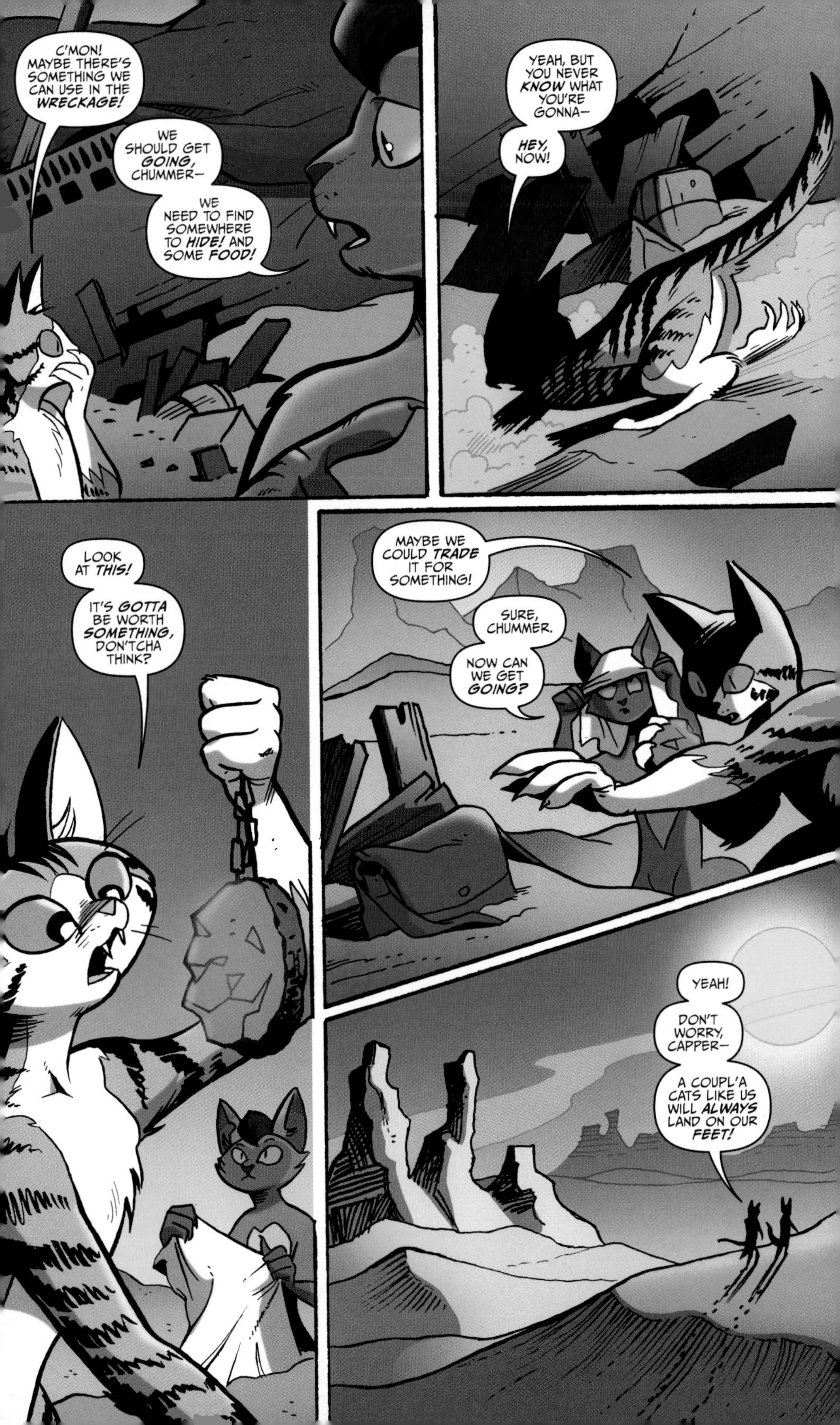
C'MON! MAYBE THERE'S SOMETHING WE CAN USE IN THE WRECKAGE!
WE SHOULD GET GOING, CHUMMER–
WE NEED TO FIND SOMEWHERE TO HIDE! AND SOME FOOD!
YEAH, BUT YOU NEVER KNOW WHAT YOU'RE GONNA–
HEY, NOW!
LOOK AT THIS!
IT'S GOTTA BE WORTH SOMETHING, DON'TCHA THINK?
MAYBE WE COULD TRADE IT FOR SOMETHING!
SURE, CHUMMER.
NOW CAN WE GET GOING?
YEAH!
DON'T WORRY, CAPPER–
A COUPL'A CATS LIKE US WILL ALWAYS LAND ON OUR FEET!

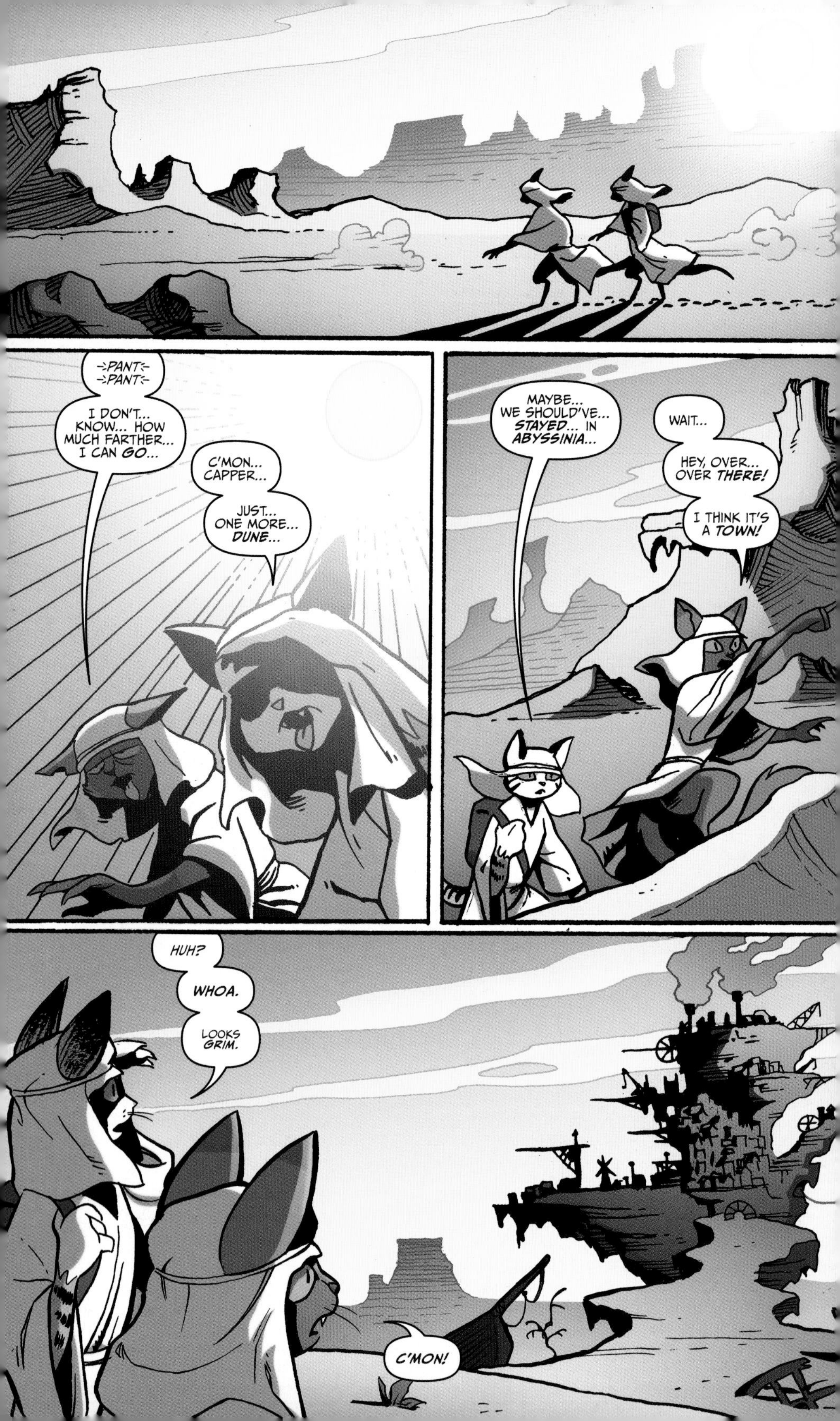

-PANT-
-PANT-
I DON'T... KNOW... HOW MUCH FARTHER... I CAN GO...
C'MON... CAPPER...
JUST... ONE MORE... DUNE...
MAYBE... WE SHOULD'VE... STAYED... IN ABYSSINIA...
WAIT...
HEY, OVER... OVER THERE!
I THINK IT'S A TOWN!
HUH?
WHOA.
LOOKS GRIM.
C'MON!

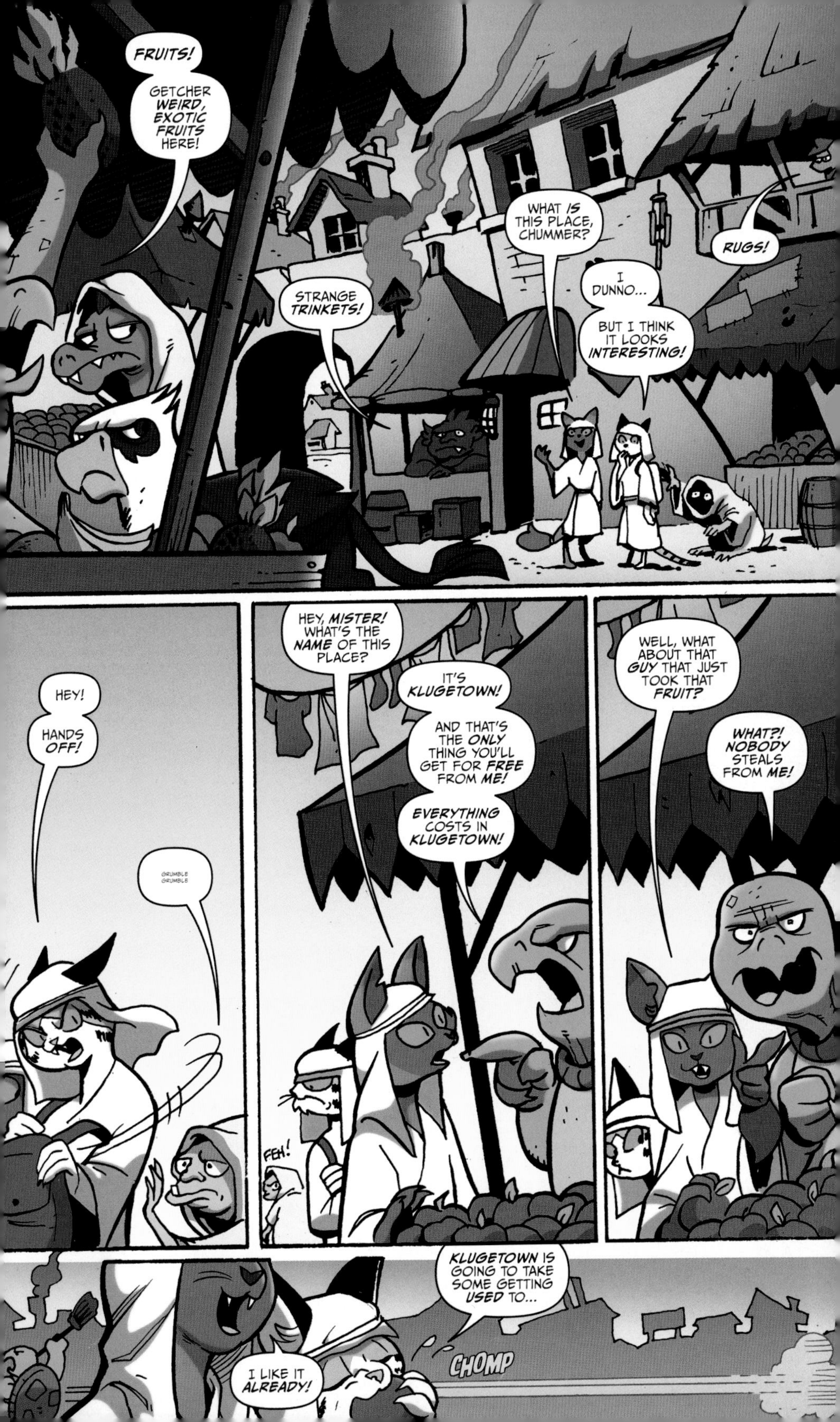
FRUITS!
GETCHER WEIRD, EXOTIC FRUITS HERE!
STRANGE TRINKETS!
WHAT IS THIS PLACE, CHUMMER?
I DUNNO...
BUT I THINK IT LOOKS INTERESTING!
RUGS!
HEY!
HANDS OFF!
GRUMBLE GRUMBLE
HEY, MISTER! WHAT'S THE NAME OF THIS PLACE?
IT'S KLUGETOWN!
AND THAT'S THE ONLY THING YOU'LL GET FOR FREE FROM ME!
EVERYTHING COSTS IN KLUGETOWN!
FEH!
WELL, WHAT ABOUT THAT GUY THAT JUST TOOK THAT FRUIT?
WHAT?! NOBODY STEALS FROM ME!
KLUGETOWN IS GOING TO TAKE SOME GETTING USED TO...
CHOMP
I LIKE IT ALREADY!

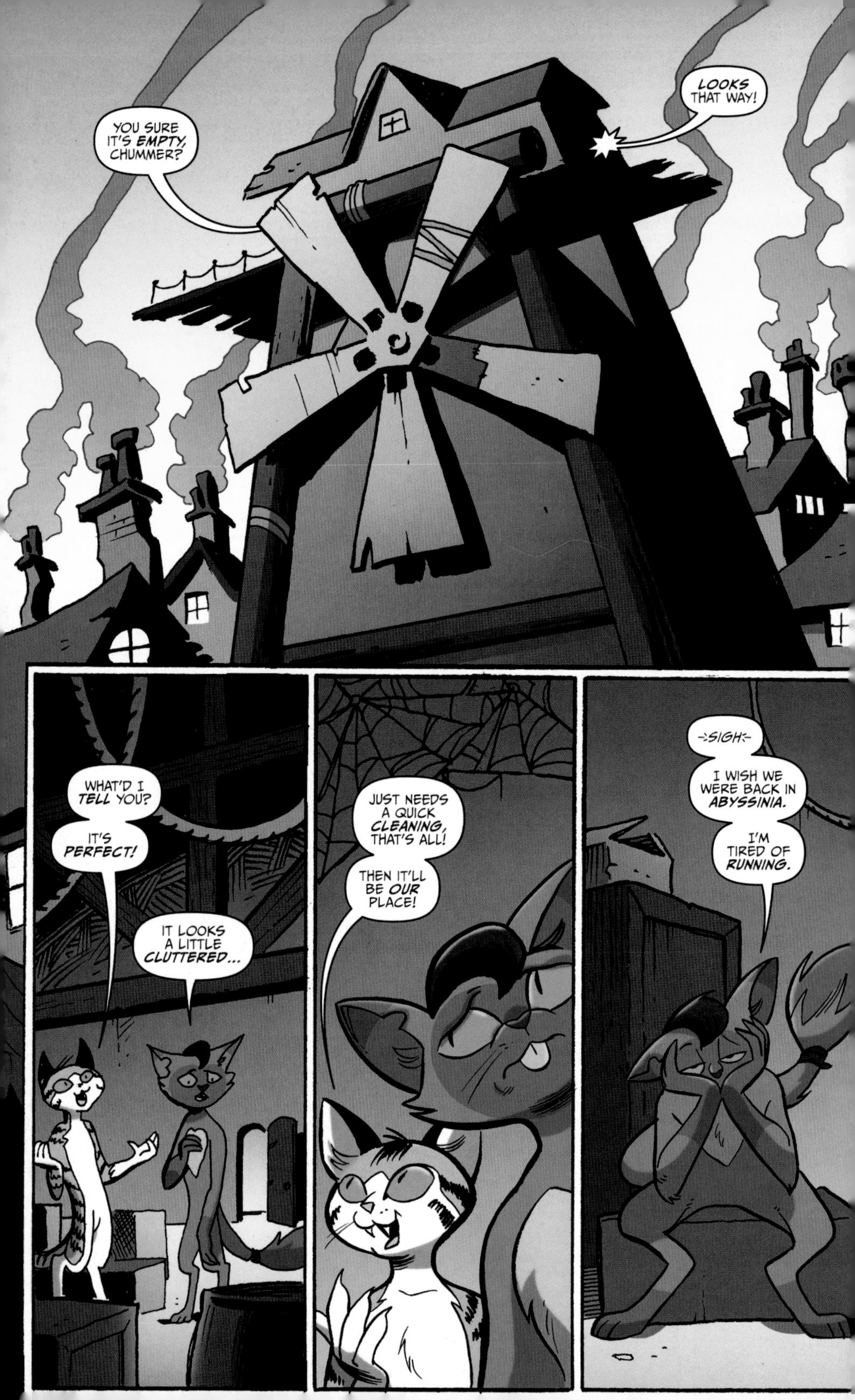

YOU SURE IT'S EMPTY, CHUMMER?
LOOKS THAT WAY!
WHAT'D I TELL YOU?
IT'S PERFECT!
IT LOOKS A LITTLE CLUTTERED...
JUST NEEDS A QUICK CLEANING, THAT'S ALL!
THEN IT'LL BE OUR PLACE!
-SIGH-
I WISH WE WERE BACK IN ABYSSINIA.
I'M TIRED OF RUNNING.

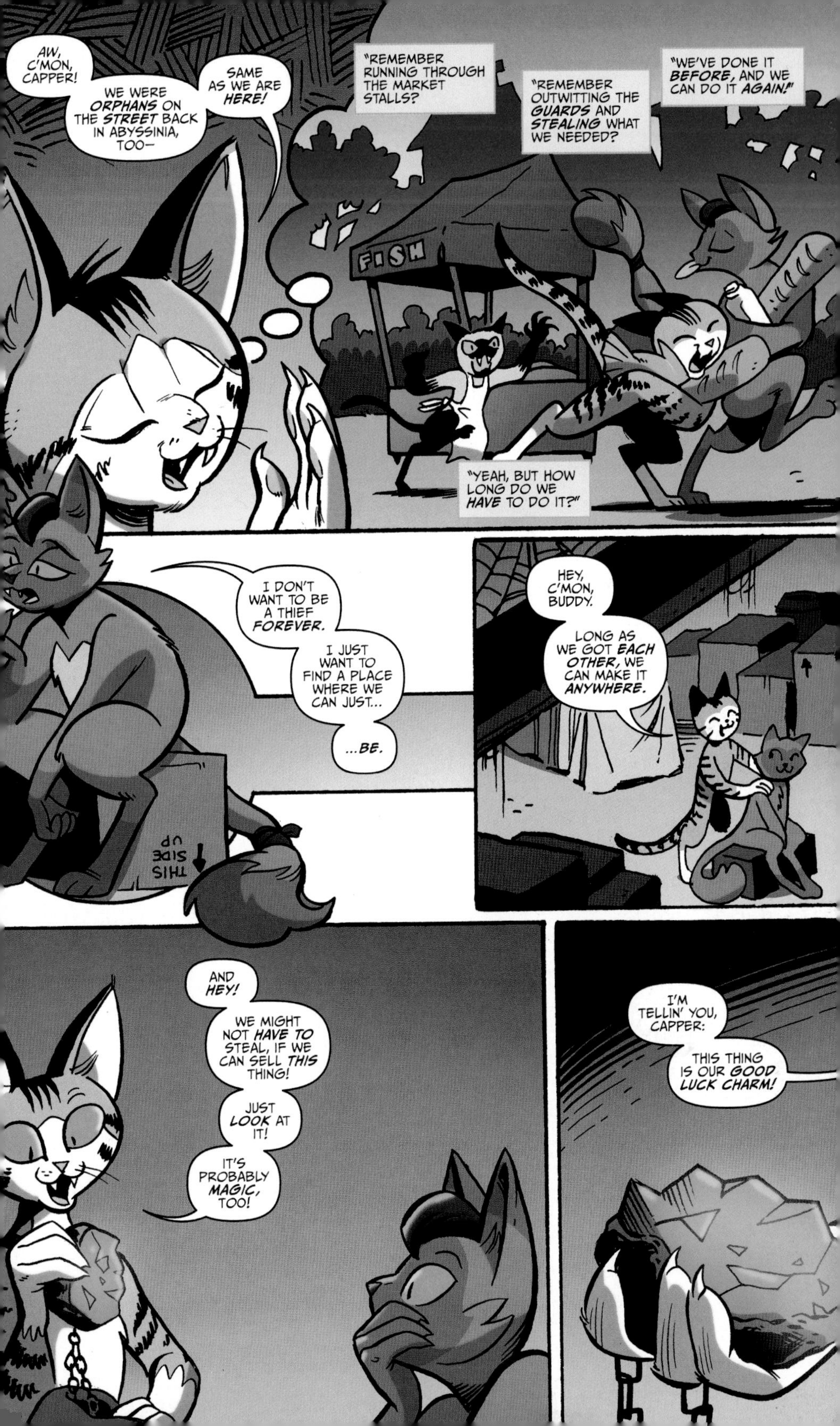
AW, C'MON, CAPPER!
WE WERE ORPHANS ON THE STREET BACK IN ABYSSINIA, TOO—
SAME AS WE ARE HERE!
"REMEMBER RUNNING THROUGH THE MARKET STALLS?
"REMEMBER OUTWITTING THE GUARDS AND STEALING WHAT WE NEEDED?
"WE'VE DONE IT BEFORE, AND WE CAN DO IT AGAIN!"
FISH
"YEAH, BUT HOW LONG DO WE HAVE TO DO IT?"
I DON'T WANT TO BE A THIEF FOREVER.
I JUST WANT TO FIND A PLACE WHERE WE CAN JUST...
...BE.
THIS SIDE UP
HEY, C'MON, BUDDY.
LONG AS WE GOT EACH OTHER, WE CAN MAKE IT ANYWHERE.
AND HEY!
WE MIGHT NOT HAVE TO STEAL, IF WE CAN SELL THIS THING!
JUST LOOK AT IT!
IT'S PROBABLY MAGIC, TOO!
I'M TELLIN' YOU, CAPPER:
THIS THING IS OUR GOOD LUCK CHARM!

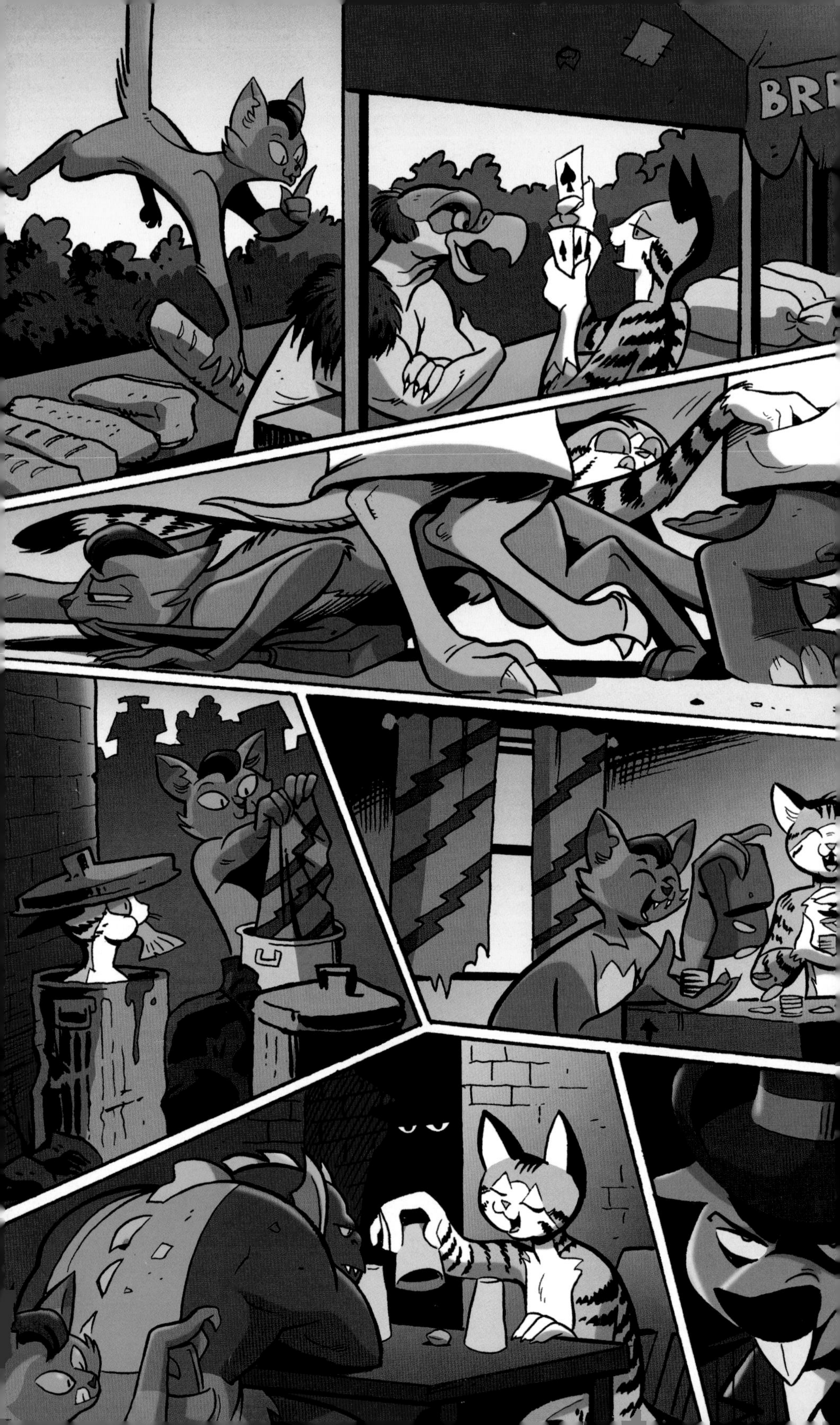
BRE

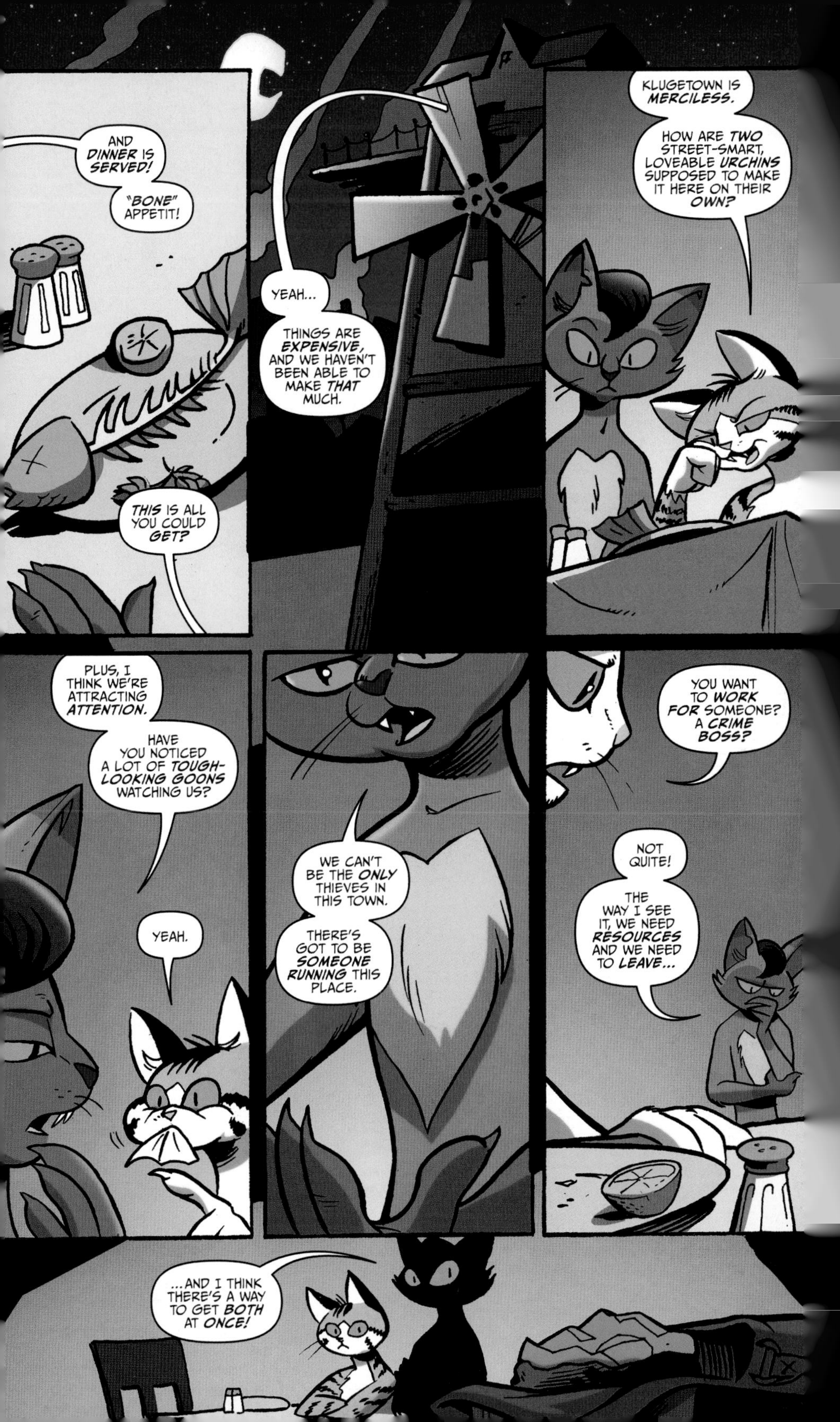
AND DINNER IS SERVED!
"BONE" APPETIT!
THIS IS ALL YOU COULD GET?
YEAH...
THINGS ARE EXPENSIVE, AND WE HAVEN'T BEEN ABLE TO MAKE THAT MUCH.
KLUGETOWN IS MERCILESS.
HOW ARE TWO STREET-SMART, LOVEABLE URCHINS SUPPOSED TO MAKE IT HERE ON THEIR OWN?
PLUS, I THINK WE'RE ATTRACTING ATTENTION.
HAVE YOU NOTICED A LOT OF TOUGH-LOOKING GOONS WATCHING US?
YEAH.
WE CAN'T BE THE ONLY THIEVES IN THIS TOWN.
THERE'S GOT TO BE SOMEONE RUNNING THIS PLACE.
YOU WANT TO WORK FOR SOMEONE? A CRIME BOSS?
NOT QUITE!
THE WAY I SEE IT, WE NEED RESOURCES AND WE NEED TO LEAVE...
...AND I THINK THERE'S A WAY TO GET BOTH AT ONCE!

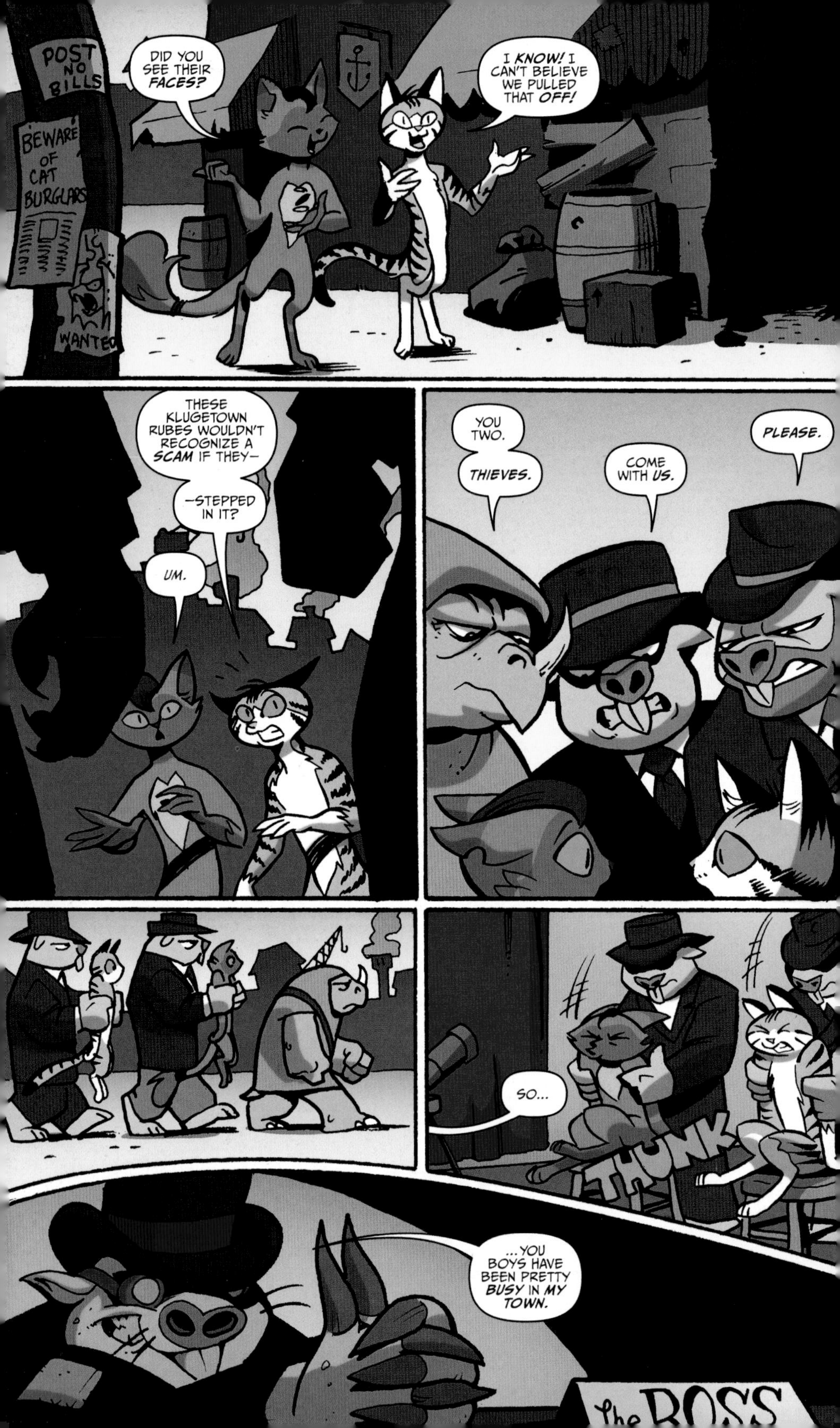

POST NO BILLS
BEWARE OF CAT BURGLARS
WANTED
DID YOU SEE THEIR *FACES?*
I *KNOW!* I CAN'T BELIEVE WE PULLED THAT *OFF!*
THESE KLUGETOWN RUBES WOULDN'T RECOGNIZE A *SCAM* IF THEY—
—STEPPED IN IT?
UM.
YOU TWO.
THIEVES.
COME WITH *US.*
PLEASE.
SO...
THUNK
...YOU BOYS HAVE BEEN PRETTY *BUSY* IN *MY TOWN.*
The BOSS

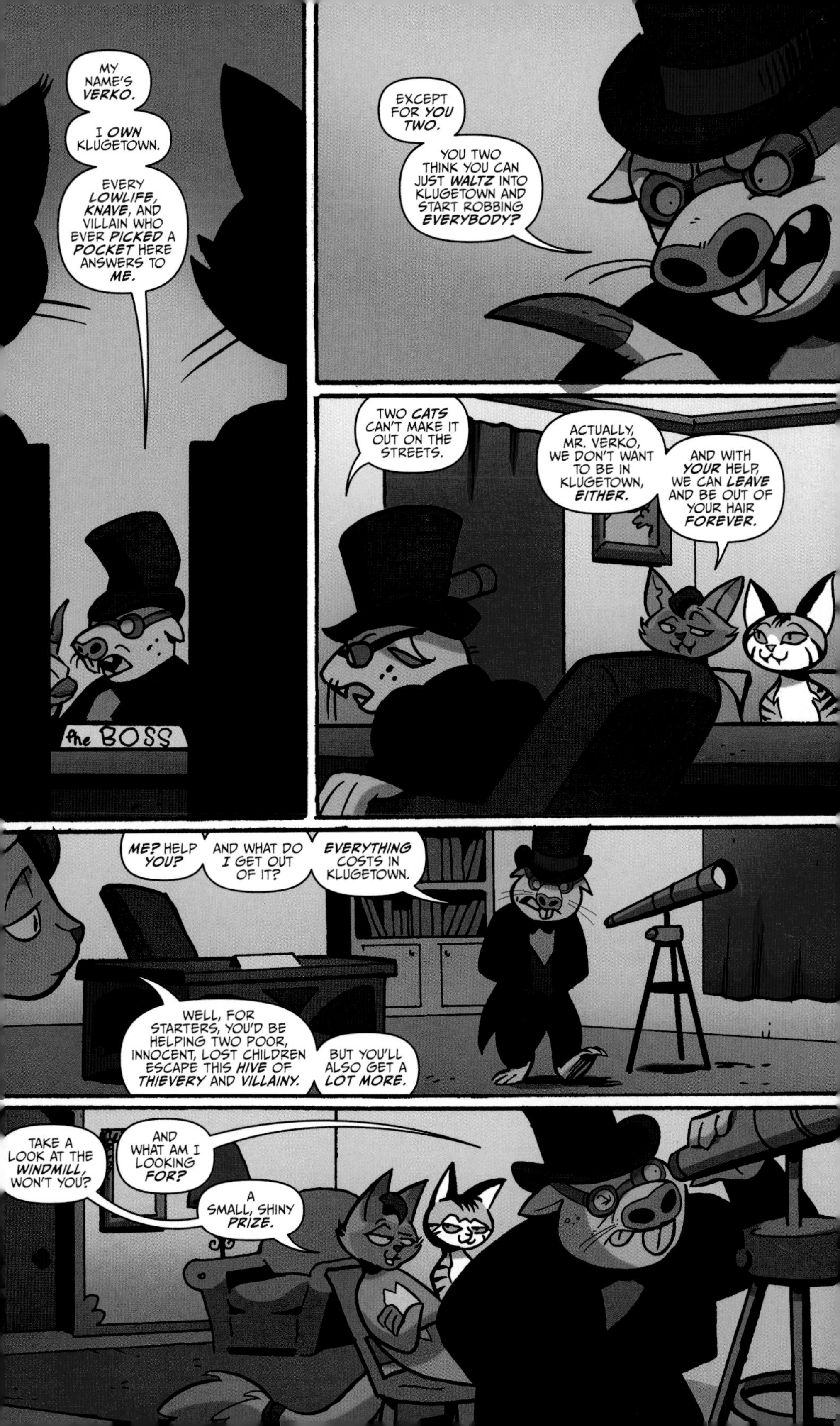
MY NAME'S VERKO.
I OWN KLUGETOWN.
EVERY LOWLIFE, KNAVE, AND VILLAIN WHO EVER PICKED A POCKET HERE ANSWERS TO ME.
the BOSS
EXCEPT FOR YOU TWO.
YOU TWO THINK YOU CAN JUST WALTZ INTO KLUGETOWN AND START ROBBING EVERYBODY?
TWO CATS CAN'T MAKE IT OUT ON THE STREETS.
ACTUALLY, MR. VERKO, WE DON'T WANT TO BE IN KLUGETOWN, EITHER.
AND WITH YOUR HELP, WE CAN LEAVE AND BE OUT OF YOUR HAIR FOREVER.
ME? HELP YOU?
AND WHAT DO I GET OUT OF IT?
EVERYTHING COSTS IN KLUGETOWN.
WELL, FOR STARTERS, YOU'D BE HELPING TWO POOR, INNOCENT, LOST CHILDREN ESCAPE THIS HIVE OF THIEVERY AND VILLAINY.
BUT YOU'LL ALSO GET A LOT MORE.
TAKE A LOOK AT THE WINDMILL, WON'T YOU?
AND WHAT AM I LOOKING FOR?
A SMALL, SHINY PRIZE.

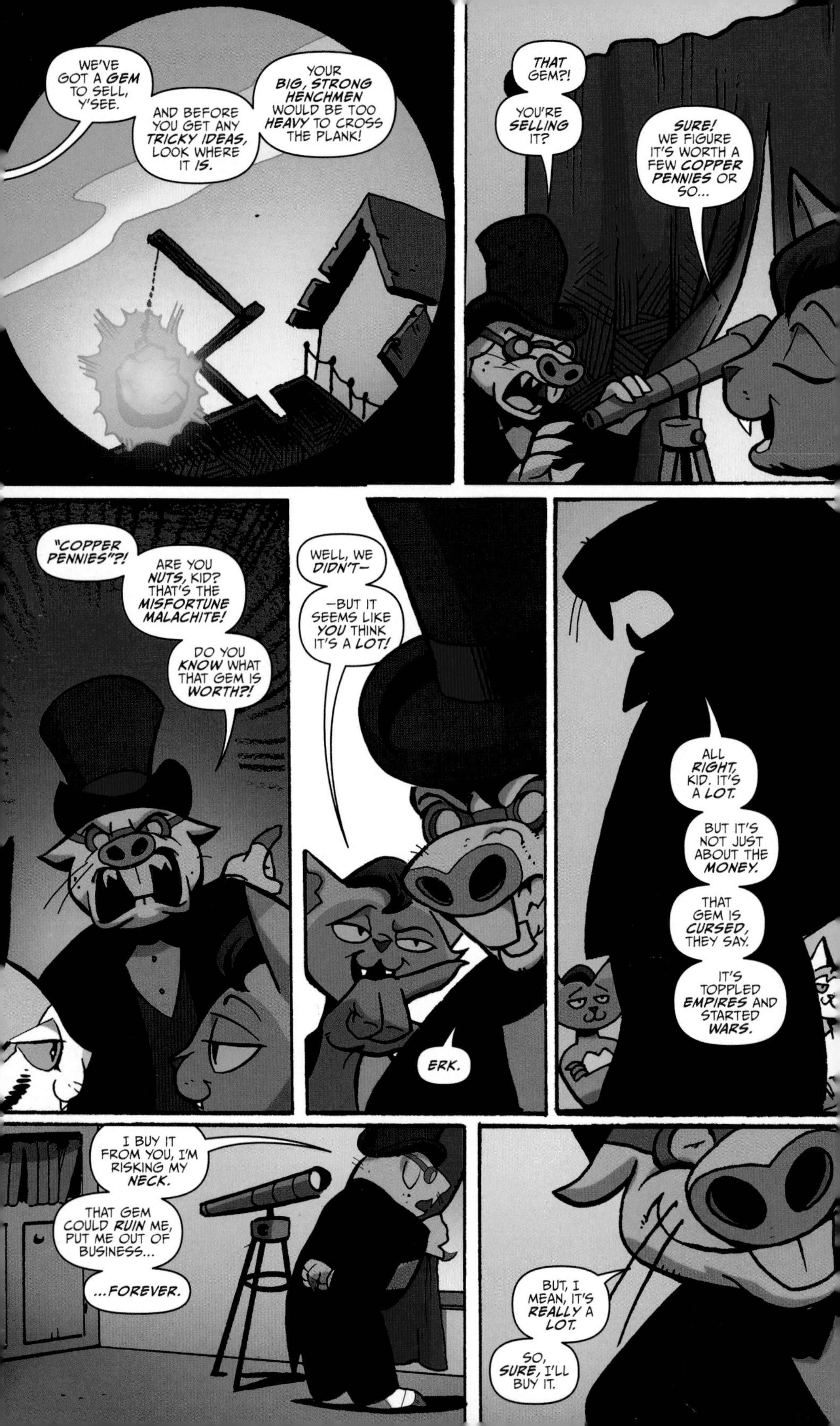
WE'VE GOT A GEM TO SELL, Y'SEE.
AND BEFORE YOU GET ANY TRICKY IDEAS, LOOK WHERE IT IS.
YOUR BIG, STRONG HENCHMEN WOULD BE TOO HEAVY TO CROSS THE PLANK!
THAT GEM?!
YOU'RE SELLING IT?
SURE! WE FIGURE IT'S WORTH A FEW COPPER PENNIES OR SO...
"COPPER PENNIES"?!
ARE YOU NUTS, KID? THAT'S THE MISFORTUNE MALACHITE!
DO YOU KNOW WHAT THAT GEM IS WORTH?!
WELL, WE DIDN'T—
—BUT IT SEEMS LIKE YOU THINK IT'S A LOT!
ERK.
ALL RIGHT, KID. IT'S A LOT.
BUT IT'S NOT JUST ABOUT THE MONEY.
THAT GEM IS CURSED, THEY SAY.
IT'S TOPPLED EMPIRES AND STARTED WARS.
I BUY IT FROM YOU, I'M RISKING MY NECK.
THAT GEM COULD RUIN ME, PUT ME OUT OF BUSINESS...
...FOREVER.
BUT, I MEAN, IT'S REALLY A LOT.
SO, SURE, I'LL BUY IT.

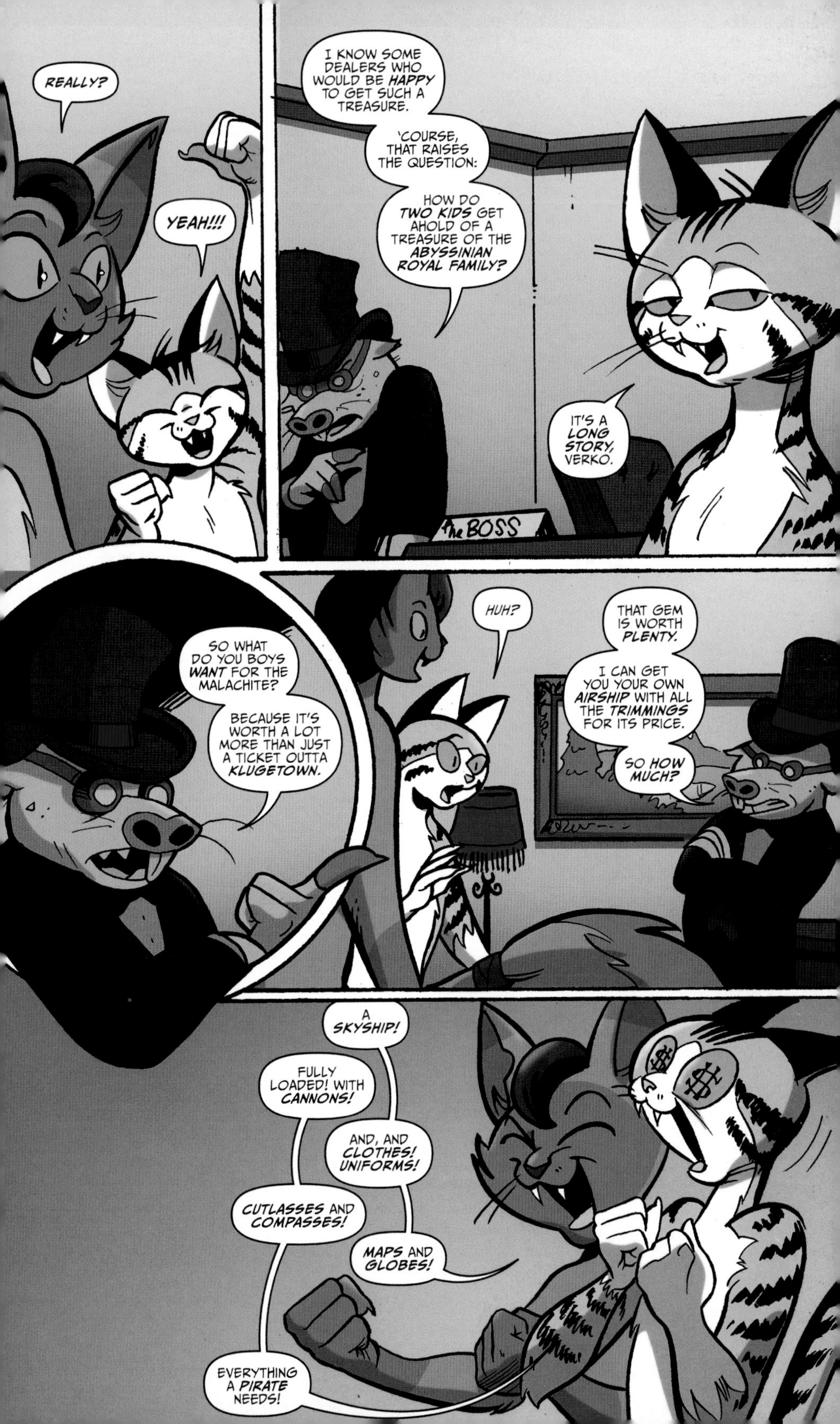
REALLY?
YEAH!!!
I KNOW SOME DEALERS WHO WOULD BE HAPPY TO GET SUCH A TREASURE.
'COURSE, THAT RAISES THE QUESTION:
HOW DO TWO KIDS GET AHOLD OF A TREASURE OF THE ABYSSINIAN ROYAL FAMILY?
IT'S A LONG STORY, VERKO.
The BOSS
SO WHAT DO YOU BOYS WANT FOR THE MALACHITE?
BECAUSE IT'S WORTH A LOT MORE THAN JUST A TICKET OUTTA KLUGETOWN.
HUH?
THAT GEM IS WORTH PLENTY.
I CAN GET YOU YOUR OWN AIRSHIP WITH ALL THE TRIMMINGS FOR ITS PRICE.
SO HOW MUCH?
A SKYSHIP!
FULLY LOADED! WITH CANNONS!
AND, AND CLOTHES! UNIFORMS!
CUTLASSES AND COMPASSES!
MAPS AND GLOBES!
EVERYTHING A PIRATE NEEDS!

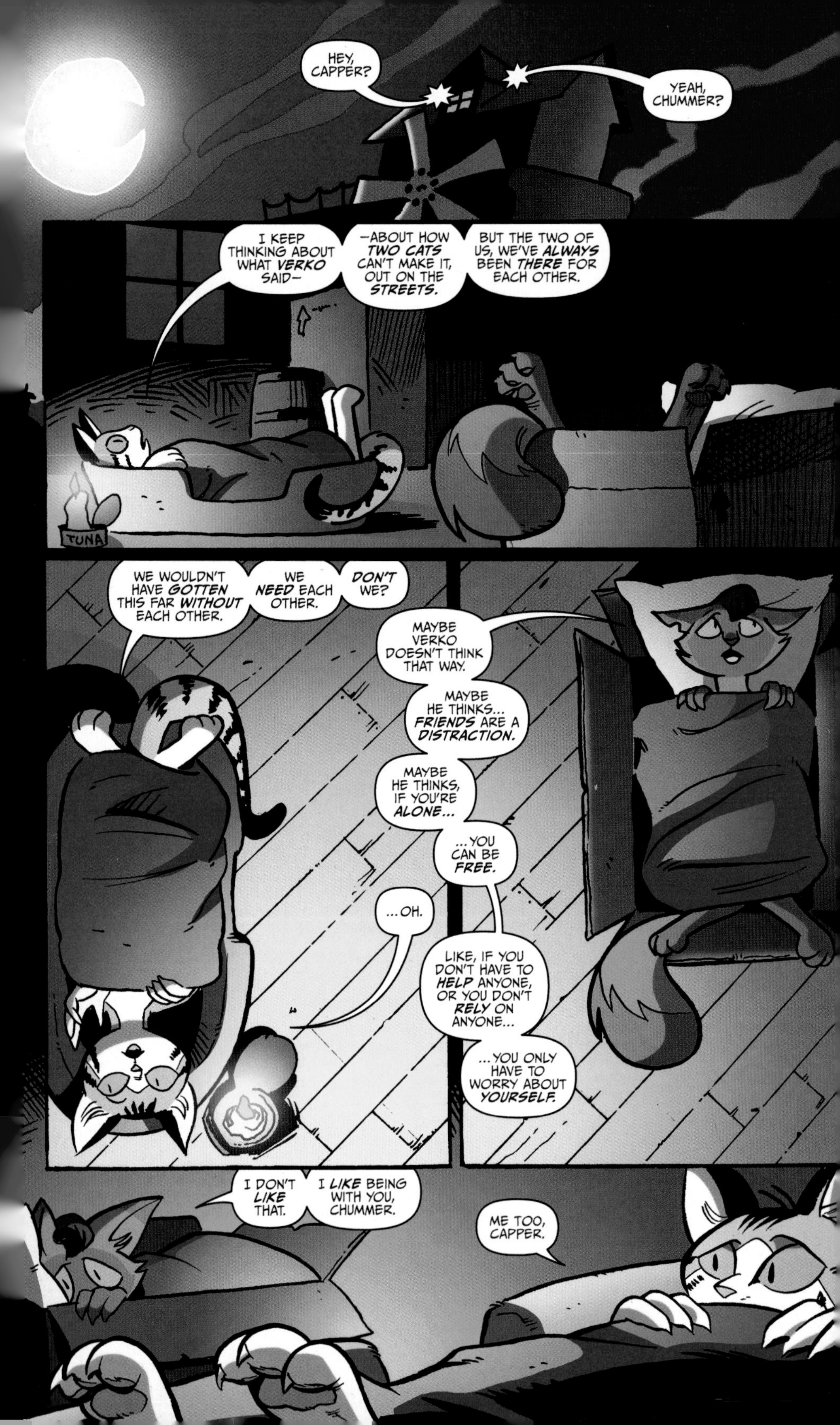
HEY, CAPPER?
YEAH, CHUMMER?
I KEEP THINKING ABOUT WHAT VERKO SAID—
—ABOUT HOW TWO CATS CAN'T MAKE IT, OUT ON THE STREETS.
BUT THE TWO OF US, WE'VE ALWAYS BEEN THERE FOR EACH OTHER.
TUNA
WE WOULDN'T HAVE GOTTEN THIS FAR WITHOUT EACH OTHER.
WE NEED EACH OTHER.
DON'T WE?
MAYBE VERKO DOESN'T THINK THAT WAY.
MAYBE HE THINKS... FRIENDS ARE A DISTRACTION.
MAYBE HE THINKS, IF YOU'RE ALONE...
...YOU CAN BE FREE.
...OH.
LIKE, IF YOU DON'T HAVE TO HELP ANYONE, OR YOU DON'T RELY ON ANYONE...
...YOU ONLY HAVE TO WORRY ABOUT YOURSELF.
I DON'T LIKE THAT.
I LIKE BEING WITH YOU, CHUMMER.
ME TOO, CAPPER.

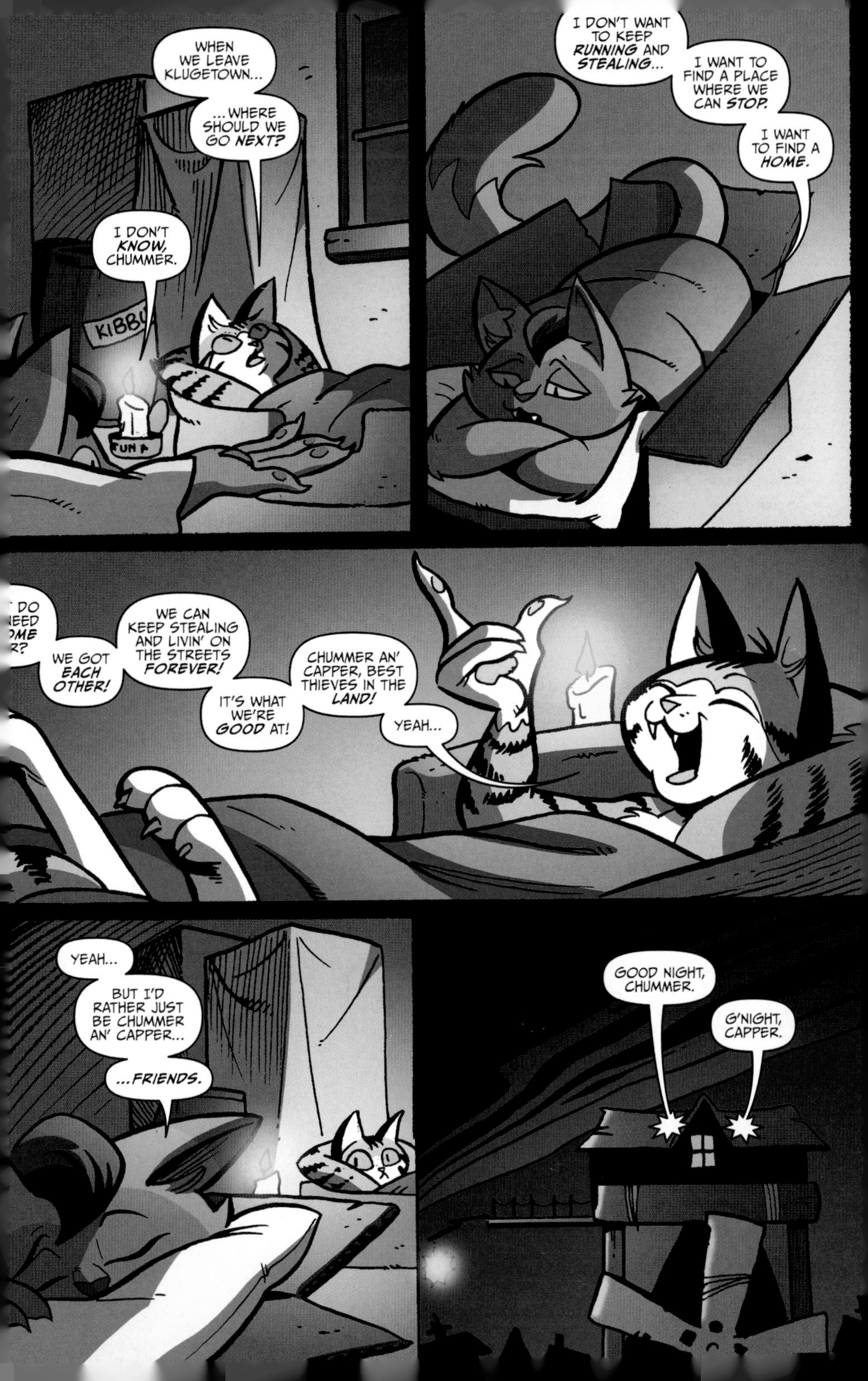

WHEN WE LEAVE KLUGETOWN...
...WHERE SHOULD WE GO NEXT?
I DON'T KNOW, CHUMMER.
I DON'T WANT TO KEEP RUNNING AND STEALING...
I WANT TO FIND A PLACE WHERE WE CAN STOP.
I WANT TO FIND A HOME.
WE GOT EACH OTHER!
WE CAN KEEP STEALING AND LIVIN' ON THE STREETS FOREVER!
IT'S WHAT WE'RE GOOD AT!
CHUMMER AN' CAPPER, BEST THIEVES IN THE LAND!
YEAH...
YEAH...
BUT I'D RATHER JUST BE CHUMMER AN' CAPPER...
...FRIENDS.
GOOD NIGHT, CHUMMER.
G'NIGHT, CAPPER.

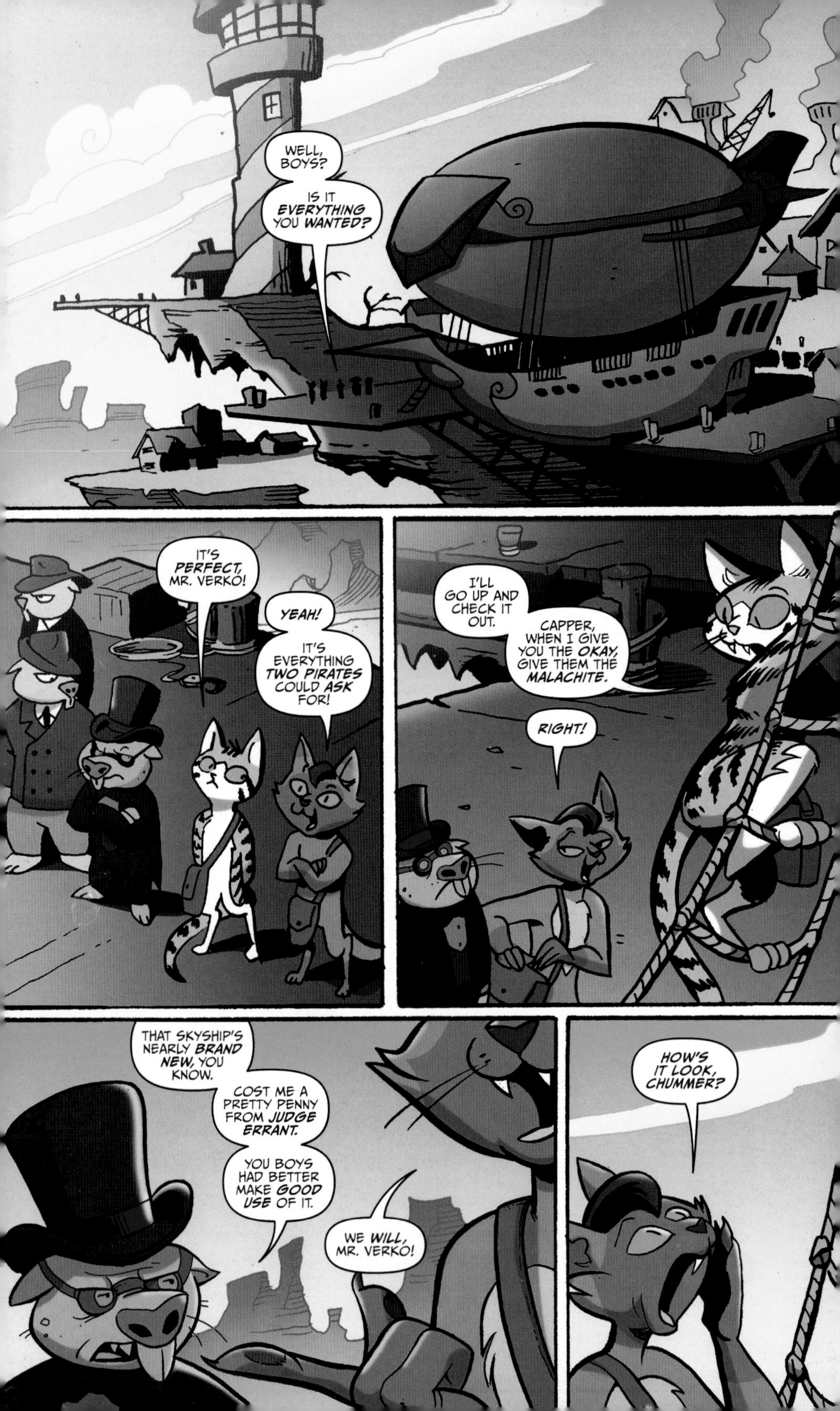
WELL, BOYS?
IS IT EVERYTHING YOU WANTED?
IT'S PERFECT, MR. VERKO!
YEAH!
IT'S EVERYTHING TWO PIRATES COULD ASK FOR!
I'LL GO UP AND CHECK IT OUT.
CAPPER, WHEN I GIVE YOU THE OKAY, GIVE THEM THE MALACHITE.
RIGHT!
THAT SKYSHIP'S NEARLY BRAND NEW, YOU KNOW.
COST ME A PRETTY PENNY FROM JUDGE ERRANT.
YOU BOYS HAD BETTER MAKE GOOD USE OF IT.
WE WILL, MR. VERKO!
HOW'S IT LOOK, CHUMMER?

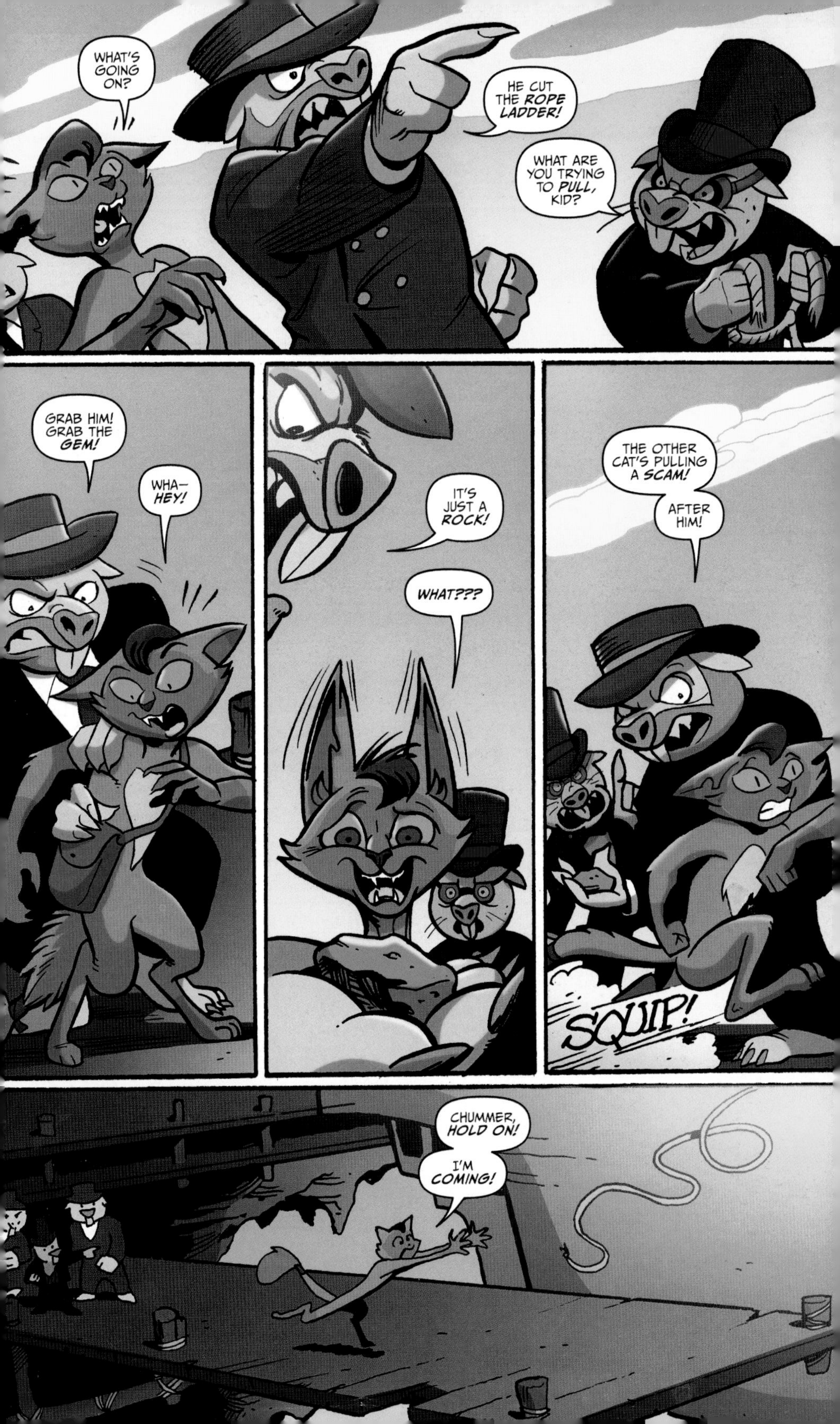
WHAT'S GOING ON?
HE CUT THE ROPE LADDER!
WHAT ARE YOU TRYING TO PULL, KID?
GRAB HIM! GRAB THE GEM!
WHA— HEY!
IT'S JUST A ROCK!
WHAT???
THE OTHER CAT'S PULLING A SCAM!
AFTER HIM!
SQUIP!
CHUMMER, HOLD ON!
I'M COMING!

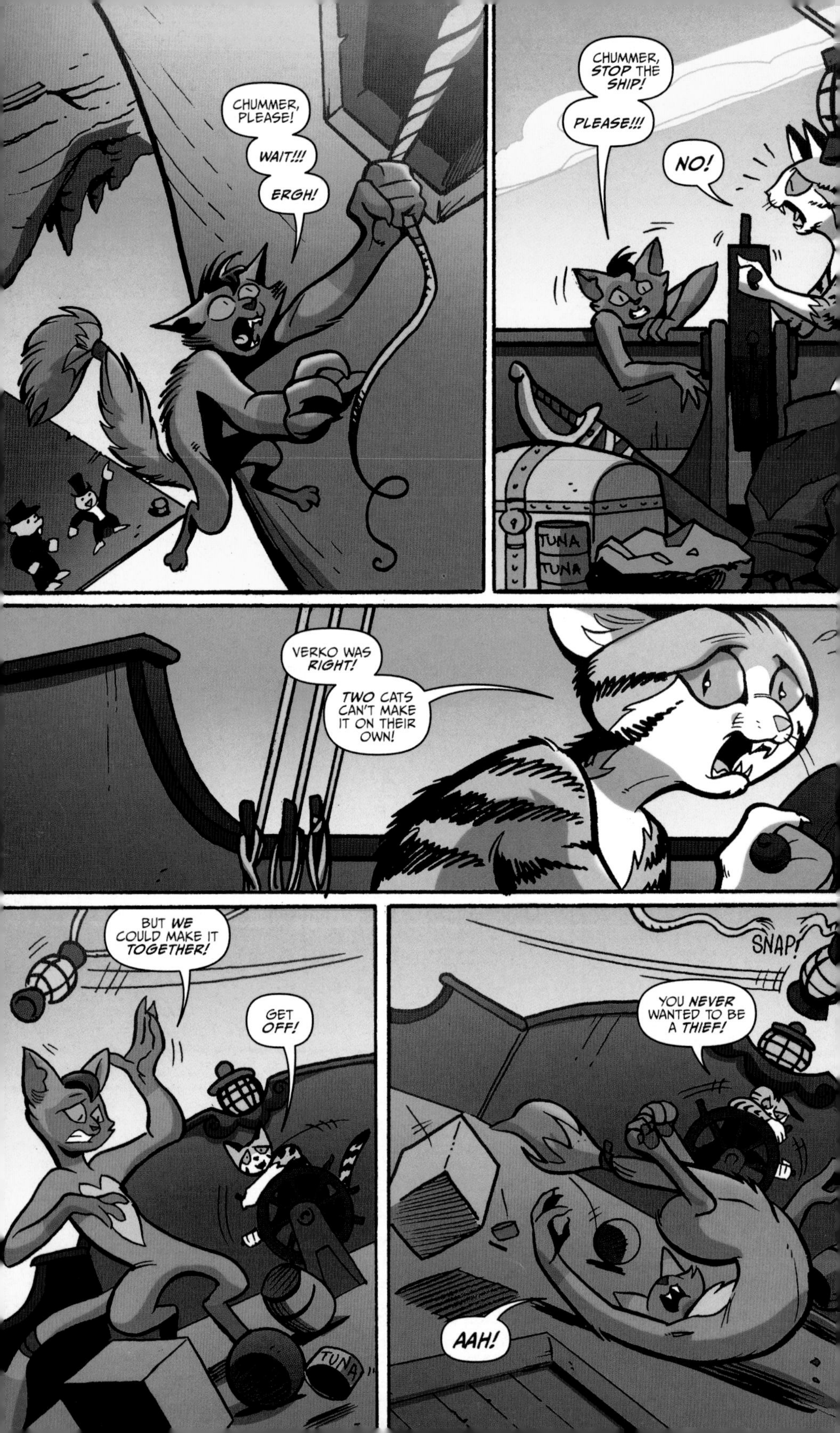
CHUMMER, PLEASE!
WAIT!!!
ERGH!
CHUMMER, STOP THE SHIP!
PLEASE!!!
NO!
TUNA
TUNA
VERKO WAS RIGHT!
TWO CATS CAN'T MAKE IT ON THEIR OWN!
BUT WE COULD MAKE IT TOGETHER!
GET OFF!
TUNA
SNAP!
YOU NEVER WANTED TO BE A THIEF!
AAH!

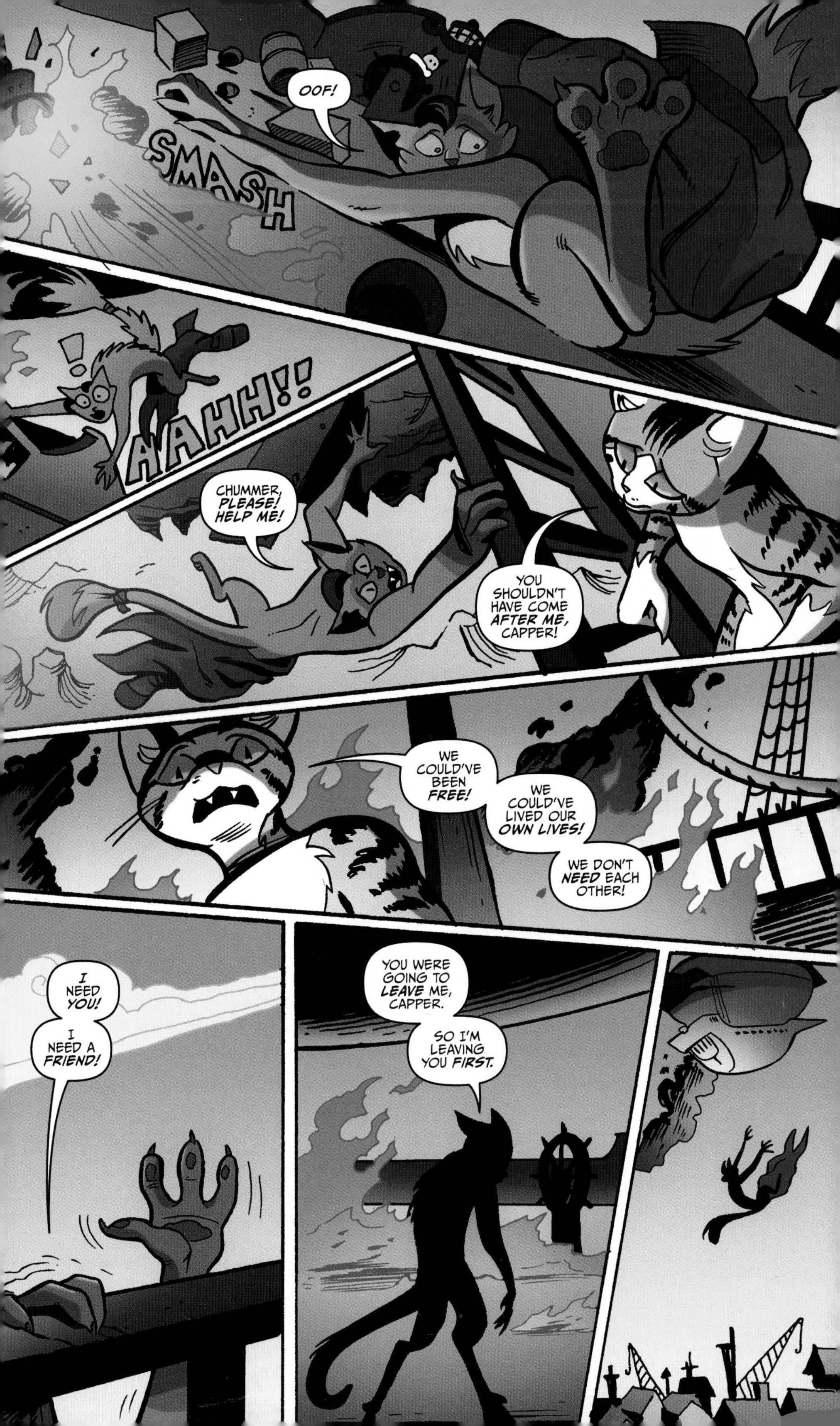
OOF!
SMASH
AAHH!!
CHUMMER, PLEASE! HELP ME!
YOU SHOULDN'T HAVE COME AFTER ME, CAPPER!
WE COULD'VE BEEN FREE!
WE COULD'VE LIVED OUR OWN LIVES!
WE DON'T NEED EACH OTHER!
I NEED YOU!
I NEED A FRIEND!
YOU WERE GOING TO LEAVE ME, CAPPER.
SO I'M LEAVING YOU FIRST.

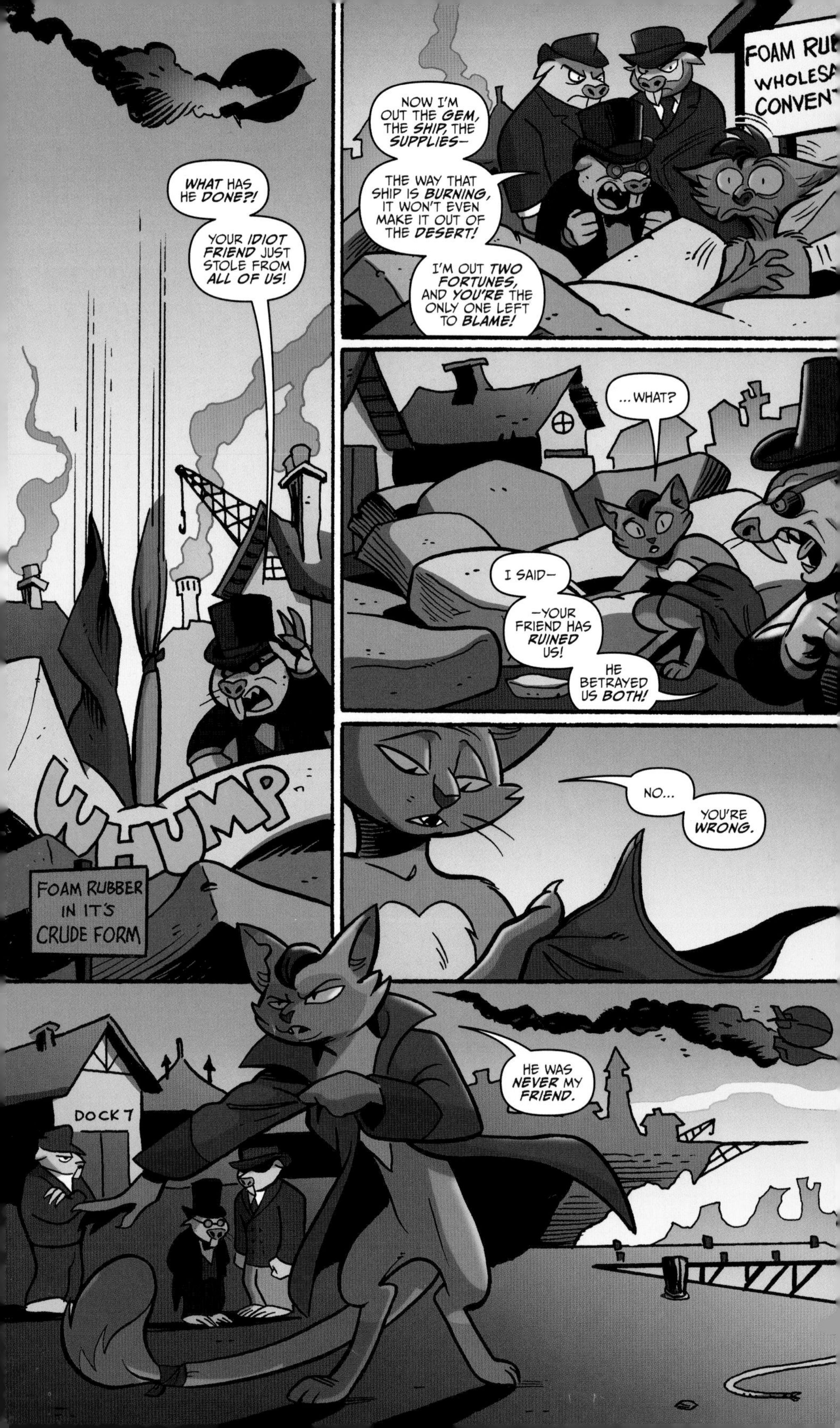
WHAT HAS HE DONE?!
YOUR IDIOT FRIEND JUST STOLE FROM ALL OF US!
WHUMP
FOAM RUBBER IN IT'S CRUDE FORM
FOAM RU WHOLESA CONVENT
NOW I'M OUT THE GEM, THE SHIP, THE SUPPLIES—
THE WAY THAT SHIP IS BURNING, IT WON'T EVEN MAKE IT OUT OF THE DESERT!
I'M OUT TWO FORTUNES, AND YOU'RE THE ONLY ONE LEFT TO BLAME!
...WHAT?
I SAID—
—YOUR FRIEND HAS RUINED US!
HE BETRAYED US BOTH!
NO...
YOU'RE WRONG.
DOCK 7
HE WAS NEVER MY FRIEND.

Art by **TONY FLEECS**

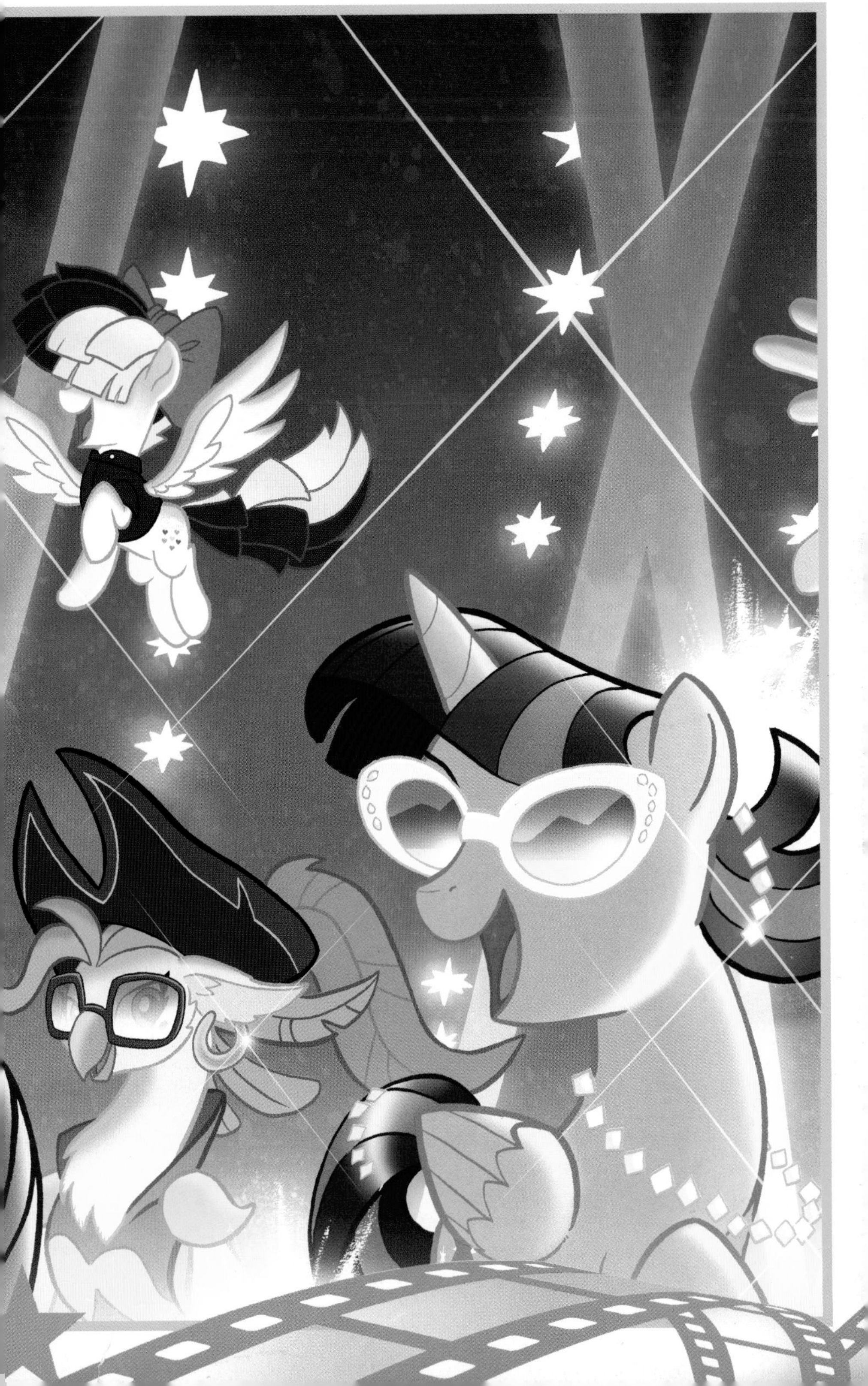

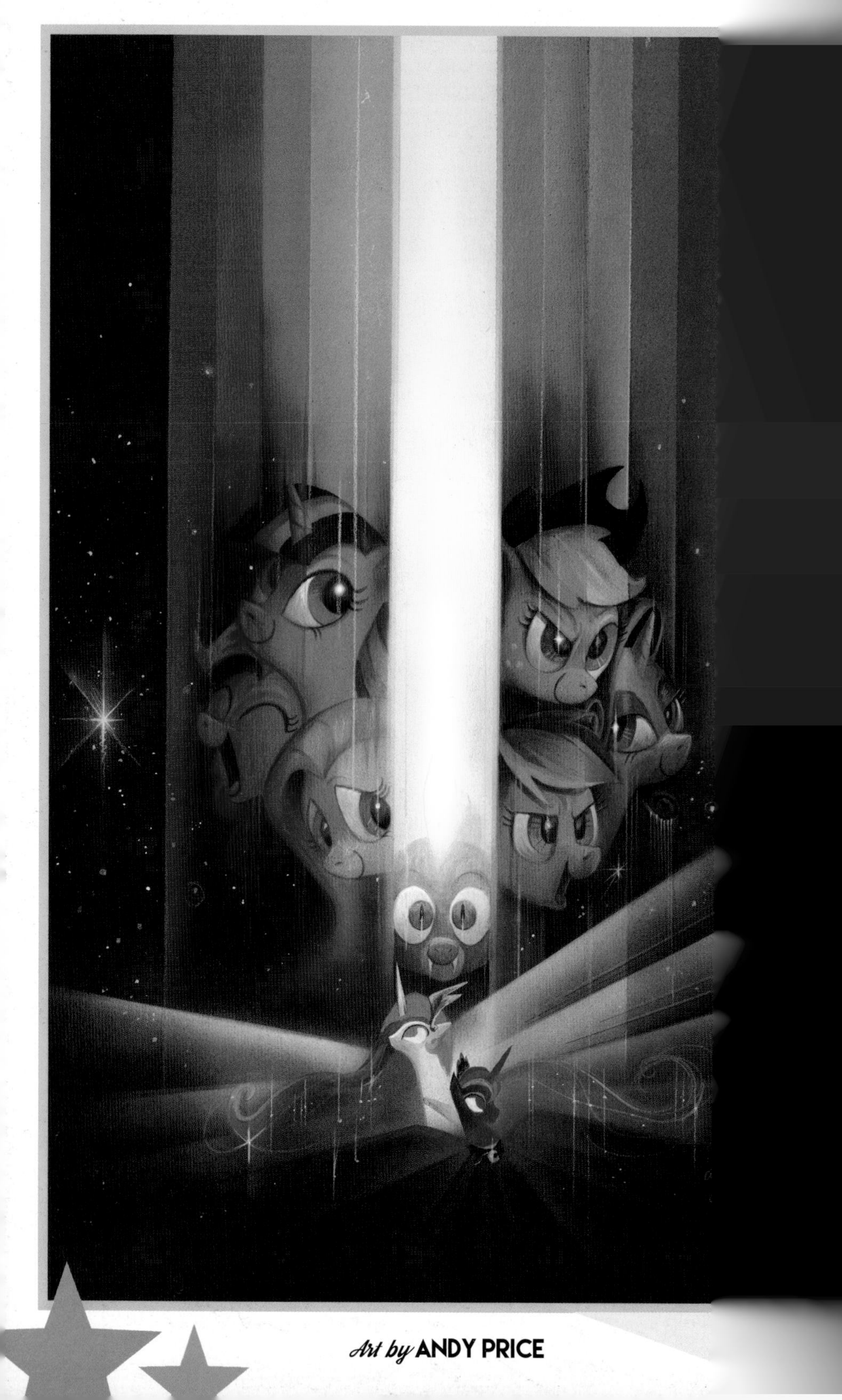

Art by **ANDY PRICE**

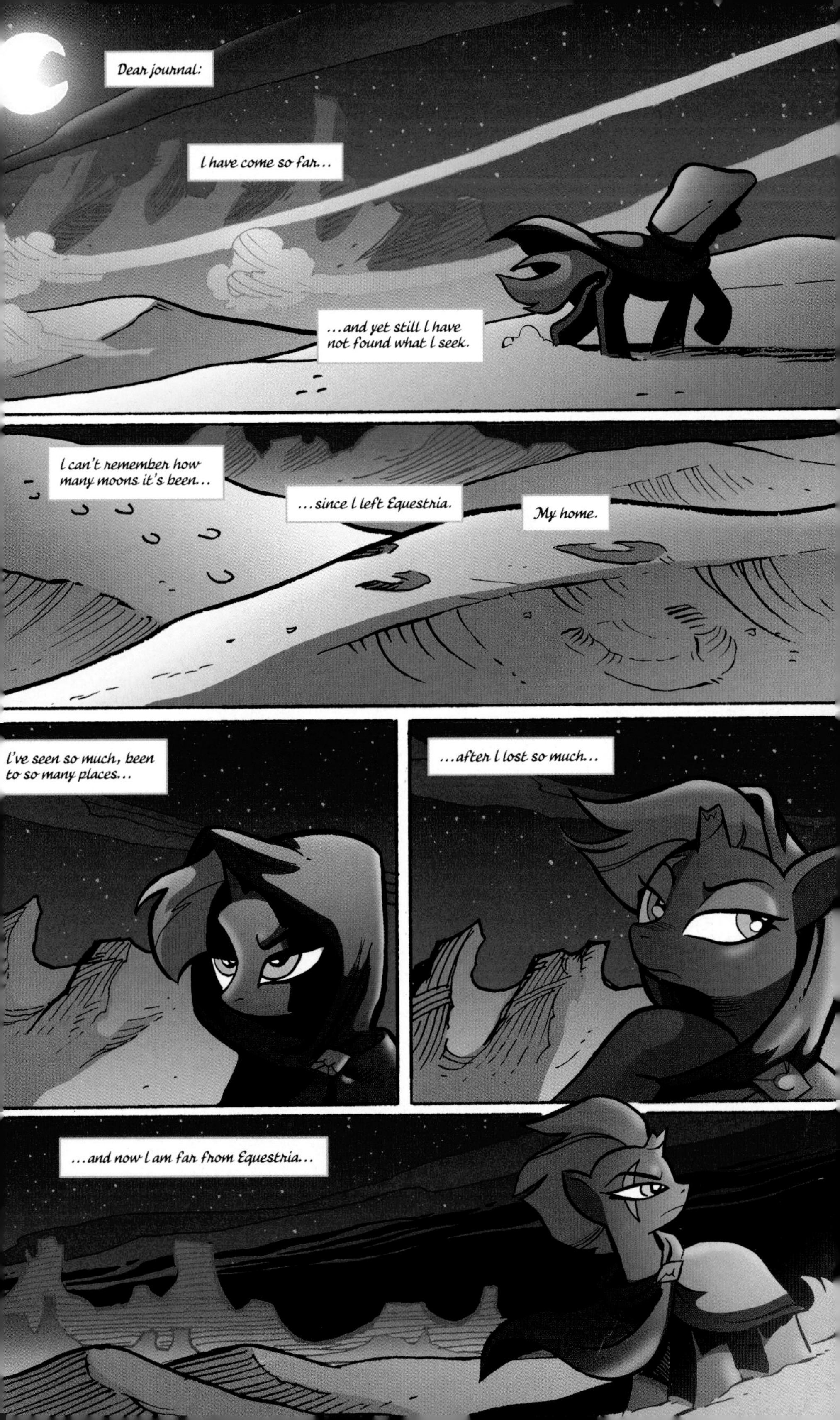
Dear journal:
I have come so far...
...and yet still I have not found what I seek.
I can't remember how many moons it's been...
...since I left Equestria.
My home.
I've seen so much, been to so many places...
...after I lost so much...
...and now I am far from Equestria...

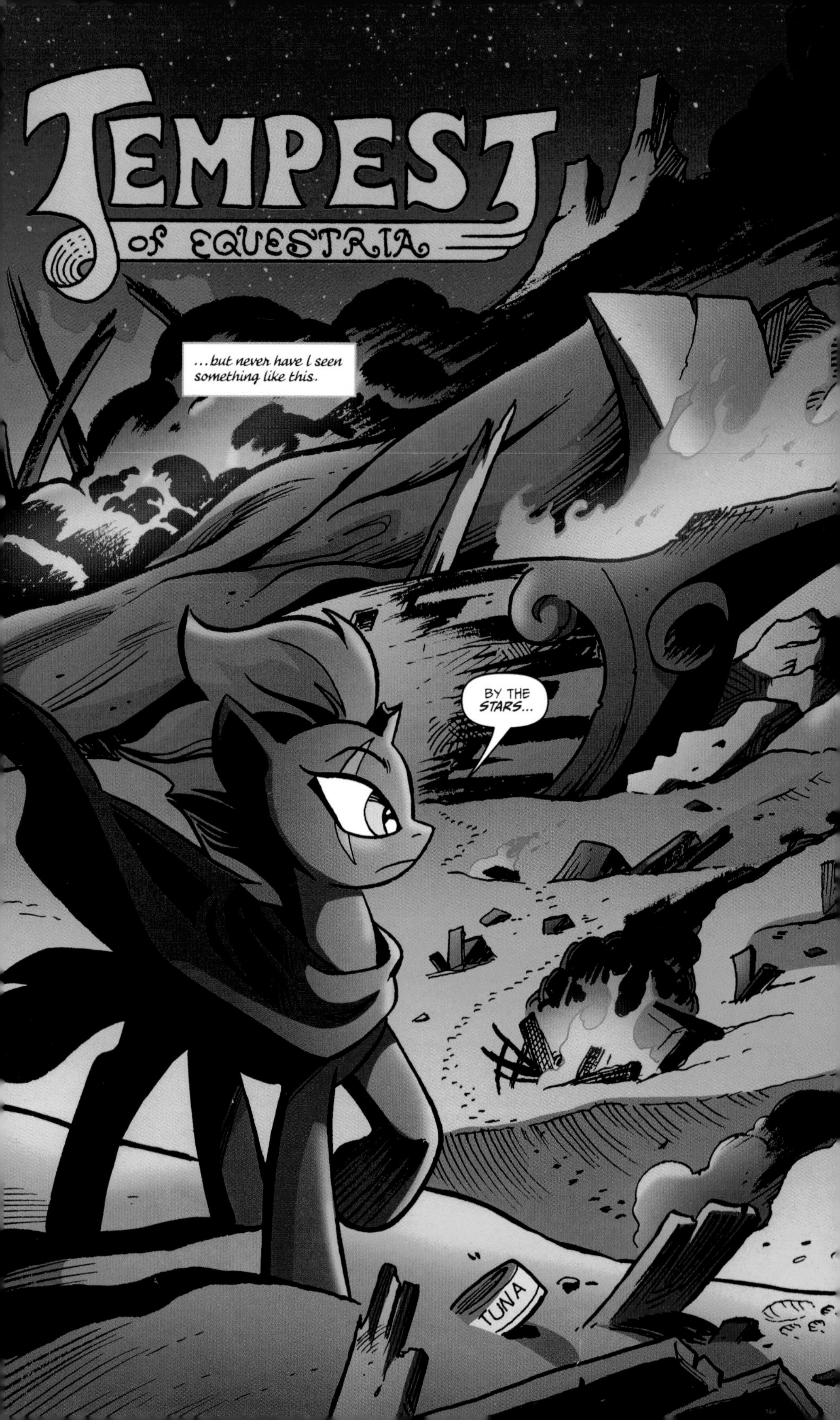
TEMPEST of EQUESTRIA
...but never have I seen something like this.
BY THE STARS...
TUNA

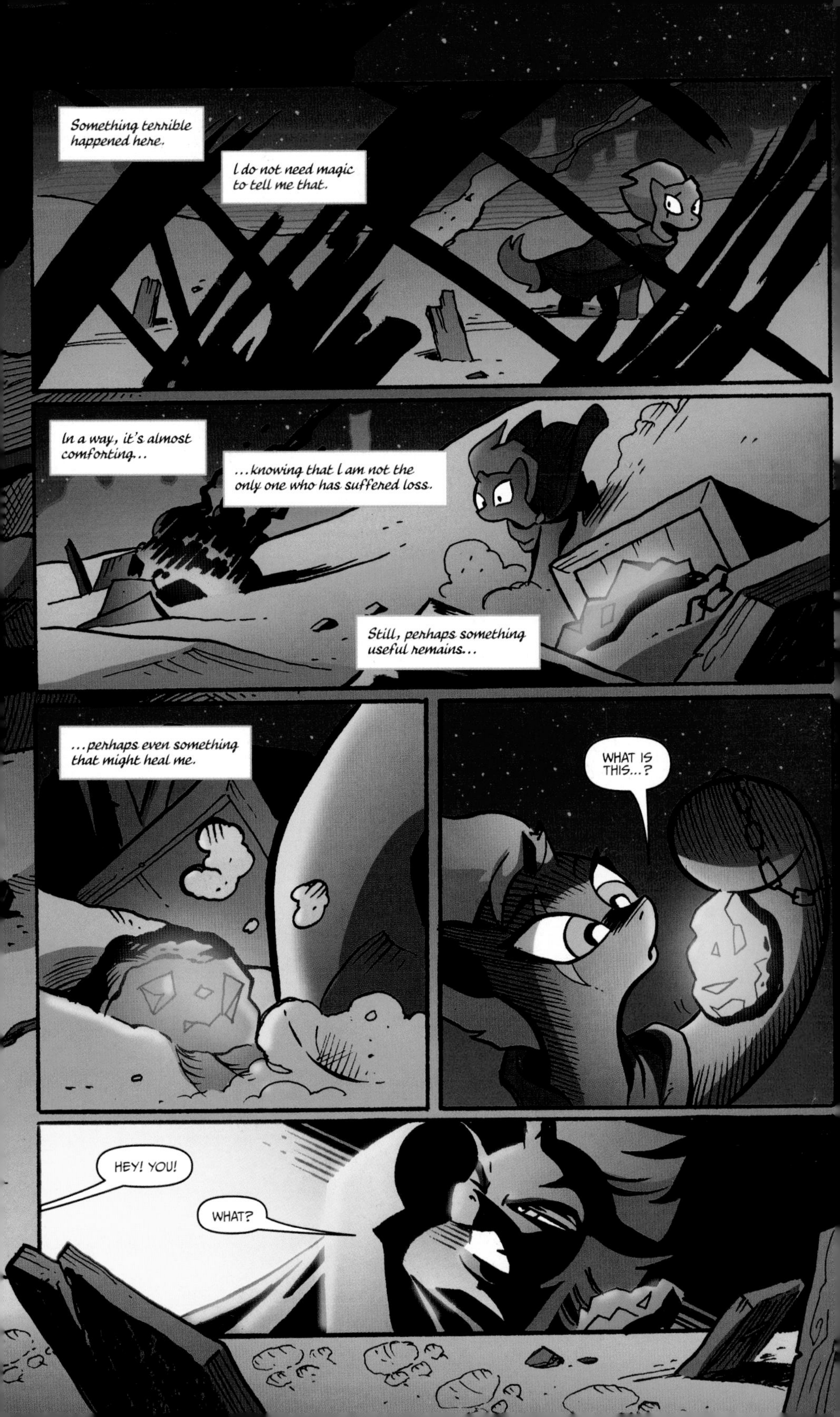

Something terrible happened here.
I do not need magic to tell me that.
In a way, it's almost comforting...
...knowing that I am not the only one who has suffered loss.
Still, perhaps something useful remains...
...perhaps even something that might heal me.
WHAT IS THIS...?
HEY! YOU!
WHAT?

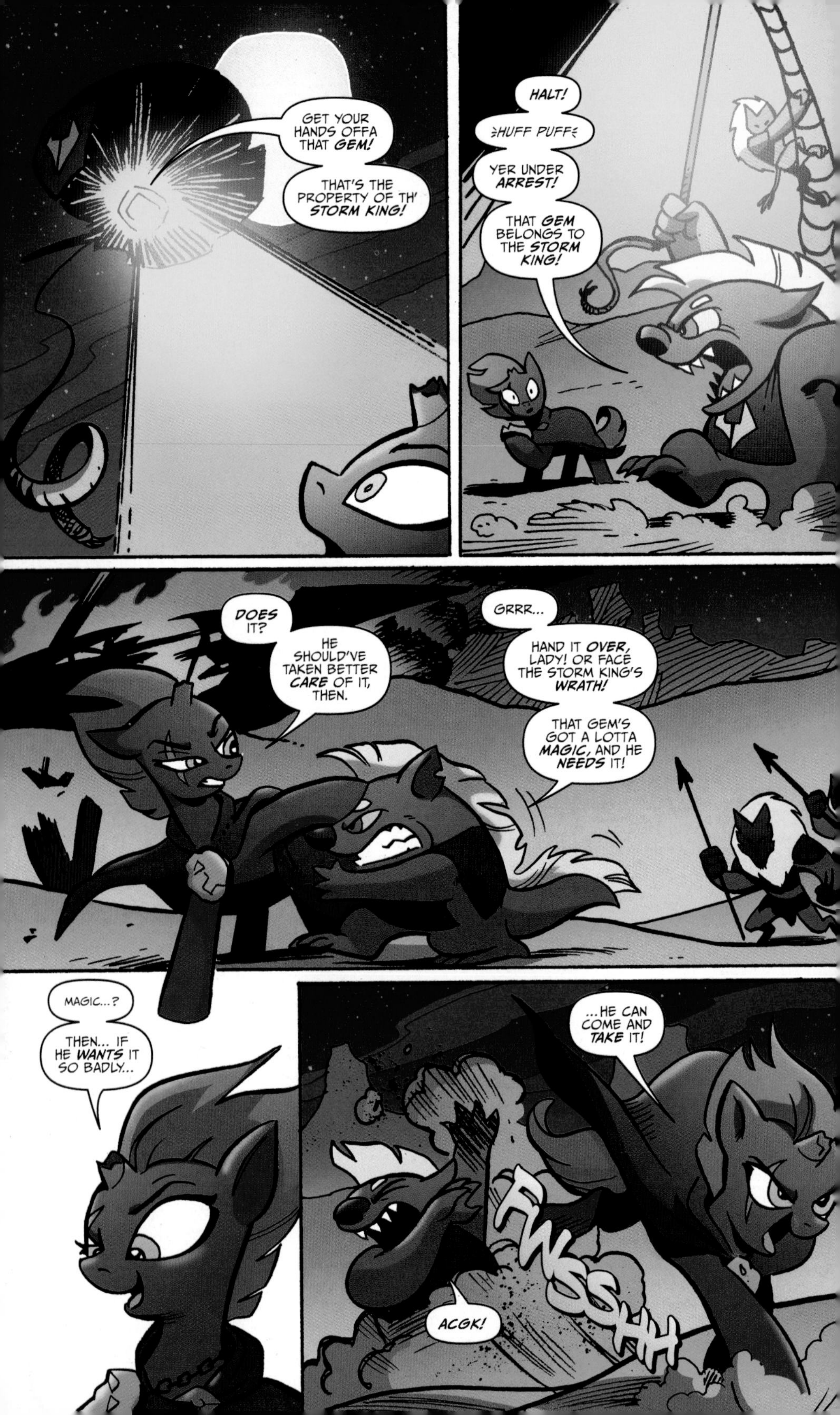
GET YOUR HANDS OFFA THAT GEM!
THAT'S THE PROPERTY OF TH' STORM KING!
HALT!
HUFF PUFF
YER UNDER ARREST!
THAT GEM BELONGS TO THE STORM KING!
DOES IT?
HE SHOULD'VE TAKEN BETTER CARE OF IT, THEN.
GRRR...
HAND IT OVER, LADY! OR FACE THE STORM KING'S WRATH!
THAT GEM'S GOT A LOTTA MAGIC, AND HE NEEDS IT!
MAGIC...?
THEN... IF HE WANTS IT SO BADLY...
...HE CAN COME AND TAKE IT!
FWSSHH
ACGK!

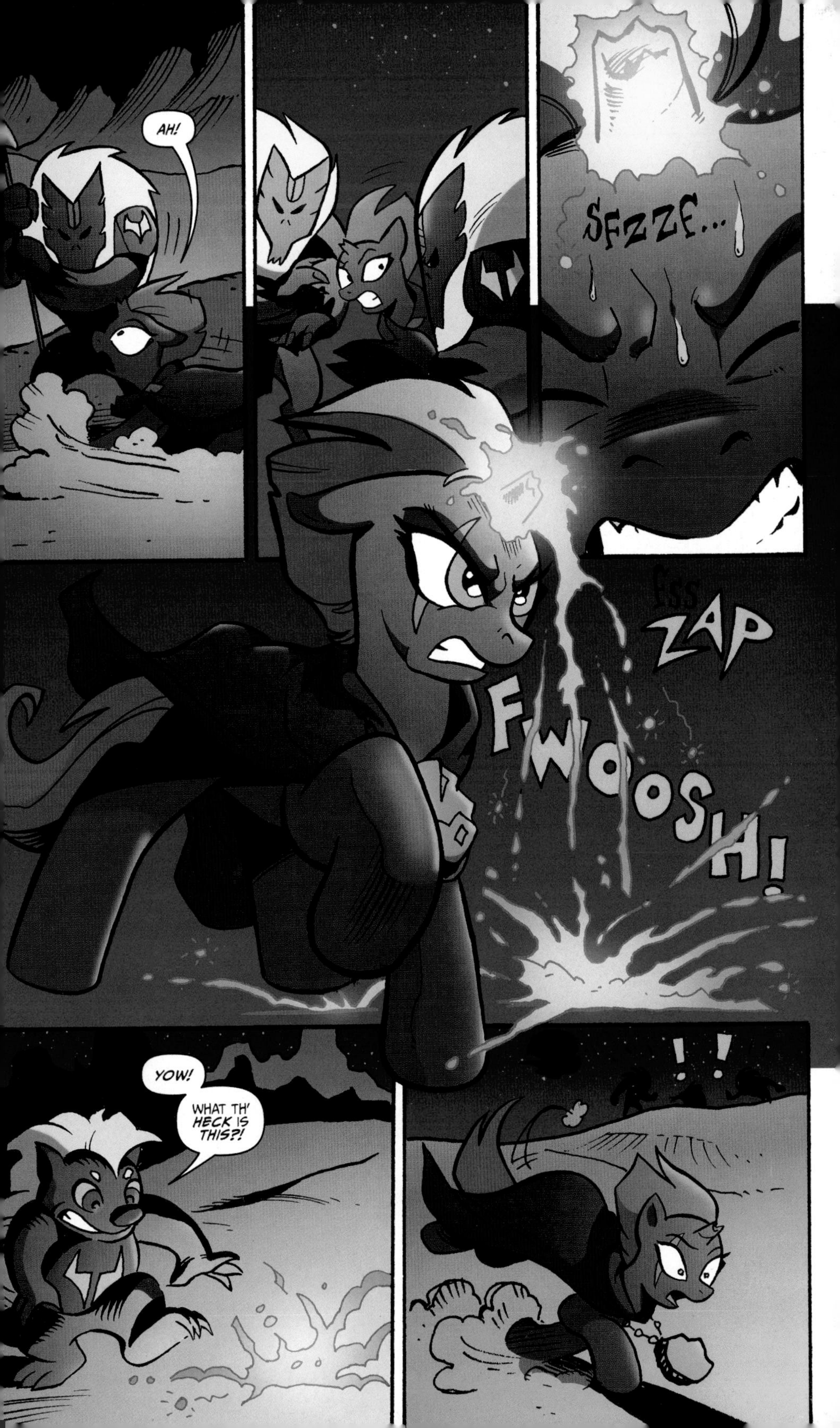

AH!
SFZZF...
FSS
ZAP
FWOOSH!
YOW!
WHAT TH' HECK IS THIS?!
!!

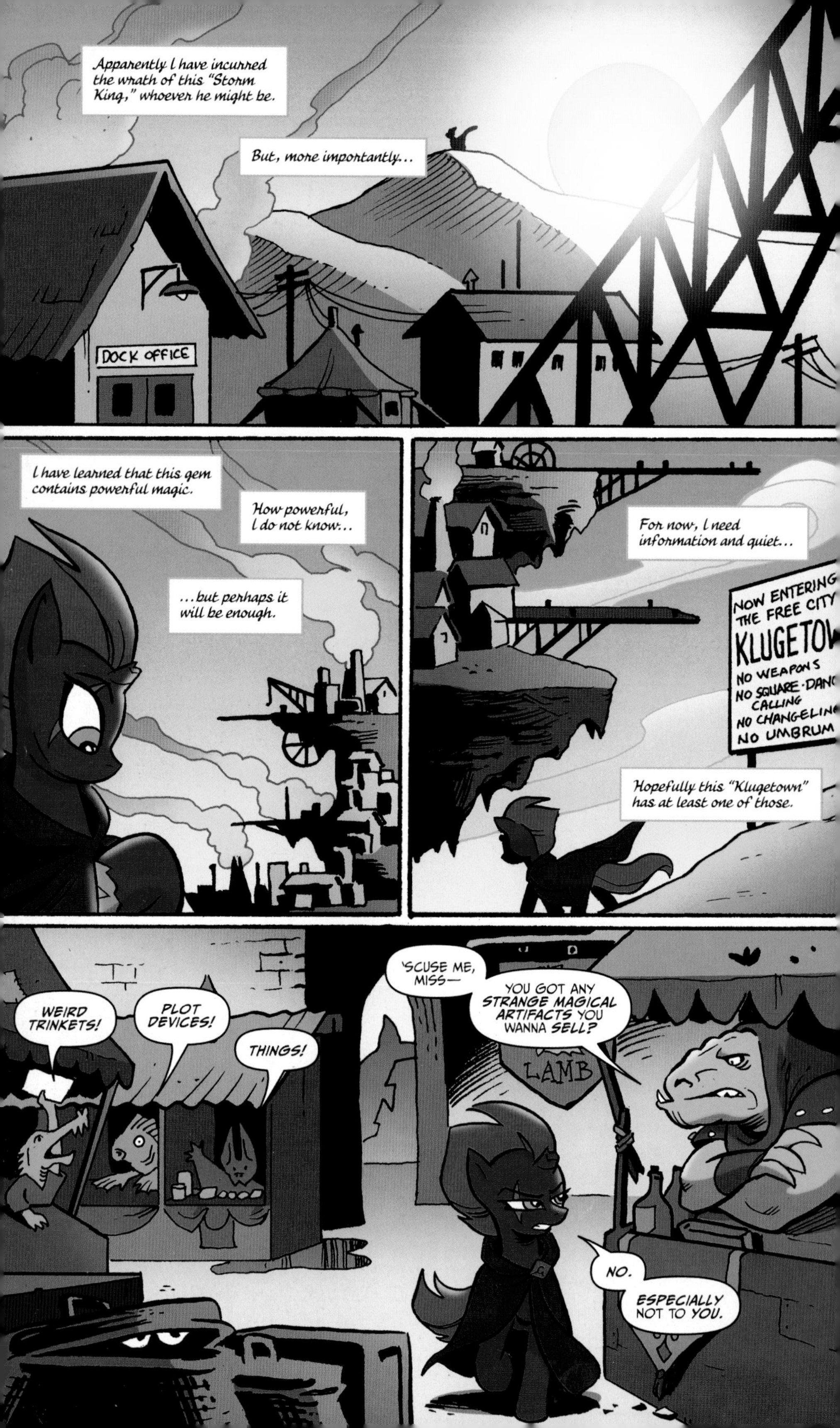

Apparently I have incurred the wrath of this "Storm King," whoever he might be.
But, more importantly...
DOCK OFFICE
I have learned that this gem contains powerful magic.
How powerful, I do not know...
...but perhaps it will be enough.
For now, I need information and quiet...
NOW ENTERING THE FREE CITY KLUGETOW
NO WEAPONS
NO SQUARE-DANC CALLING
NO CHANGELIN
NO UMBRUM
Hopefully this "Klugetown" has at least one of those.
WEIRD TRINKETS!
PLOT DEVICES!
THINGS!
'SCUSE ME, MISS—
YOU GOT ANY STRANGE MAGICAL ARTIFACTS YOU WANNA SELL?
LAMB
NO.
ESPECIALLY NOT TO YOU.

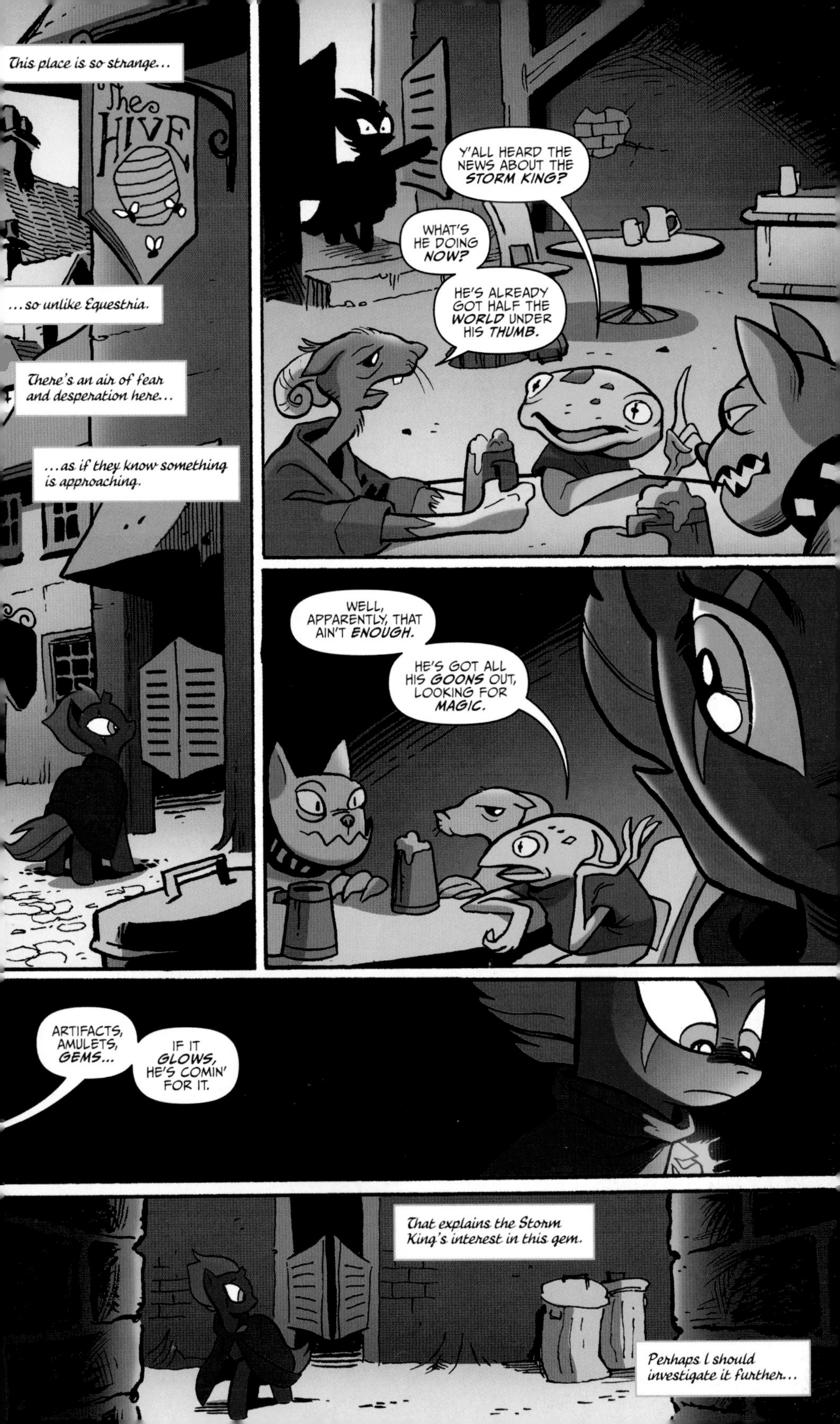
This place is so strange...
The HIVE
...so unlike Equestria.
There's an air of fear and desperation here...
...as if they know something is approaching.
Y'ALL HEARD THE NEWS ABOUT THE STORM KING?
WHAT'S HE DOING NOW?
HE'S ALREADY GOT HALF THE WORLD UNDER HIS THUMB.
WELL, APPARENTLY, THAT AIN'T ENOUGH.
HE'S GOT ALL HIS GOONS OUT, LOOKING FOR MAGIC.
ARTIFACTS, AMULETS, GEMS...
IF IT GLOWS, HE'S COMIN' FOR IT.
That explains the Storm King's interest in this gem.
Perhaps I should investigate it further...

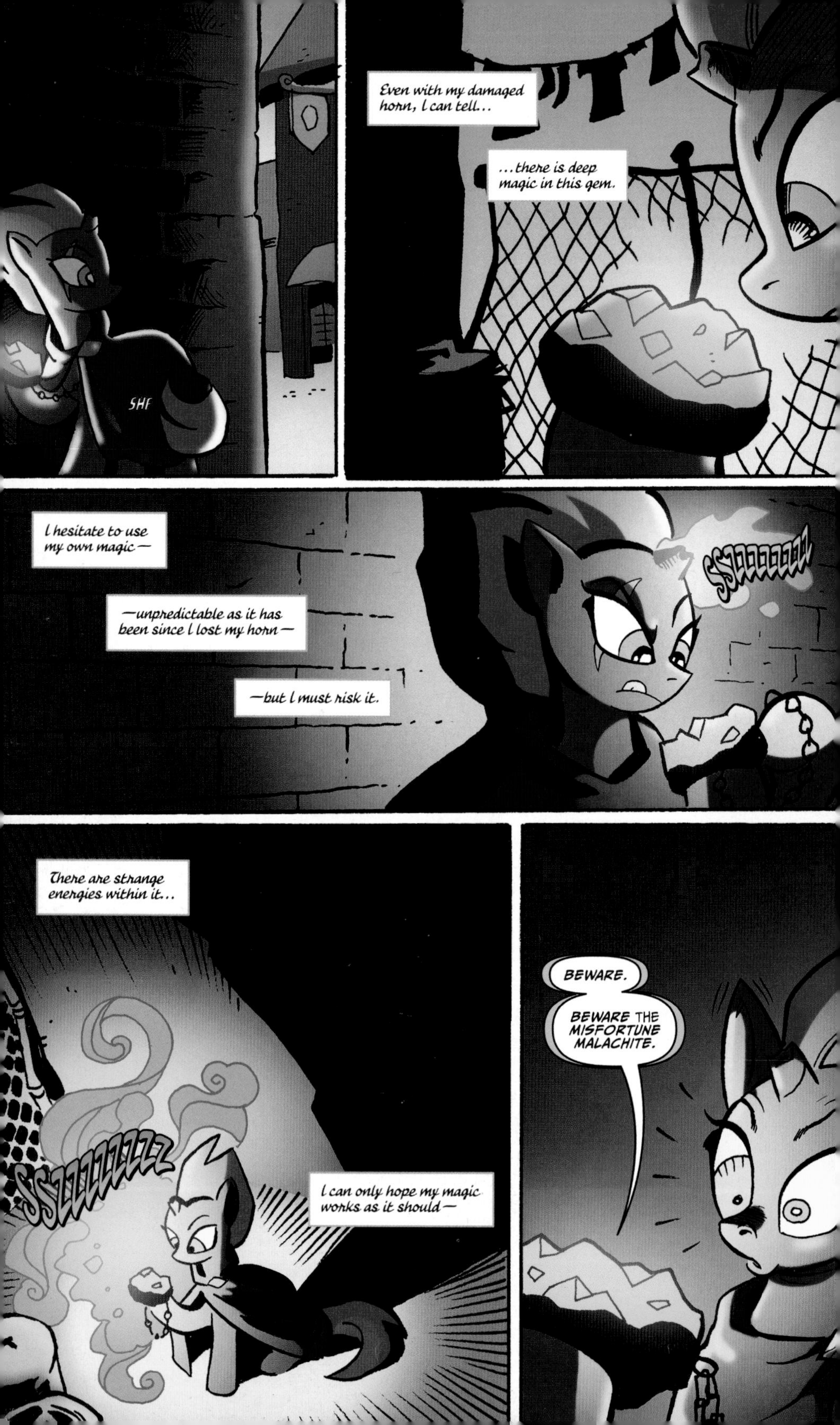
SHF
Even with my damaged horn, I can tell...
...there is deep magic in this gem.
I hesitate to use my own magic—
SSZZZZZZZ
—unpredictable as it has been since I lost my horn—
—but I must risk it.
There are strange energies within it...
SSZZZZZZZZ
I can only hope my magic works as it should—
BEWARE.
BEWARE THE MISFORTUNE MALACHITE.

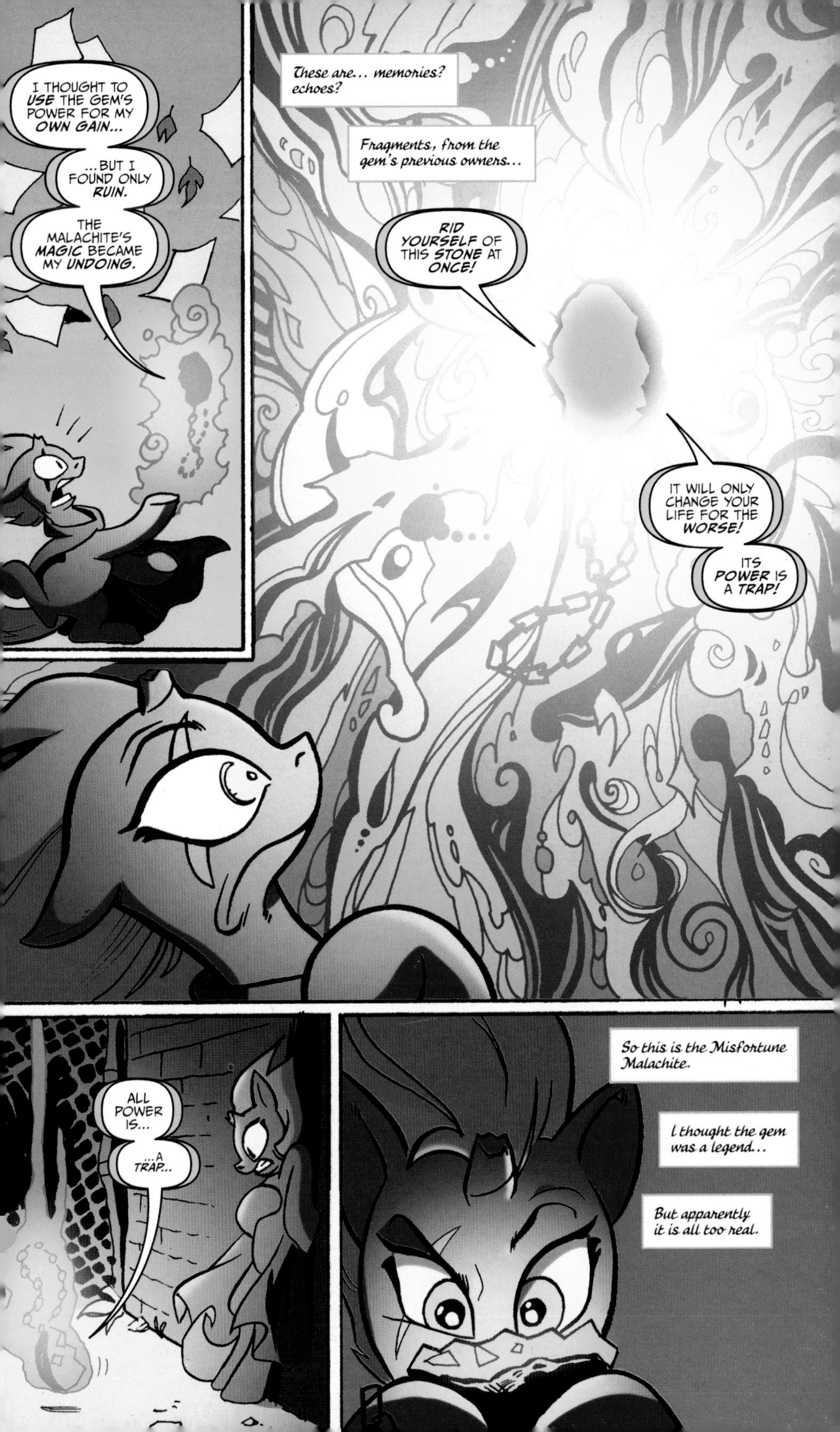
I THOUGHT TO USE THE GEM'S POWER FOR MY OWN GAIN...
...BUT I FOUND ONLY RUIN.
THE MALACHITE'S MAGIC BECAME MY UNDOING.
These are... memories? echoes?
Fragments, from the gem's previous owners...
RID YOURSELF OF THIS STONE AT ONCE!
IT WILL ONLY CHANGE YOUR LIFE FOR THE WORSE!
ITS POWER IS A TRAP!
ALL POWER IS...
...A TRAP...
So this is the Misfortune Malachite.
I thought the gem was a legend...
But apparently it is all too real.

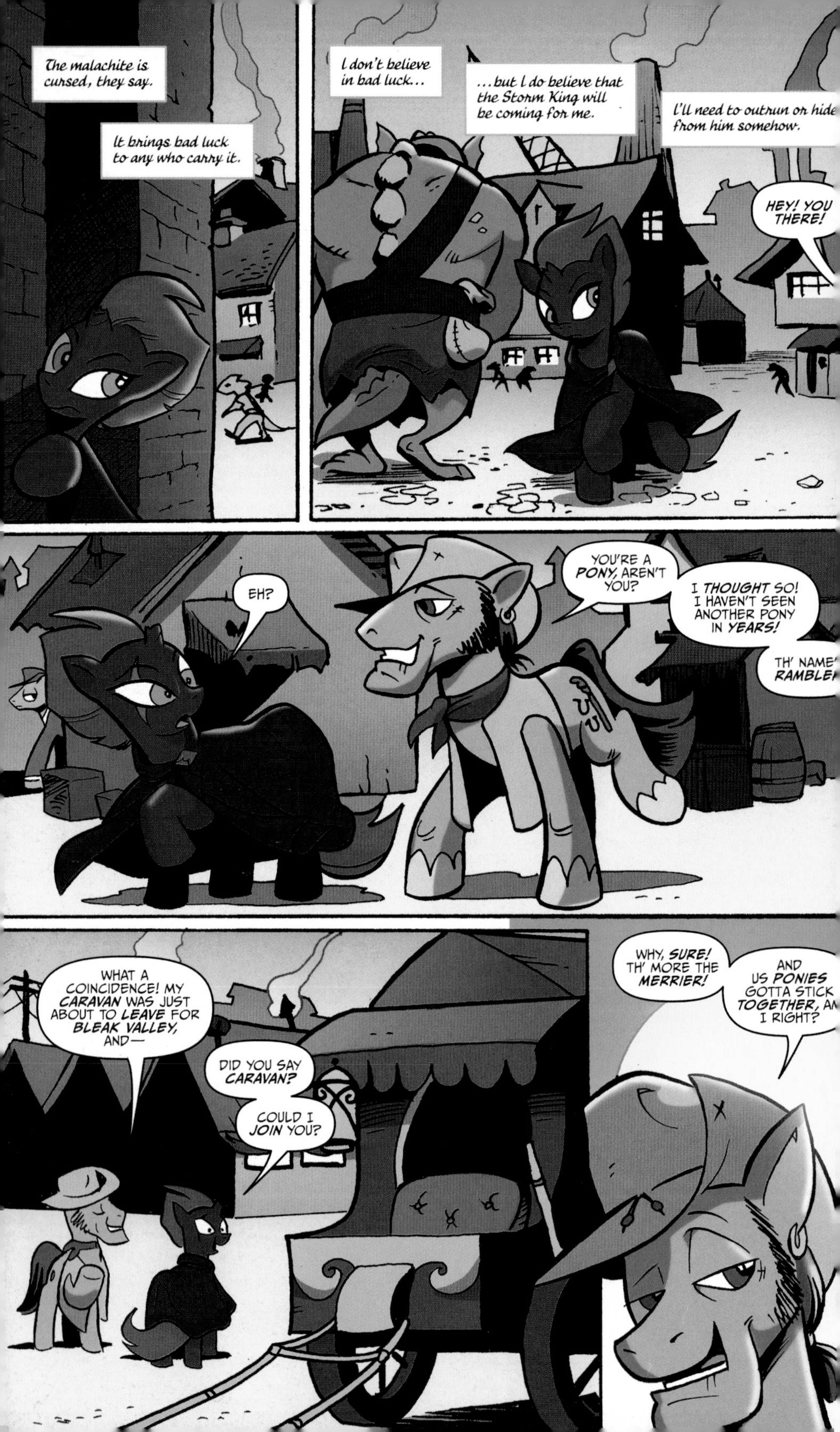
The malachite is cursed, they say.
It brings bad luck to any who carry it.
I don't believe in bad luck...
...but I do believe that the Storm King will be coming for me.
I'll need to outrun or hide from him somehow.
HEY! YOU THERE!
EH?
YOU'RE A PONY, AREN'T YOU?
I THOUGHT SO! I HAVEN'T SEEN ANOTHER PONY IN YEARS!
WHAT A COINCIDENCE! MY CARAVAN WAS JUST ABOUT TO LEAVE FOR BLEAK VALLEY, AND—
DID YOU SAY CARAVAN?
COULD I JOIN YOU?
WHY, SURE! TH' MORE THE MERRIER!

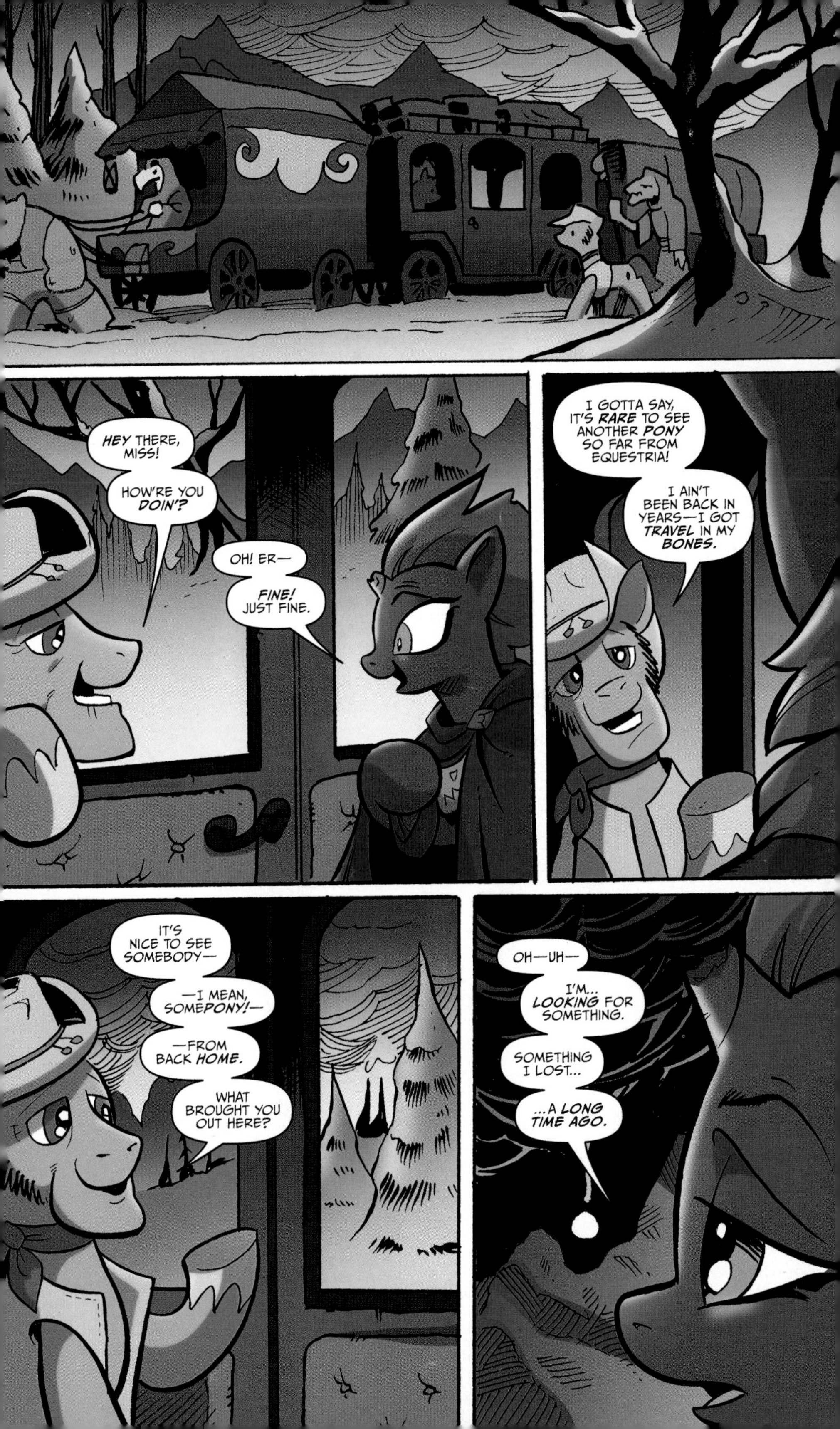
HEY THERE, MISS!
HOW'RE YOU DOIN'?
OH! ER—
FINE! JUST FINE.
I GOTTA SAY, IT'S RARE TO SEE ANOTHER PONY SO FAR FROM EQUESTRIA!
I AIN'T BEEN BACK IN YEARS—I GOT TRAVEL IN MY BONES.
IT'S NICE TO SEE SOMEBODY—
—I MEAN, SOMEPONY!—
—FROM BACK HOME.
WHAT BROUGHT YOU OUT HERE?
OH—UH—
I'M... LOOKING FOR SOMETHING.
SOMETHING I LOST...
...A LONG TIME AGO.

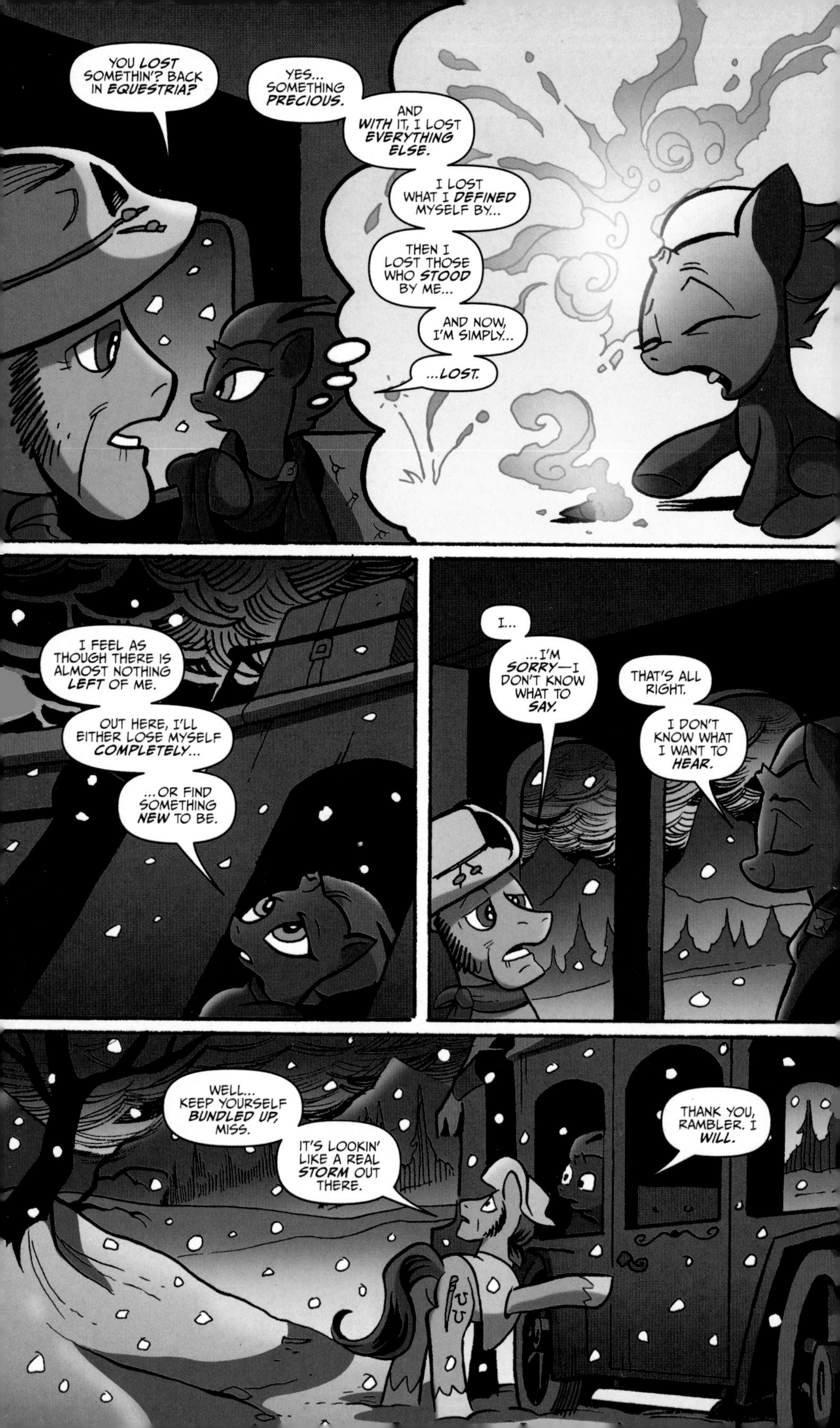
YOU LOST SOMETHIN'? BACK IN EQUESTRIA?
YES... SOMETHING PRECIOUS.
AND WITH IT, I LOST EVERYTHING ELSE.
I LOST WHAT I DEFINED MYSELF BY...
THEN I LOST THOSE WHO STOOD BY ME...
AND NOW, I'M SIMPLY...
...LOST.
I FEEL AS THOUGH THERE IS ALMOST NOTHING LEFT OF ME.
OUT HERE, I'LL EITHER LOSE MYSELF COMPLETELY...
...OR FIND SOMETHING NEW TO BE.
I...
...I'M SORRY—I DON'T KNOW WHAT TO SAY.
THAT'S ALL RIGHT.
I DON'T KNOW WHAT I WANT TO HEAR.
WELL... KEEP YOURSELF BUNDLED UP, MISS.
IT'S LOOKIN' LIKE A REAL STORM OUT THERE.
THANK YOU, RAMBLER. I WILL.

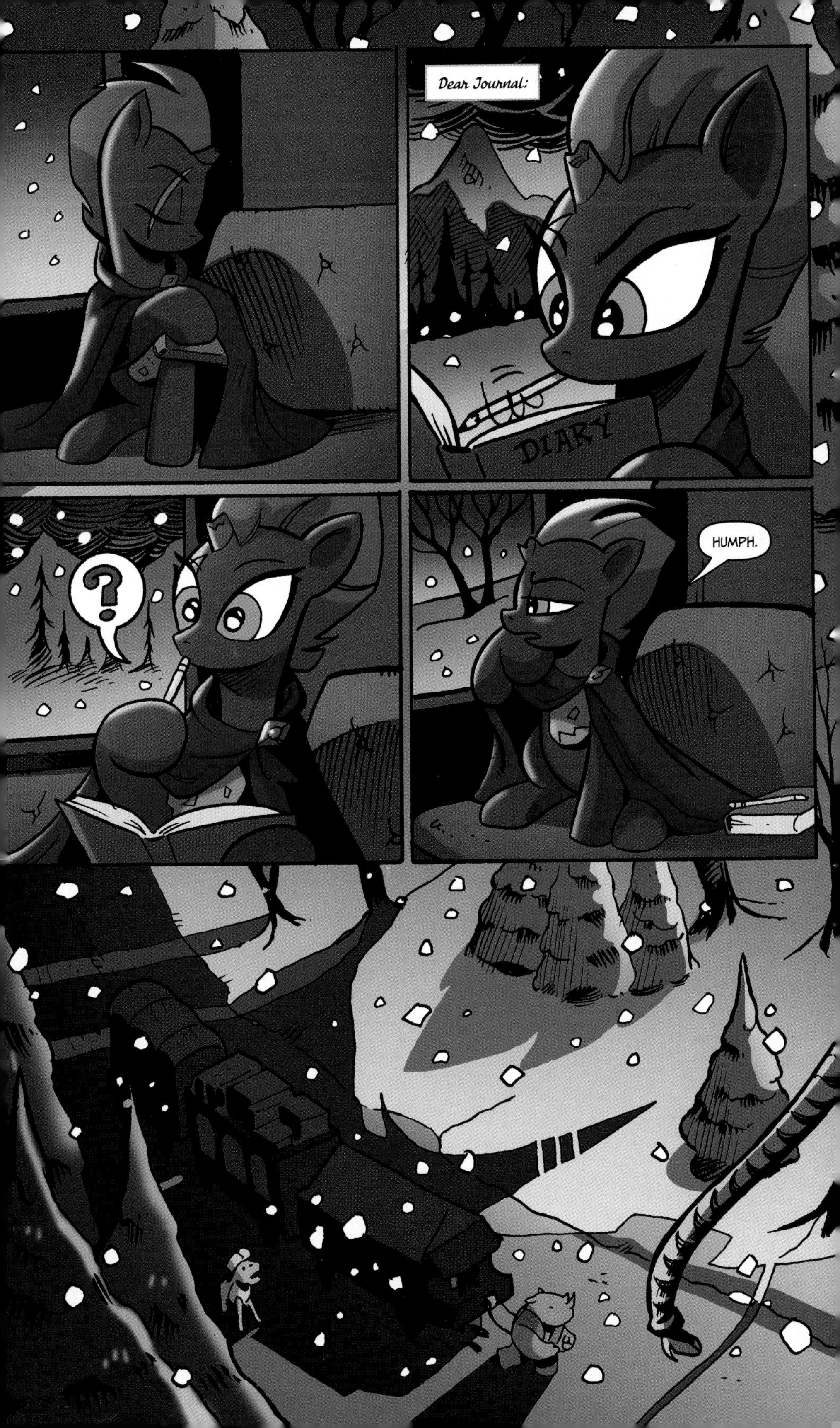
Dear Journal:
DIARY
?
HUMPH.

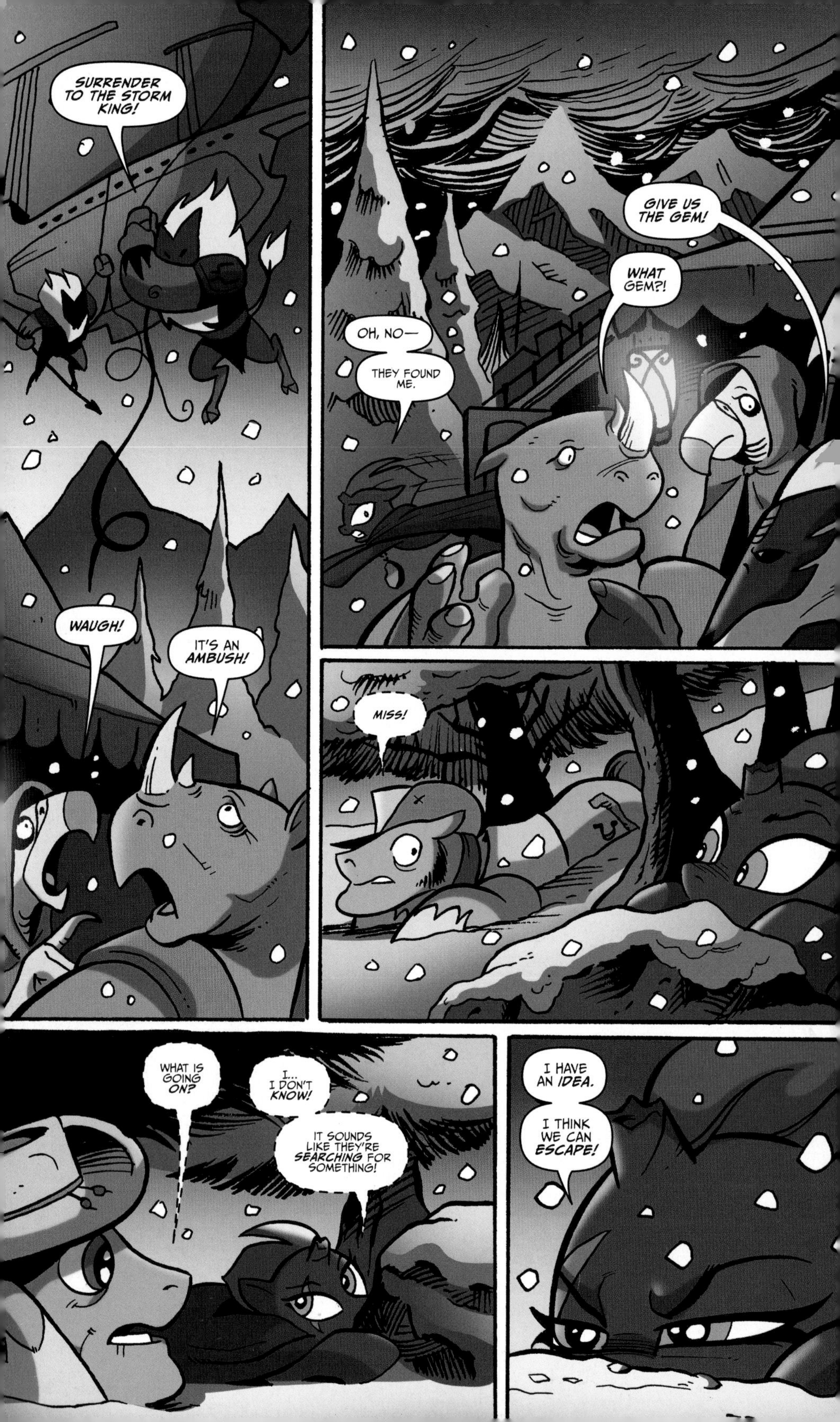
SURRENDER TO THE STORM KING!
WAUGH!
IT'S AN AMBUSH!
GIVE US THE GEM!
WHAT GEM?!
OH, NO—
THEY FOUND ME.
MISS!
WHAT IS GOING ON?
I... I DON'T KNOW!
IT SOUNDS LIKE THEY'RE SEARCHING FOR SOMETHING!
I HAVE AN IDEA.
I THINK WE CAN ESCAPE!

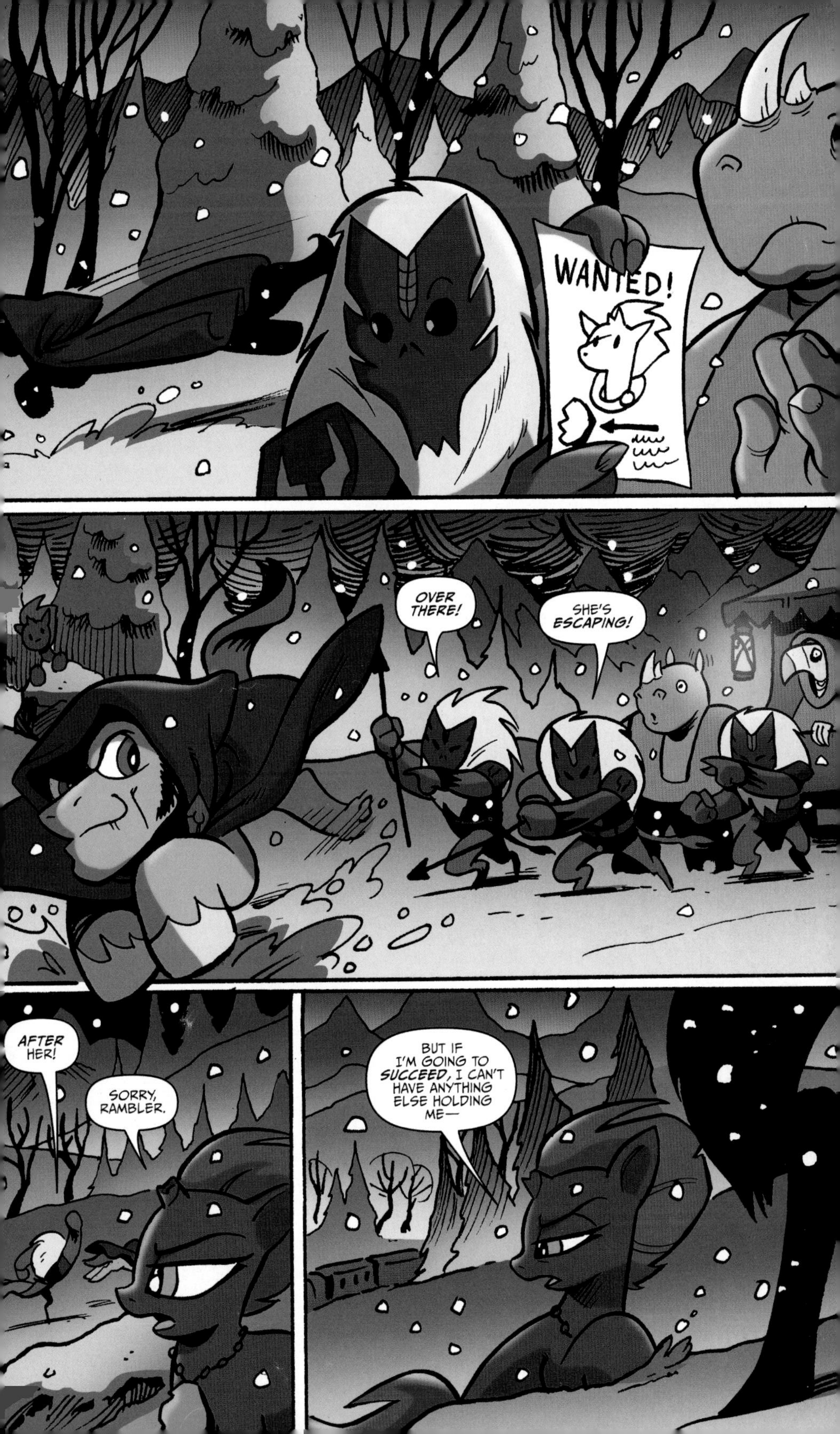
WANTED!
OVER THERE!
SHE'S ESCAPING!
AFTER HER!
SORRY, RAMBLER.
BUT IF I'M GOING TO *SUCCEED*, I CAN'T HAVE ANYTHING ELSE HOLDING ME—

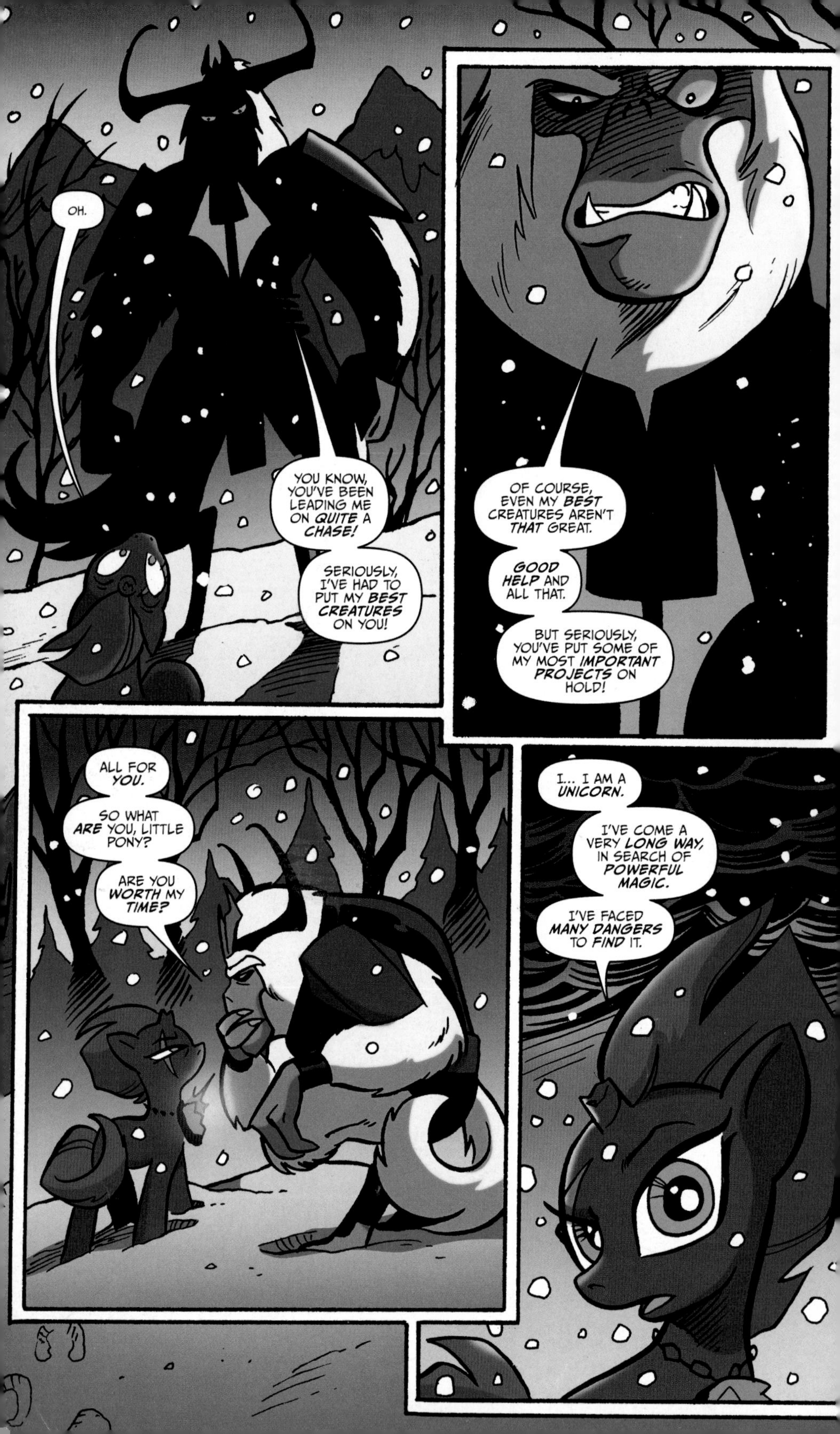
OH.
YOU KNOW, YOU'VE BEEN LEADING ME ON QUITE A CHASE!
SERIOUSLY, I'VE HAD TO PUT MY BEST CREATURES ON YOU!
OF COURSE, EVEN MY BEST CREATURES AREN'T THAT GREAT.
GOOD HELP AND ALL THAT.
BUT SERIOUSLY, YOU'VE PUT SOME OF MY MOST IMPORTANT PROJECTS ON HOLD!
ALL FOR YOU.
SO WHAT ARE YOU, LITTLE PONY?
ARE YOU WORTH MY TIME?
I... I AM A UNICORN.
I'VE COME A VERY LONG WAY, IN SEARCH OF POWERFUL MAGIC.
I'VE FACED MANY DANGERS TO FIND IT.

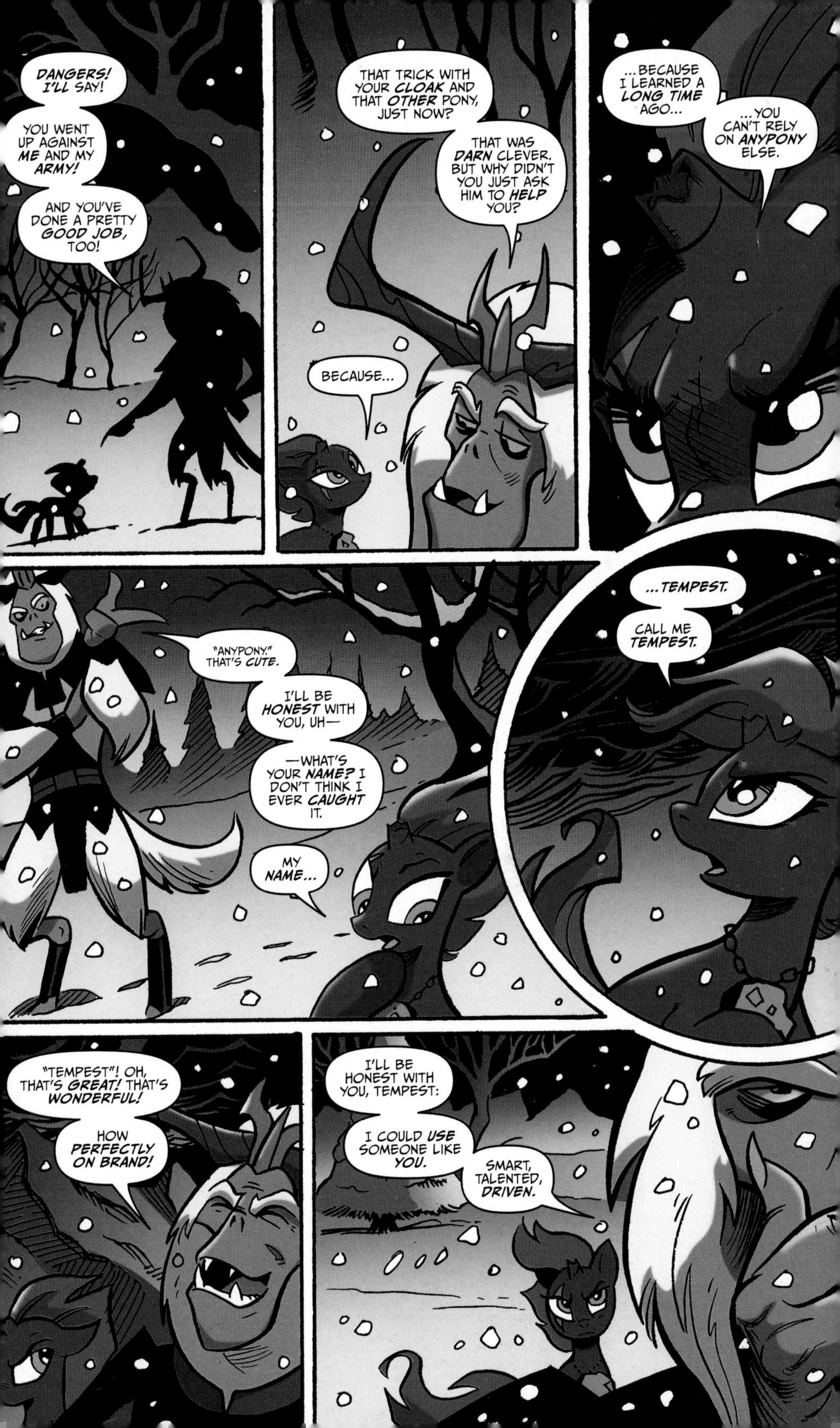
DANGERS! I'LL SAY!
YOU WENT UP AGAINST ME AND MY ARMY!
AND YOU'VE DONE A PRETTY GOOD JOB, TOO!
THAT TRICK WITH YOUR CLOAK AND THAT OTHER PONY, JUST NOW?
THAT WAS DARN CLEVER. BUT WHY DIDN'T YOU JUST ASK HIM TO HELP YOU?
BECAUSE...
...BECAUSE I LEARNED A LONG TIME AGO...
...YOU CAN'T RELY ON ANYPONY ELSE.
"ANYPONY." THAT'S CUTE.
I'LL BE HONEST WITH YOU, UH—
—WHAT'S YOUR NAME? I DON'T THINK I EVER CAUGHT IT.
MY NAME...
...TEMPEST.
CALL ME TEMPEST.
"TEMPEST"! OH, THAT'S GREAT! THAT'S WONDERFUL!
HOW PERFECTLY ON BRAND!
I'LL BE HONEST WITH YOU, TEMPEST:
I COULD USE SOMEONE LIKE YOU.
SMART, TALENTED, DRIVEN.

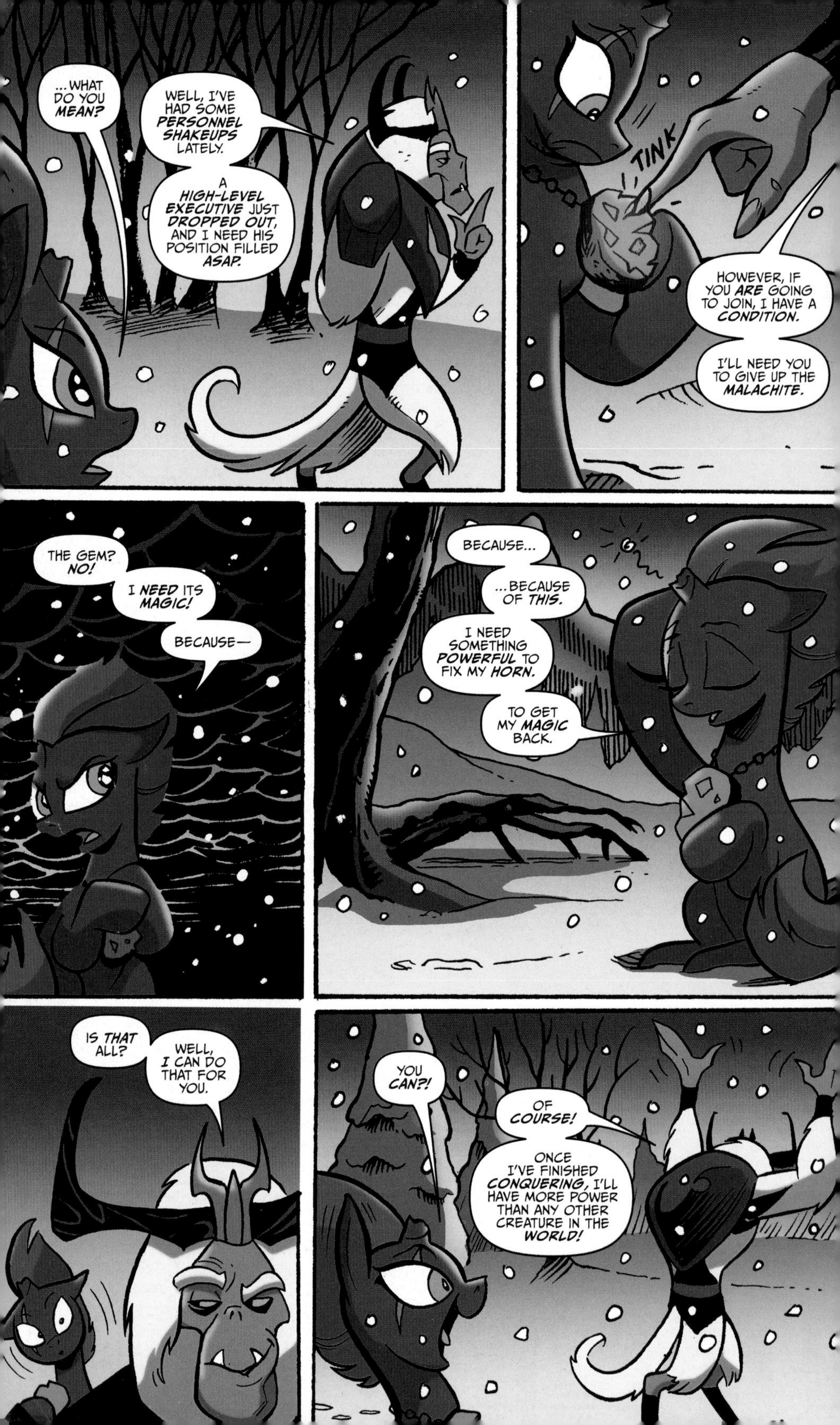
...WHAT DO YOU MEAN?
WELL, I'VE HAD SOME PERSONNEL SHAKEUPS LATELY.
A HIGH-LEVEL EXECUTIVE JUST DROPPED OUT, AND I NEED HIS POSITION FILLED ASAP.
TINK
HOWEVER, IF YOU ARE GOING TO JOIN, I HAVE A CONDITION.
I'LL NEED YOU TO GIVE UP THE MALACHITE.
THE GEM? NO!
I NEED ITS MAGIC!
BECAUSE—
BECAUSE...
...BECAUSE OF THIS.
I NEED SOMETHING POWERFUL TO FIX MY HORN.
TO GET MY MAGIC BACK.
IS THAT ALL?
WELL, I CAN DO THAT FOR YOU.
YOU CAN?!
OF COURSE!
ONCE I'VE FINISHED CONQUERING, I'LL HAVE MORE POWER THAN ANY OTHER CREATURE IN THE WORLD!

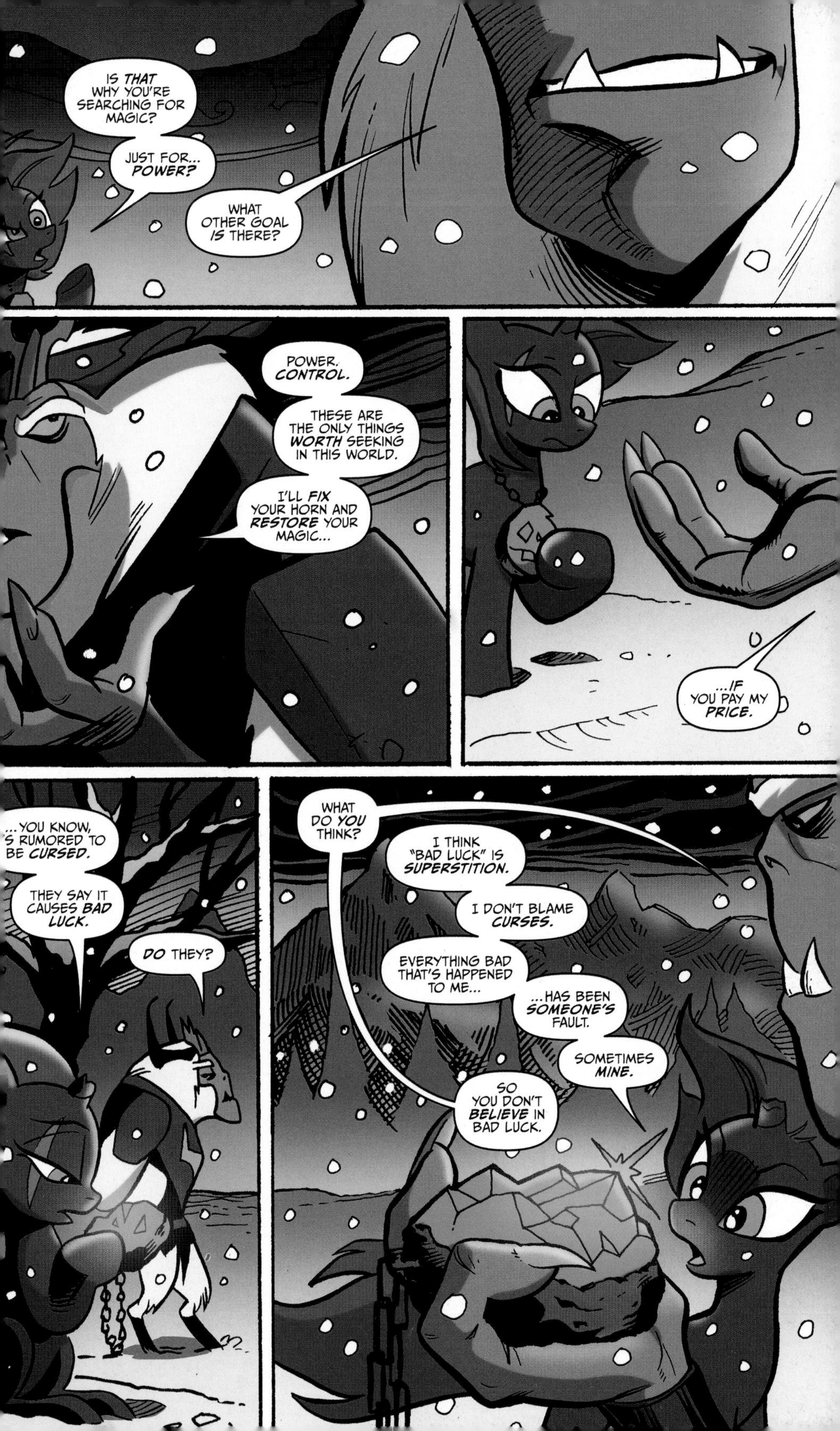
IS THAT WHY YOU'RE SEARCHING FOR MAGIC?
JUST FOR... POWER?
WHAT OTHER GOAL IS THERE?
POWER. CONTROL.
THESE ARE THE ONLY THINGS WORTH SEEKING IN THIS WORLD.
I'LL FIX YOUR HORN AND RESTORE YOUR MAGIC...
...IF YOU PAY MY PRICE.
...YOU KNOW, 'S RUMORED TO BE CURSED.
THEY SAY IT CAUSES BAD LUCK.
DO THEY?
WHAT DO YOU THINK?
I THINK "BAD LUCK" IS SUPERSTITION.
I DON'T BLAME CURSES.
EVERYTHING BAD THAT'S HAPPENED TO ME...
...HAS BEEN SOMEONE'S FAULT.
SOMETIMES MINE.
SO YOU DON'T BELIEVE IN BAD LUCK.

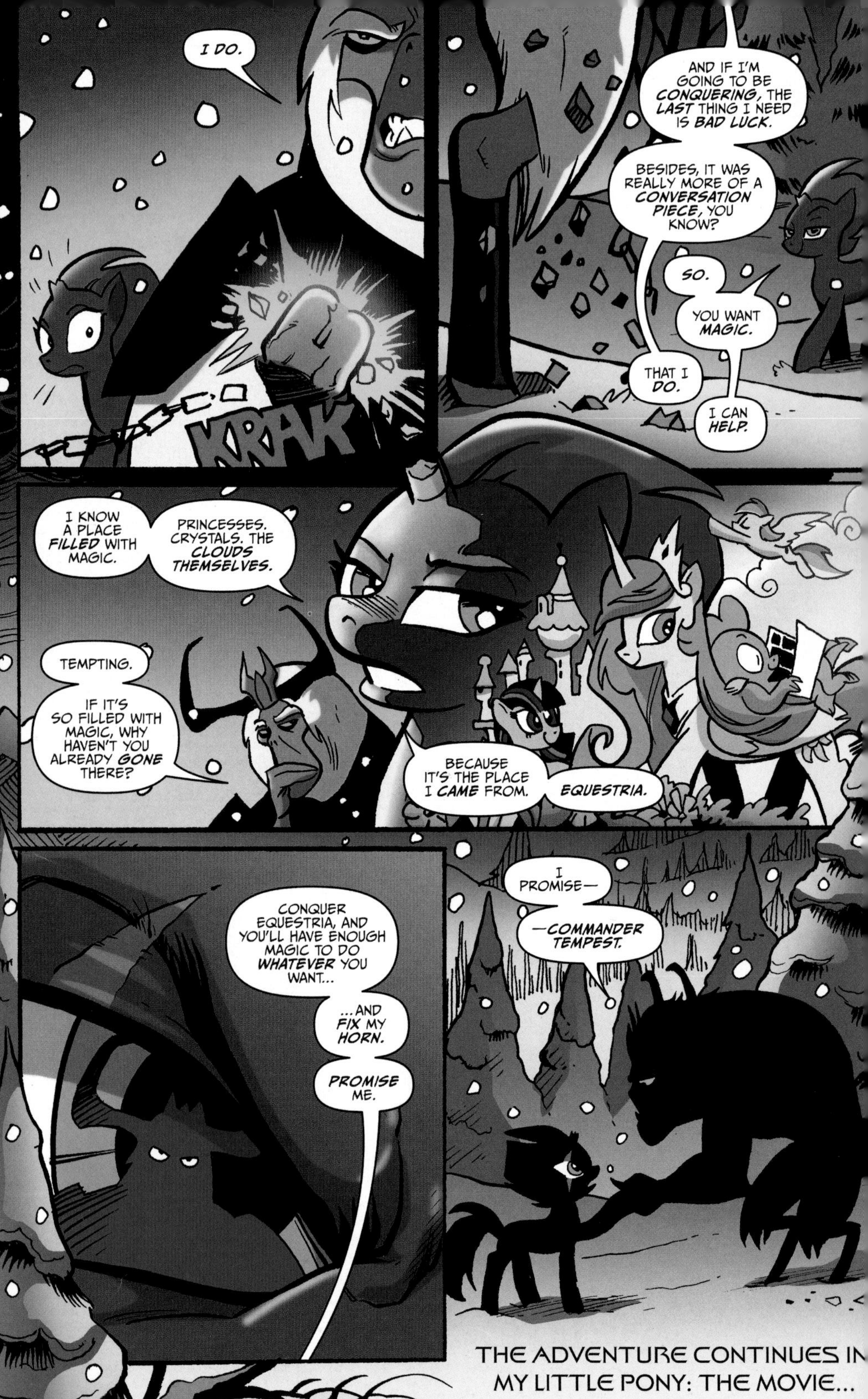
I DO.
KRAK
AND IF I'M GOING TO BE CONQUERING, THE LAST THING I NEED IS BAD LUCK.
BESIDES, IT WAS REALLY MORE OF A CONVERSATION PIECE, YOU KNOW?
SO.
YOU WANT MAGIC.
THAT I DO.
I CAN HELP.
I KNOW A PLACE FILLED WITH MAGIC.
PRINCESSES. CRYSTALS. THE CLOUDS THEMSELVES.
TEMPTING.
IF IT'S SO FILLED WITH MAGIC, WHY HAVEN'T YOU ALREADY GONE THERE?
BECAUSE IT'S THE PLACE I CAME FROM.
EQUESTRIA.
CONQUER EQUESTRIA, AND YOU'LL HAVE ENOUGH MAGIC TO DO WHATEVER YOU WANT...
...AND FIX MY HORN.
PROMISE ME.
I PROMISE—
—COMMANDER TEMPEST.

THE ADVENTURE CONTINUES IN
MY LITTLE PONY: THE MOVIE...

Art by **TONY FLEECS**

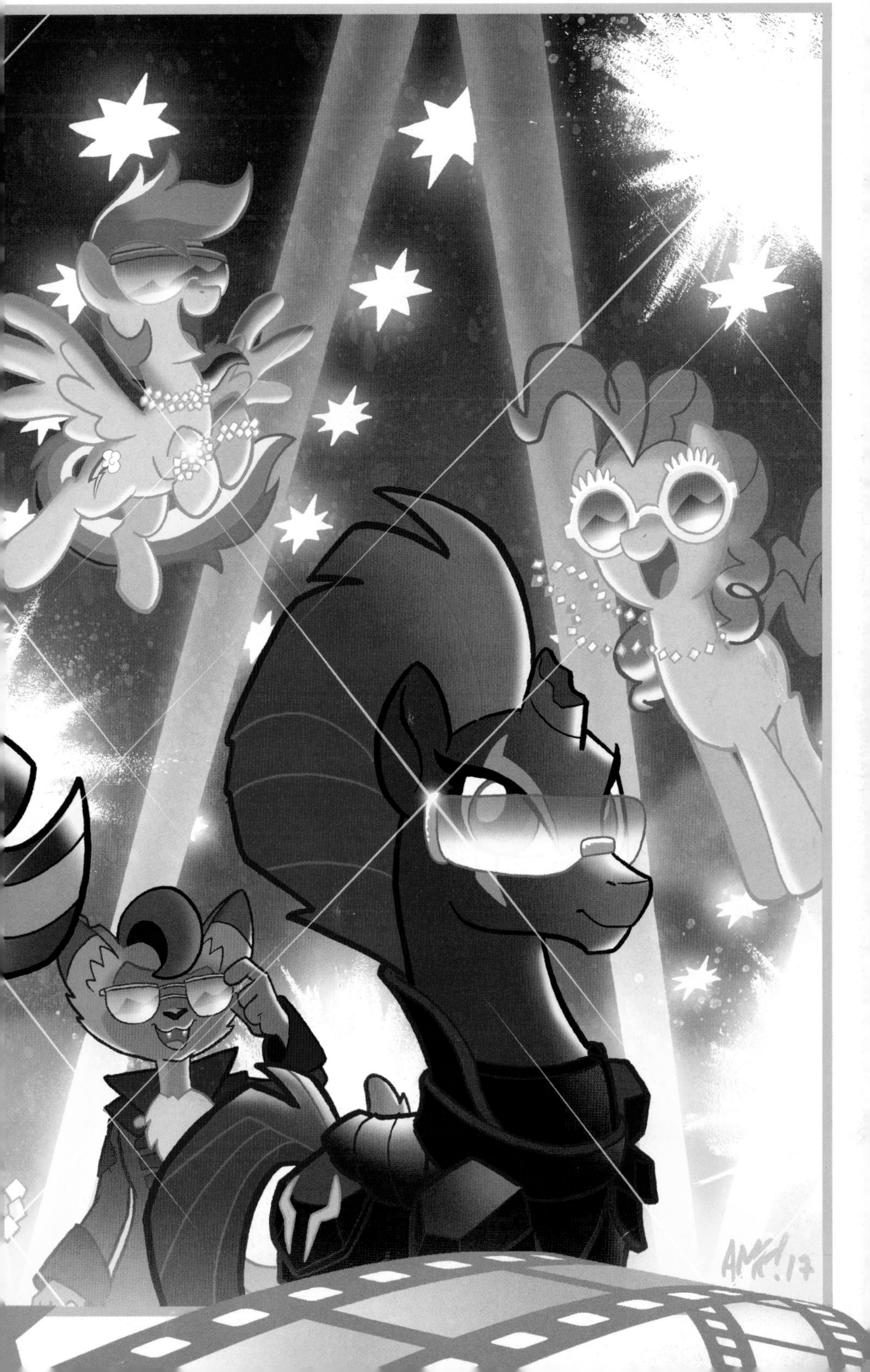

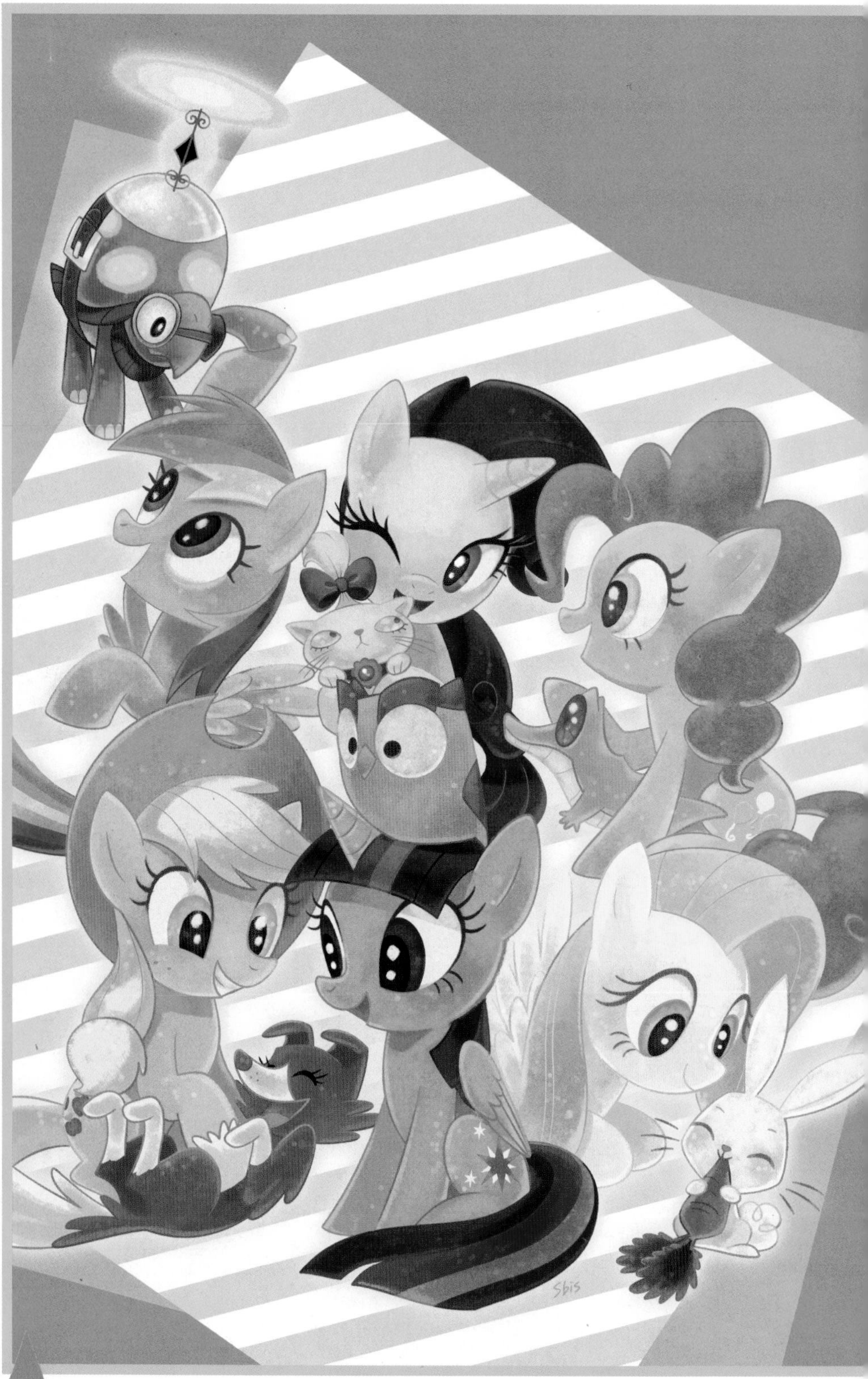
Sbis

Art by **KAORI MATSUO**

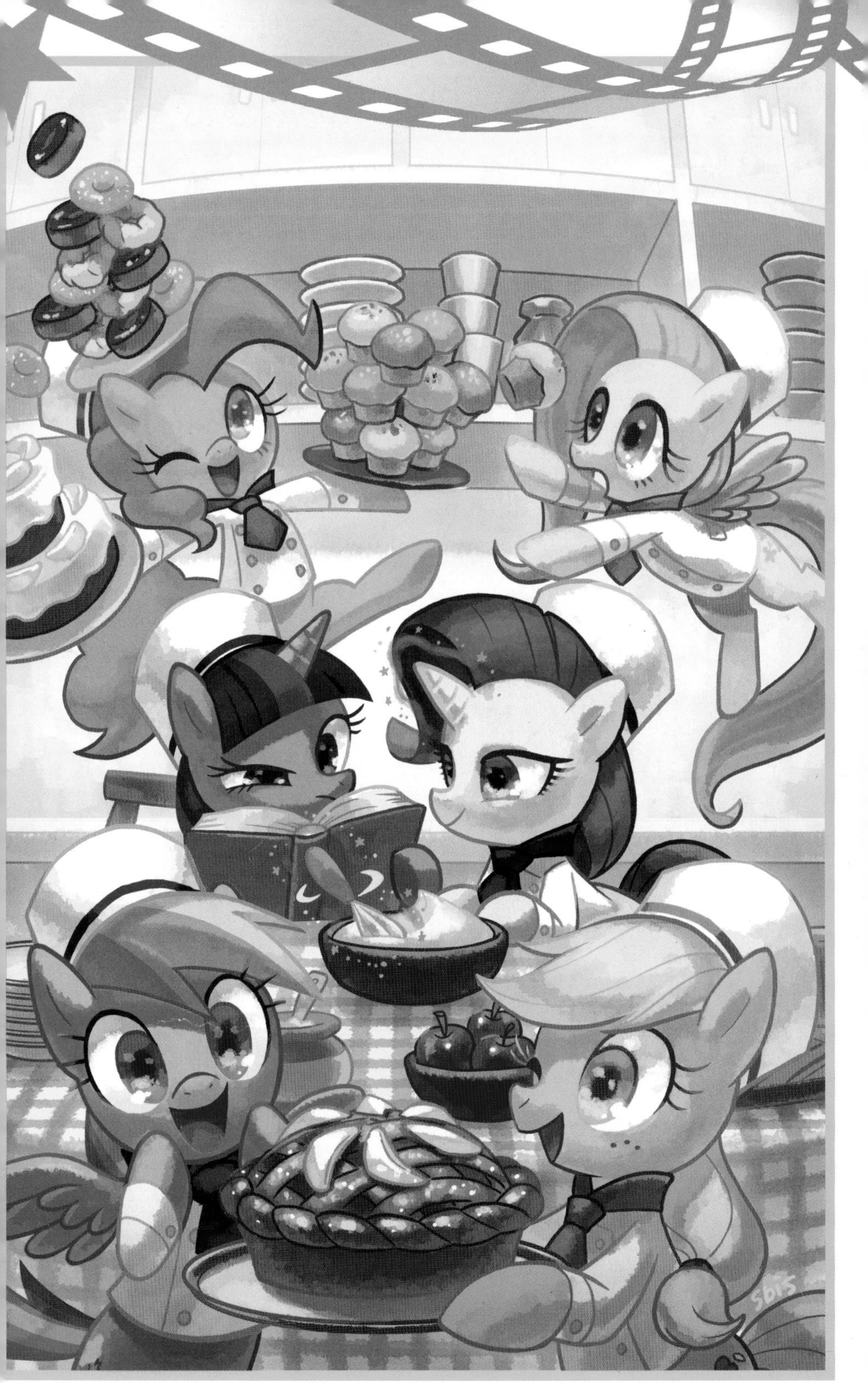

Art by **KAORI MATSUO**

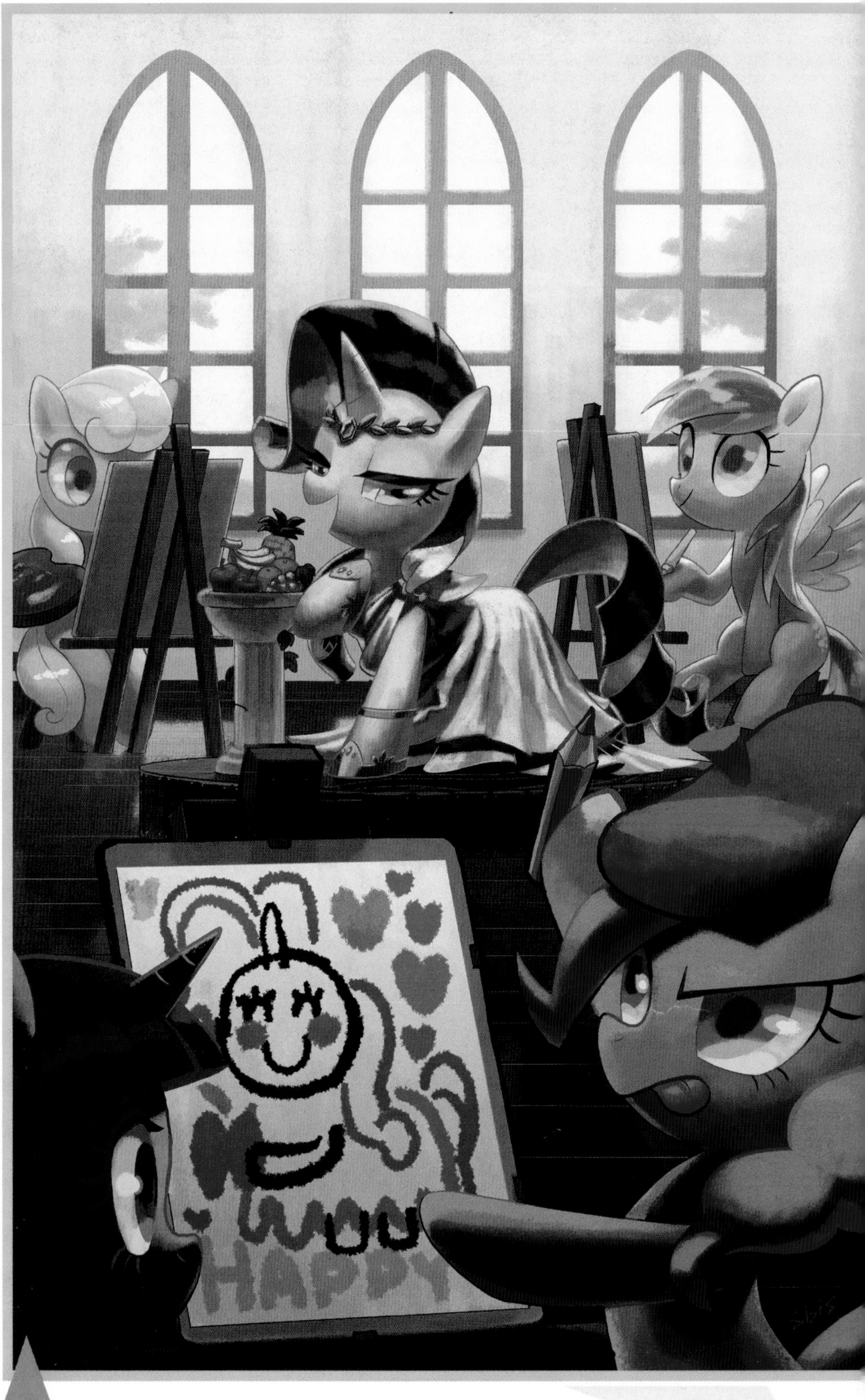
HAPPY

Art by **KAORI MATSUO**

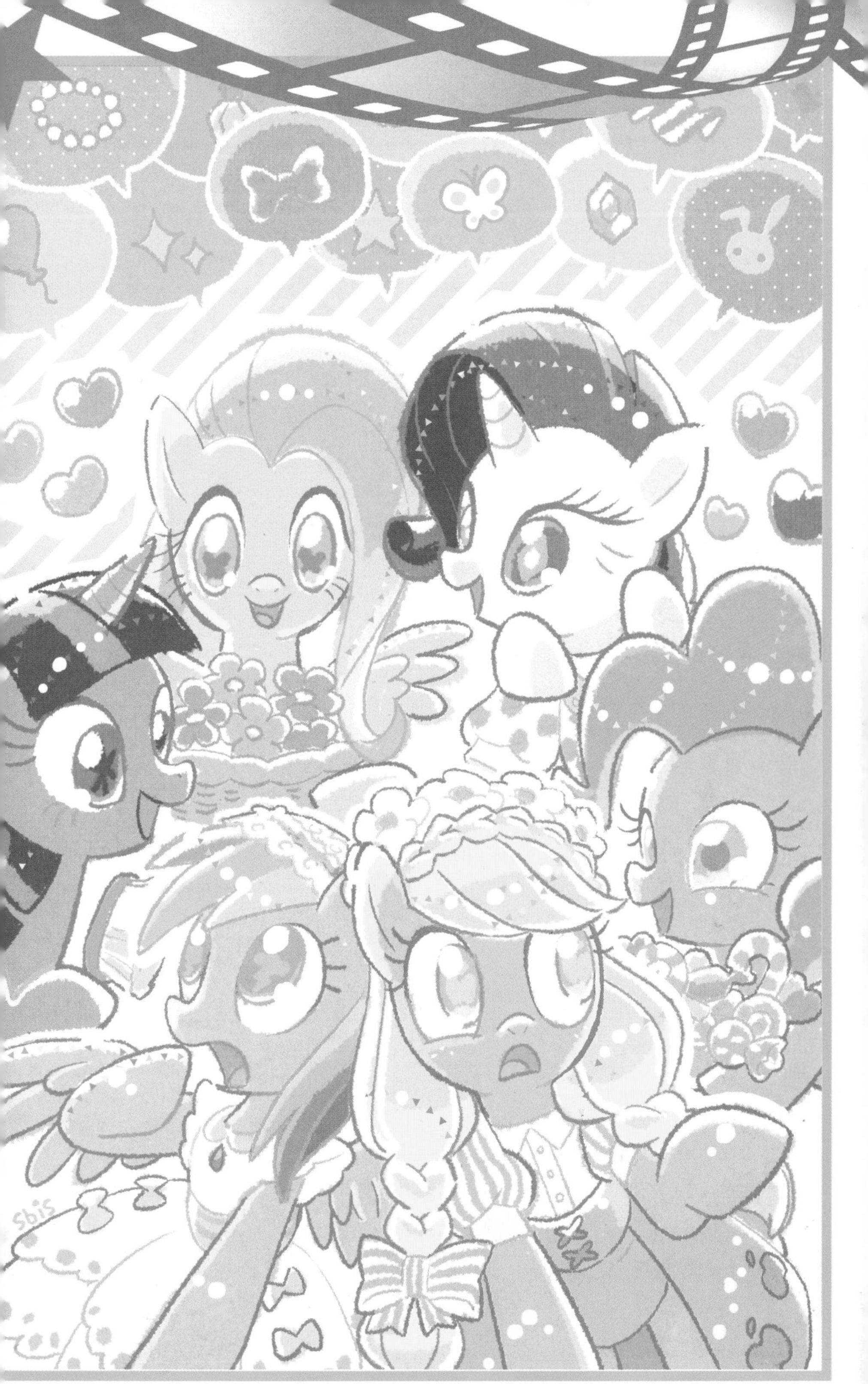

Art by KAORI MATSUO

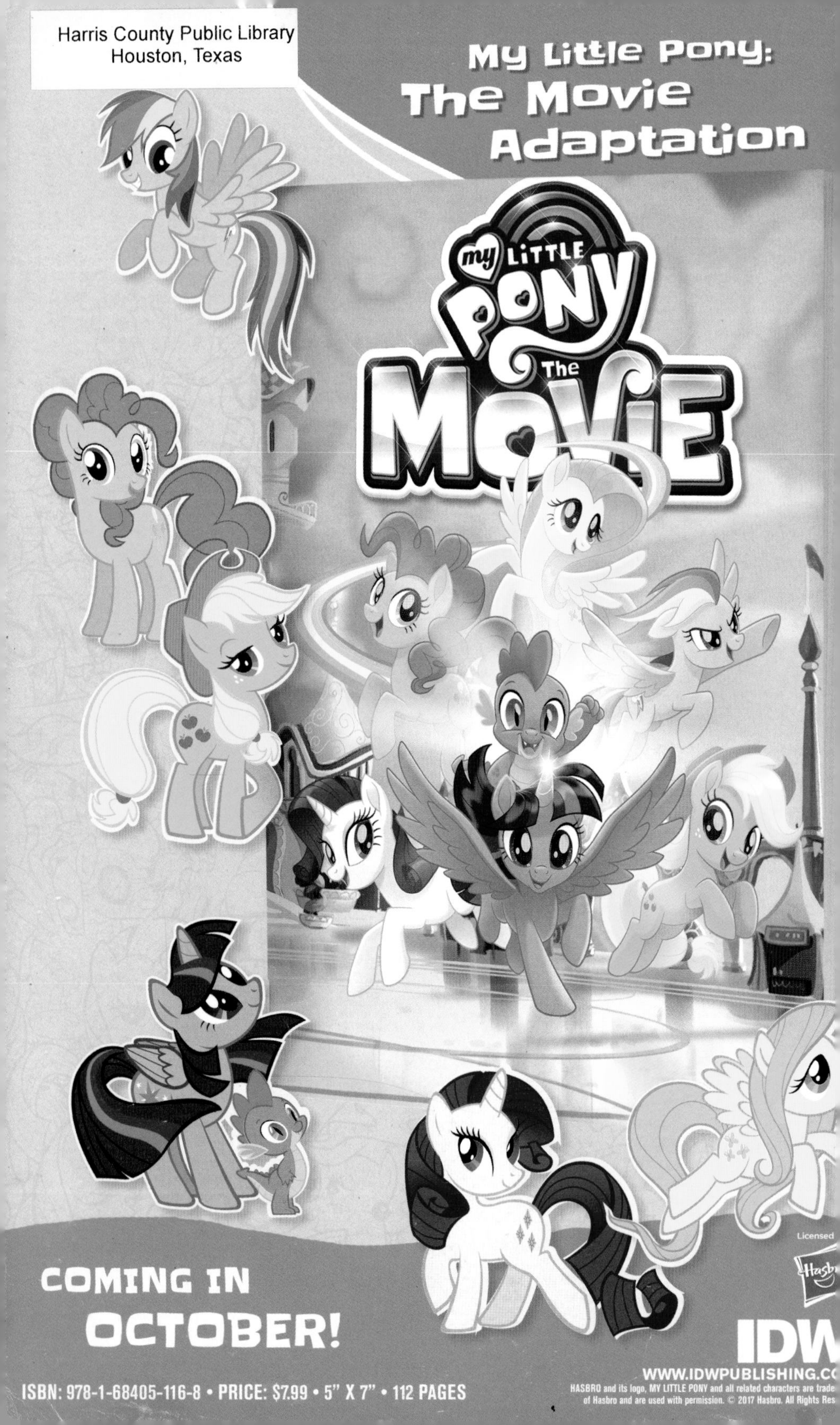
My Little Pony:
The Movie
Adaptation
my LITTLE PONY
The MOVIE
COMING IN
OCTOBER!
Licensed
IDW
WWW.IDWPUBLISHING.CO
ISBN: 978-1-68405-116-8 • PRICE: $7.99 • 5" X 7" • 112 PAGES
HASBRO and its logo, MY LITTLE PONY and all related characters are trade
of Hasbro and are used with permission. © 2017 Hasbro. All Rights Res